Dark Room Secrets

THIS IS A REVISED VERSION OF, 'The Girl in The Dark' WITH SOME NEW MATERIAL. THE NOVEL WAS FIRST PUBLISHED IN 2017 BY ENDEAVOUR PRESS.

Kim was surrounded by herself
   She gaped at the photographs of herself covering the two walls. They were images from throughout her life. She wondered why he'd put this collection together.
   Looking more closely, she noticed that her husband and bridesmaids had been cut from her wedding photos. She stood alone in her wedding gown.
   Kim shivered and glanced nervously over her shoulder. None of this feels right.
   She struggled not to panic.

Chapter One

Kim Nicholson sat in the photography studio with the owner, Sidney, discussing a new contract to style fruit and vegetables for a shoot. Kim had worked for Sidney many times over the years as a freelance food stylist and knew him on a personal level as he'd been a close friend to her late husband, David. Sidney had just finished explaining his need to employ an assistant to help in the studio when Kim turned to look at a man entering the reception area.

Sidney jumped from his chair. 'And speak of the devil, here he is now,' he said, hurrying over to greet him.

Kim watched Sidney shake the man's hand. When they walked back towards where she sat in the corner of the room, she gasped at the sight of this stranger, he was enormous. Kim reckoned he must be well over six foot, with huge biceps and a broad chest which strained against his tight-fitting brown shirt.

Sidney introduced them. 'Kim, this is Alex, my new assistant.'

Alex walked towards her and held out his hand. He cast a shadow in the sunlight shining through the window and Kim caught her breath when she saw him up close.

Kim was not short, five-foot eight in her stocking feet, but she felt as though he towered over her. She could feel her cheeks flush as she stood up and he took her small hand in his. Staring down at the large powerful hand holding hers, Kim noticed how gently he had woven his fingers around hers. Almost as though he was holding a delicate piece of porcelain.

Maybe this is what's meant by the phrase, a gentle giant, she thought and raised her eyes to his face.

His eyebrows were so black and thick that they would give the impression of a permanent frown if it weren't for the shine in his deep green eyes. Kim gulped. The faint scent of sandalwood after-shave filled the air, and she couldn't help but smile with pleasure.

'Hello,' he said smiling. 'Nice to meet you at last. Sidney's told me all about you, and especially how you do fabulous things with food.'

His low voice had a mellow tone which broke her reverie. She shook herself out of the trance-like state.

Kim struggled to find her voice. 'W...well, I think Sidney is exaggerating my talents somewhat,' she murmured. 'But hello, it's nice to meet you too.'

She looked down at her hand still lying in his palm and felt a sense of security and warm comfort flood through her.

Hovering in the background with a cafetière in his hand, Sidney offered Alex coffee. Alex turned to walk back across the room towards him, and Kim felt bereft. It was as if she'd had a special gift snatched from under her nose and rubbed her hand which felt strangely cold without Alex's warm fingers.

With her coffee left to go cold, Kim stared at the backs of the two men and wondered what had just happened. She felt shocked to the core, her mouth was dry, and she swallowed hard. She didn't usually react like this to men. It wasn't in her nature. But for some inexplicable reason, this guy was having a strange effect on her. He's not my type, she thought watching him run a hand through his thick black hair. But there again, what was her type now?

Kim thought of her beloved David, who she'd nursed for nearly a year while prostate cancer ravaged his body. She had met him at university aged eighteen and he was the only man she'd ever known. David had only been five-foot seven, with a lean athletic build before his illness, and the total opposite of Alex. In fact, David had been more like Sidney in physique and certainly nothing like this giant of a man who was now sipping his coffee and smiling at her.

Sidney topped up his coffee mug while they chatted amicably and then returned to the small table where Kim began to stack piles of photographic materials to one side. She gathered a bundle of coloured marker pens when Alex joined them and sat down opposite to her. Alex lifted a Microsoft tablet from his leather briefcase and flicked out the stand while Sidney pulled up a chair to the table.

The recently re-vamped studio had a new round wooden table and slim high-backed chairs with small cushion pads. Kim stared at Alex's massive thighs hanging over the sides and prayed the chair would be strong enough to hold him.

Sidney began, 'So, today is more of a meet-and-greet session ahead of our first day's work tomorrow. And if it's okay, I thought we could start at ten tomorrow and brainstorm a pool of ideas.'

Kim smiled at Sidney's attempt at workplace jargon that sounded strange coming from his slightly eccentric manner of speech. When he'd rung earlier to offer her the contract, he had raved about a new management course he had recently attended. It was just like him to be impressed with all the trendy-speak he'd heard.

She nodded and tucked a strand of blonde hair behind her ear. 'That's fine with me, Sidney,' she said. 'But can you tell us the brief from the retailer now so that I can think about things tonight and come up with some ideas. All you said on the phone was that it's for fruit and vegetables.'

Having opened his tablet, Alex grinned at them both. 'Couldn't agree more, Kim,' he said. 'I'm raring to go.'

There was something about the way he'd said her name. It was as if he was trying it out for the first time to see if it fitted around his tongue. She knew he was staring at her because she could feel his eyes boring into her face. She looked down and fiddled with a paper clip on the table.

Sidney ran his tongue along the length of his wiry grey moustache and read aloud the email with the request for fresh vegetables and peeled fruit photographs and the extent of the photo shoot.

'And, as the client isn't attending for these shoots, we have Kim, our food stylist, on board. So, if we don't have any issues, we should be able to wrap these photographs and headline descriptions up within four or five days. But if there's other work to slot in between, then maybe eight days at the most, I'd say.'

Alex nodded and Kim looked up at him, but his eyes were downcast reading something on the tablet.

Kim tried to smooth the creases out of her blue linen trousers as if she could magically make them disappear. The creases had formed since she left the house only a few hours ago, and when she glanced down at the frequently worn T-shirt, she'd chosen, she wanted to kick herself. Knowing from experience that it was often hot and stuffy in the studio at this time of year she had chosen her clothes to keep cool and comfortable. She'd been under the impression that it was just a quick chat and coffee with Sidney then frowned. If she had known it was to be in the company of such a gorgeous guy, she would have chosen something else to wear.

Sidney pushed his gold-rimmed glasses further up onto his nose and continued, 'I thought we could take a minute to introduce each other and maybe say a little bit about ourselves.'

Kim shook the thoughts from her head and felt her previous high spirits drop. She'd hated having to talk about herself in front of strangers since school days, and the thought of being tongue-tied in front of Alex made her cringe. She folded her hands under the table and locked her fingers remembering previous work situations when she'd felt intimidated. She never quite knew what to say about herself. Although she knew she was good at her job, she often felt that her humdrum life sounded pathetic compared to other women's high-flying careers.

'Oh, Sidney,' she groaned. 'You know I hate talking about myself like this. Can't we just chat while we work and get to know each other that way?'

Sidney shuffled the printed emails in his hand and Kim heard Alex chortle slightly. She wondered if he felt the same.

Sidney reached across the table and covered Kim's hand with his. 'But, sweetheart,' he said. 'We're all friends and it's just an intimate gathering. There's nothing to feel anxious about.'

Kim carefully slid her hand from under his. He always had sweaty palms no matter what the season. She wrinkled her nose deciding it wasn't a pleasant experience.

Silence settled between them until Alex spoke out. 'Okay,' he said with a smile. 'As I'm the outsider who neither of you two know anything about, I'll start.'

Kim nodded. She relaxed her shoulders and sat further back into the chair ready to listen. She wondered what size shirt he needed for his huge chest, XXXL? Was there such a size? She shook herself back to focus.

In his low masculine voice, Alex began, 'Well, I'm Alex Stephenson. I'm thirty-eight and moved to Durham last Monday. I love my job and if I say so myself, you'll struggle to find a more enthusiastic photographer. I'm renting a newly built duplex apartment in St. Andrews Court, overlooking the river and Elvet Bridge, at a very reasonable rate. It has fabulous views, but the small rooms are not really my cup of tea as I do prefer older properties with bigger rooms.'

Alex looked at Sidney and raised an eyebrow. 'Is that enough?'

Sidney smiled encouragingly. 'Great, Alex,' he nodded. 'And what about outside of work?'

Alex grinned and looked as though he was enjoying the exchange. 'Well, in my spare time I used to play rugby, but had to retire early when I injured my ankle a few years ago,' he said and shuffled on his seat. His smile disappeared and was replaced with a small frown when he continued, 'I'm in the process of getting divorced from my wife, who is in Scunthorpe with my twin boys...' Alex paused and gazed towards the window obviously deep in thought. 'The boys are, well actually, they're the light of my life.'

Kim felt entranced while he spoke. She felt her bottom lip tremble. His eyes looked so sad when he mentioned his boys and she desperately wanted him to know that he had her sympathy.

'Oh, Alex, I'm so sorry to hear that,' she gushed. 'But isn't it going to be even more difficult living further away from them?'

Alex shook his head. 'Not really. To be honest it won't make much difference at the moment. My darling, soon to be ex-wife, will only let me see them every now and then until the solicitors have agreed access. It's been a bit like Chinese torture because although I knew they were close by, I still couldn't see them.'

Kim nodded gravely. It was her turn to speak out. She took a deep breath hoping to get her words about David without crying. Sometimes she could manage to say the words, David died, and some days they stuck and choked in the back of her throat rendering her speechless. If only she didn't feel so guilty, she sighed.

But, she brightened, here was this gigantic man obviously cut up about the loss of his children even though they still lived near him. Whereas it should be easier for her because David wasn't waiting around every corner for her to bump into.

The awareness of Alex's sad situation gave Kim a determined type of courage and she pulled her shoulders back. 'Well, here goes,' she began. 'I'm forty-nine. I'm a Home Economist with a great deal of experience in styling food for local photographers in the North East. I was married for thirty years to David and still live on Ravensworth Terrace in the city. It's an old rambling property with five bedrooms and an iconic view of the castle and cathedral. Sadly, we didn't have any children, and he...' she took a deep breath and looked at Alex.

Alex's eyes were shining, and he gave her the tiniest wink as if to say, keep going, you can do this.

She took a huge breath in and exhaled slowly. 'D...David died fourteen months ago from prostate cancer. I know the house is far too big for me, but I can't bear to move because all my memories with him are there. I'm saving hard for September to go to Provence for a month to visit my friend who moved to France last year.'

Kim let her shoulders droop and unclenched her hands lying in her lap. She hadn't realised how tightly she'd been squeezing them together until she saw her white knuckles.

'There now,' Sidney said fingering the green silk cravat he wore around his neck. 'That wasn't too bad, Kim, was it?'

Bad enough, Kim wanted to mutter at his patronising tone, but instead she gave him a winning smile of relief.

Sidney continued, 'And now it's my turn. However, before I start, and for the benefit of Alex, my name is Sidney Palfrey. I say this because people love to shorten names, which I dislike immensely. I was christened, Sidney, and not Sid.'

Alex nodded and jiggled one of his bushy eyebrows at Kim, making her want to giggle. She stifled the bubble in her throat and turned her head away from Alex's obvious amusement to give Sidney her full attention.

Sidney cleared his throat, 'Well, I'm certainly the oldest in our little team, at fifty-eight, and have had the studio for many years now. But upon my own admission, I'm struggling in the new digital era. Therefore, as Alex is a genius at digital photography and IT, in the future we should be well ahead of the game. I consider myself fortunate to have found him. The main core of my business has always been photographing food and products for retailer's magazines, local businesses, and big Christmas hampers. And wherever possible I've used Kim to help me as she is a wiz at making food look its best,' he said then paused. He put his head on one side. 'And at the same time, I just wanted to say that I was good friends with David because we were at university together.'

Both men looked at Kim and she nodded with gratitude at their obvious respect. She knew that in his slightly eccentric way, Sidney was fond of her and he was easy to work with. And, above all else, he was a generous, kind-hearted man. When David had first died, he'd been a good friend and she knew that he too, still missed David.

Alex broke her train of thought by asking what good restaurants there were in Durham and all three relaxed and discussed their favourite meals, deciding unanimously that Indian food was at the top of their list.

'Great,' Alex said. 'So maybe towards the end of the week we could all eat curry somewhere?'

Kim agreed and smiled while Sidney told them that he would have to check his diary as socially he did have a busy week ahead. Kim frowned, wondering about this newfound social life because he usually came across as being incredibly lonely and had previously pestered her into meeting him for dinner on a weekly basis.

Two months after the funeral however, she'd started to decline his invitations because she didn't want to give him, or anyone else for that matter, the wrong impression. It wasn't that she wanted to portray herself as a grieving miserable widow, but she did strive to have what her sister, Patricia would call a modicum of decent behaviour. Patricia often said, widowhood should be expressed in a lengthy bereavement period.

Kim had wanted to shout at her sister that they weren't living in the Victorian era, however, she knew it would have no sway. Their parents had been killed in a car accident when they were teenagers, and as the elder, Patricia wouldn't pay the slightest attention to her opinion. She never had and never would.

'So, Kim, it looks like it's just you and me,' Alex said. 'Could you put up with me for a couple of hours at dinner? My table manners are good, and I do like to share. I'm not one of those people who stands guard over their naan bread.'

Kim giggled. 'Yeah, I know what you mean. People do tend to get very precious over their Indian food.'

Alex stood and straightened up, then folded over his tablet ready to put it into the briefcase. 'Good,' he answered. 'So that's a date then?'

Kim's heart leapt. Did he mean a date as though she was simply a casual dinner partner to eat curry with, or a proper date between two adults who were obviously attracted to each other? Although she didn't know the first thing about the dating scene now-a-days, she hoped what she saw shining in his eyes was the same attraction she was feeling.

Try and keep it casual, she thought and pulled her linen jacket from the back of the chair. 'Great,' she said smiling. 'I'll look forward to that.'

Alex strode ahead calling goodbye as he left the studio and Kim bid Sidney farewell at the same time. She agreed to be prompt at ten the following morning.

***

Kim wandered down the narrow pavement on Sadler Street avoiding the cobbles in the centre of the narrow old road in her open-toed sandals. She couldn't wipe the smile from her face. The street was busy with workers and shoppers hurrying home with their bags and occasionally she stepped carefully on to the cobbles to avoid bumping into people. She thought of the last few hours and gently shook her head in amazement at how quickly things could happen in life.

Three hours ago, she'd been in her usual frame of mind thinking sadly of David and making her work plan for the next few weeks to include Sidney's new contract. But after meeting Alex, her stomach churned with excitement and anticipation of the week ahead.

When Sidney had said she was a wiz at styling food she'd felt her ego rise and knew that once they got started, she would throw herself into the contract. Already her mind was buzzing with ideas. But she pushed these ideas aside and thought about Alex.

Recapping every moment from the second he strode into the studio until he left a few minutes ago, Kim decided that the effect he'd had on her had been like a tornado. She remembered the feeling when her hand lay in his. The warm touch of his skin. And how he'd clung onto it for longer than necessary. His gaze had roved over her body with a small smile as though he liked what he saw which had made her quiver in expectation.

Hurrying up Ravenscroft Road, Kim turned into her gate and towards the front door smiling all the while. Sexual feelings had been the furthest thing from her mind when she'd left home that morning. She honestly couldn't remember the last time she'd even thought of sex. It simply never entered her mind.

Turning the key in the lock on the shiny black door, Kim thought of all the feelings she'd experienced during the last few years. The overwhelming grief and sadness associated with losing the man she loved. Frustration and anger at losing him at such an early age. But feelings of sexual attraction and desire hadn't been on her radar since long before David was diagnosed.

She picked up a bundle of junk mail from the mat and hurried along the long hallway into the kitchen. She struggled to remember the last time they'd actually made love. It had to be at least three years ago because David had been so worn out, he'd hardly had the energy to climb the stairs let alone anything else.

Kim switched on the kettle, and while spooning coffee granules into a mug, she remembered the warm sensuous feelings that had flooded her body when Alex held her hand and their skin touched. It was like a bomb exploding inside her. It had reawakened senses and feelings she'd thought were long gone.

Pouring milk into the bottom of a coffee mug, she frowned. But what if she had misread the signs and Alex was like this with all women. He could be nothing short of a resounding flirt. Or maybe he hadn't felt the same attraction she had. And if that's the case, she thought pouring boiling water into the mug, how on earth was she going to work alongside him?

She sipped her coffee and mused. Hmm, this certainly wasn't going to be a run of the mill contract. She knew somewhere deep inside that it was going to be special in more ways than one.

Chapter Two

Kim's eyes travelled further down the photographs on the wall and she gasped in shock. In these wedding shots, he had replaced her late husband with a photograph of himself wearing a black suit with a flower in the lapel. She wondered if this was the suit he had worn on his own wedding day? She gulped hard; what did it mean?

When Kim woke the following morning, well before the eight o'clock alarm, the first thoughts in her mind were about the previous day and meeting Alex. She smiled looking around the large bedroom and over to where the sun shone through the slats in the wood shutters deciding it was going to be another lovely spring day. She squeezed her eyes tight shut and felt ridiculously happy then excited at the thought of seeing Alex later that morning.

Kim threw back the quilt and swung her long legs out of bed. She noticed the slight stubble which had grown on her legs during the last few days. And that, Kim thought purposefully striding into the bathroom, was the first thing that needed attention.

The black and white ceramic tiles on the bathroom floor were cool under her bare feet and she pulled the white shower curtain across the bath. Using a favourite musky body wash she lathered herself and inhaled the delightful aromas then washed her hair with a generous dollop of shampoo while singing a chorus she'd heard on the radio, 'Because I'm happy, clap along if you know what happiness is to you.'

With her legs shaved and teeth brushed, Kim felt refreshed and invigorated. She skipped down the wide staircase longing for a mug of hot coffee.

At the bottom of the stairs, she paused to see the local cricket magazine lying on the mat and instantly realised it was the first delivery of the magazine that David had liked to read during the summer months. Kim gulped and felt the usual crushing sadness descend upon her.

Following his death, she hadn't been able to cope with cancelling the magazine. She'd tried a couple of times, but on both occasions the words had stuck in her throat and she had fled the newsagent's shop, red-faced and choking back tears. She still struggled to find the right words when telling people what had happened. Did she simply say, my husband is dead now, so he doesn't need the magazine anymore? Or did she avoid the upsetting words and invent an excuse to cancel. She had rehearsed, David has a new hobby now, but this held its own set of problems as the newsagent might offer her another magazine for this imaginary hobby.

Hence, the magazine was still being delivered along with her two food magazines and she was still paying the bill. Patricia had already told her it was perfectly ridiculous. In this she had to agree with her sister, who, of course, was right.

Kim bent to pick up the magazine from the mat and as she placed it on the hallstand she frowned. If she told Patricia the real reason why she still liked it to be delivered she would probably have her committed.

Tracing her finger along his name printed on the cover she sighed. It was simply because she found comfort in seeing his name, Mr David Nicholson, on the address label. It said to her, yes, David had existed, he had been her husband, and yes, he had lived at this address.

After he'd died Kim had been determined that everything in their home would remain the same. She couldn't bear any changes to the house, décor, furniture, or her daily routine.

Even though some well-meaning friends had told her, 'Kim, it's time you were moving on and living your own life again.' But she remained stubbornly opposed to this.

She shook her head, plodded along the hall to the kitchen and set the coffee filter in place. It was only when she opened the glass sliding doors leading out into the garden that she stopped and realised how differently she'd behaved since waking up.

Usually, she would open her eyes and roll over to the empty side of the bed thinking of David, but this morning her first thoughts had been about Alex and her cheeks flushed. She placed the cool palms of her hands on her cheeks, feeling ashamed of herself for tarnishing his memories by thinking of another man while lying in their bed.

Kim groaned in weariness at the incessant sadness she still felt then a voice of reason sprang to her mind and she banged her coffee mug down on the granite work surface.

You're just being ridiculous, she thought, there's nothing whatsoever to feel guilty about. Nothing has happened with Alex. It's only your imaginings and daydreams of meeting a man who is quite different from anyone you've ever known. And that was enough to make her feel momentarily off-kilter. The rest of her thoughts yesterday were simply rubbish. She ate her breakfast and then made her way upstairs to dress.

Kim opened the wardrobe and grimaced. It was bound to be warm in the studio again and she deliberately chose her cream shift dress. She slipped the dress over her head and felt her spirits lift. It fitted her long slim body perfectly. Bought recently for a friend's wedding Kim knew the dress wasn't old or casual, and even though she had berated herself earlier for juvenile daydreams, she did want to look her best.

Being tall, Kim always wore flat shoes. A heel meant she towered above some men and most women. At times this made her feel self-conscious about her height. She slipped her feet into plain brown leather sandals and sighed with disappointment. The sandals did nothing to make her overall appearance say, classy professional woman, which was the look she'd been aiming for. Turning from side to side in front of the mirror she fantasised about her feet in dainty stilettos, or maybe even a gold strappy sandal.

Kim had never been too interested in fashion, and especially during the misery of recent years when she'd been content to hang around in old jeans and trainers. In fact, the dress was the first new item she had bought since David's illness began. Not that he would have minded because he often urged her to spend money on herself. 'Go on, treat yourself,' he'd say. 'Buy yourself something nice.'

But that hadn't been important to her at the time.
However, as she picked up her cream handbag to
check the contents, she decided to leave home earlier
than planned and browse the city shops before going
into the studio for ten.

Kim pulled the door closed behind her and stepped
lightly down the three stone steps onto the pavement.

Her neighbour, two doors down called, 'Good
morning.'

Kim stopped at her gate and said, 'It's another
lovely Spring day.'

Her neighbour carefully placed her toddler into his
car seat and strapped him in securely. 'Yeah, it makes
me feel so much more upbeat.'

Kim nodded and put on her sunglasses then
continued down the street. She began humming the
same tune while she walked briskly, enjoying her
light-hearted mood. She determined to have a good
day no matter what it brought.

Nearing the bottom part of the city, Kim walked past
the new Gala Theatre and smiled. This had always
been a wasted area before redevelopment, but now
the beautiful theatre building led on to paved areas
with restaurants and coffee shops overlooking the
river.

It was now known as the trendy place to be in
Durham and Kim liked what the planners had
achieved. She knew Patricia wouldn't agree as she
wanted Durham to remain olde-worlde and not
venture into modernism. Kim wasn't sure whether
this was because Patricia lived in fast-paced London
and liked everything the same when she returned
home to her birthplace. But Kim loved her city with

its mixture of old and new, and knew she'd never want to live anywhere else.

She walked up towards the market square where three building labourers were laying paving stones outside Next clothes store. Kim heard one of them wolf-whistle. Automatically she looked behind to see which young girl was the centre of their attention but seeing only an old man walking slowly with his stick, she realised they must have meant the whistle for her. She grinned at them as she passed by then stopped to look in the side window of the store at the clothes and underwear.

In the centre of the window display was a model dressed in a bright orange bra and panties set. Kim gasped with pleasure at the beautiful colour. It was more like a tangerine shade and after months of dark drab winter colours this made her smile with thoughts of sunshine and the coming summer months.

Kim wondered if other women wore matching sets of underwear because she never had and entered the shop heading to the lingerie section. Fingering the silky material and delicate lace on the half-cup bra, she decided it was the tangerine colour that was capturing her imagination. She thought of her plain black and white sets of bras and panties at home and frowned. She had never, not in all the years she'd been married, bought anything as frivolous then wondered how it would feel to wear something so deliciously feminine.

Tutting under her breath at the very thought of buying them she turned and sauntered into the shoe section to look at the sandals. It's quite ridiculous, she thought, waiting for the assistant to find a pair of sandals in size seven. But while she hovered, picking up different styles of sandals on the shelves, she kept glancing back to the tangerine underwear. She simply couldn't stop herself being drawn to them. Buoyed up by the young assistant's attention and encouragement, Kim slipped her feet into a pair of cream sling-back sandals and decided to buy them.

Twirling the small sandal hanger in her hand, she stole back across the shop to the underwear. Working her way through the rack of bras she found her exact size, 32B. A small voice of sanity niggled in the back of her mind saying, you're not seriously thinking of buying it, are you?

Kim smiled at her reflection in the mirror and imagined the feel of the soft silk on her skin and the delight every time she looked at herself in the vibrant tangerine colour. She picked up a size ten in the matching panties and strode purposefully to the pay desk.

With the price ticket peeled from the bottom of the sandals Kim changed from the plain brown sandals into the new sling-backs. When she strode out of the shop and through the marketplace towards M&S she felt as though she was walking completely different. Her shoulders were pulled back in a confident posture while she gaily swung the carrier bag in her hand.

David had often commented that because she felt self-conscious about her height, she was round-shouldered or slumped. 'You should try to stride forward like a model on the catwalk,' he'd said.

Kim caught her reflection in the glass frontage of Costa coffee, and she realised she was doing just that. The sandals had only a half-inch heel, but they certainly made a vast difference and complemented her dress beautifully. She remembered the saying that a good pair of shoes makes the outfit. And in this instance, she had to agree.

Usually when she worked with Sidney, he would give her a shopping list before they started, and although she knew today was purely to brainstorm ideas, she decided to take a few key vegetables and fruits to put in the centre of the table. She often found it easier to visualise ideas if she had some basics to remind her of their shape and size so bought carrots, green beans, and fruits before walking up to the studio.

Chapter Three

'Hellooo,' Kim called out cheerfully as she entered the studio and paused in reception. She was sure the way she'd reacted to Alex yesterday was simply a figment of her imagination and none of it had happened.

Both Sidney and Alex were in the camera room, and although she could hear their muffled voices, they'd obviously not heard her enter. Quietly, Kim walked through the hall towards the camera room.

The two men were discussing the newly revamped studio and she heard Alex complimenting Sidney. 'High ceilings are vital, and fortunately these old properties in Durham are ideal.'

Sidney nodded. 'Yes, although the place doesn't have a lot of natural light, I find artificial light is sometimes better because at least you can control it.'

Kim approached the door just as Alex was suggesting how a plasma screen, where Sidney could showcase his portfolio images, would make a nice addition to the reception area.

She noticed from the usual layout of the large, airy camera room, that Sidney had put a table in the corner for Alex. Already his tablet and briefcase lay open ready to use. She poked her head around the doorframe, called another greeting and dropped the two carrier bags on the floor near the table.

'Morning to you too,' Alex said from where he sat on the edge of the table swinging his leg casually.

Kim smiled while checking out the black trousers and light grey shirt he wore. She'd forgotten how big this Arnie Schwarzenegger look-a-like actually was.

But now, as she stared at his taut thighs and broad chest, she could feel herself weakening again.

'Been shopping already?' Sidney asked, looking at the bags and fiddling with a connection on the bottom of the camera tripod.

Kim explained how she'd bought packets of carrots, green beans, and broccoli as visual props for their brainstorming ideas.

Alex's eyes danced with amusement and she decided that if he suddenly gave her a wolf whistle as the builders had done earlier, she wouldn't have been surprised.

'Hey, Kim,' Alex said. 'Another warm day on the cards, I think.'

She nodded while lifting a bag of carrots out of the carrier bag and placing them on the end of the table. She could feel Alex's eyes gazing up her dress towards her face and she shuffled her feet in the new sandals. 'Yeah, it's unusual for us to have such warm weather so early in June, but hey, who's complaining?'

Alex jumped off the desk and lifted the other carrier bag from the floor. 'It'll be the same in Scunthorpe,' he said. 'I think a lot of people are getting caught out not having their lighter clothes ready to wear. But I can tell you're not that type of woman and are dressed for summer already.'

Kim felt a little flustered, but happily so, and decided to play along with his teasing. 'Yep, that's me when I was a girl guide our motto was always, Be Prepared.'

Alex placed the second carrier bag on the table and Kim watched in horror to see the Next bag with the tangerine underwear slightly open. The small hanger with the bra straps was visible and she saw Alex look at it then the corners of his mouth twitch. 'Hmm, not only shopping for vegetables I see.'

Kim felt a flush start from her chest, up her neck and continue to her cheeks. She knew they were burning uncontrollably bright red. She grabbed the carrier bag from Alex and folded the inner bag together then cast it under the table just as Sidney joined them.

Sidney, obviously noticing her flushed appearance was concerned and hurried to open the back door of the studio. 'It'll let a little fresh air through,' he said smiling at her.

Kim was mortified to think that Alex had seen the tangerine bra and swallowed hard with a dry throat. What will he think of me? She cast her eyes downwards while fiddling with the handles on the carrier bag. Her previous good humour had vanished, and she cringed at her stupid behaviour. How could she have laid herself open to such ridicule in front of him.

She felt a warm touch on her arm, and she looked up into Alex's eyes. Tilting his head to one side he gave her a big smile and another wink. He'd given a similar wink yesterday and it was having the same steadying influence on her now.

Kim startled as Sidney placed a large bottle of chilled mineral water and three glasses on the table next to her.

'It's going to be warm today,' he said. 'And I'm sure we'll all benefit from cool drinks rather than hot coffee.'

Alex removed his hand from Kim's arm and twisted the cap to open the bottle. 'Aah,' he breathed gratefully. 'Well done, Sidney. This is perfect. I'm parched already.'

The distraction gave Kim a few seconds to compose herself and she pulled her shoulders back. So-what, if he's seen the tangerine underwear, forget about it now and concentrate on the job in hand. In the past, whenever she'd felt undermined in any way, she had relied on her food-styling knowledge and experience to pull her through a difficult situation. And this time, she decided, wouldn't be any different.

Kim gulped greedily at the water to quench her dry throat and began opening the bags of vegetables. She spread the green beans, purple sprouting broccoli and carrots onto the table.

'Well, guys,' she began. 'I've had some thoughts overnight while I was watching TV and was amazed at the new M&S adverts. Did anyone see the Easter adverts with flying liquid chocolate splattering around chocolate eggs, hand painted eggs and then dripping melted chocolate from a whisk?'

She paused as both men shook their heads and looked puzzled.

She continued, 'No? Well, how about the adverts this week for the barbecue season? Last night I watched one where the seasonings and herbs appeared to fly and stick onto the sides of salmon in a fusion of wonderful bright colours. Oh, and there was a row of extra-long matches which were simultaneously lit.'

Alex said, 'Oh, right, yes, I have seen them. The advert I saw had a sauce flowing over chicken drumsticks, covering them gradually from the outer edges inwards. Is that what you mean?'

Kim nodded. 'Exactly, but it was actually a marinade that one would use to soak and infuse the meat with flavourings for a few hours. I know we usually have still shots in our photography, but I do love the basic concept of presenting food in this way. It reminds me of how the sea covers large areas of sand on the beach,' she said and smiled.

Raising an eyebrow at Alex, she asked, 'So, how does that work? Is it simply a case of trick photography?'

Kim watched Alex pull his large shoulders back and she could tell he was delighted to bring his input into the discussion. He explained how easy it was to achieve this appearance while Kim sat quietly on the chair beside the table.

While she listened to him speak, she felt entranced by his fluid movements and mannerisms. She understood what people meant when they said they couldn't take their eyes off someone and felt just as absorbed in him as she had yesterday.

She'd forgotten that Sidney was still in the room until he spoke. 'Look, I'm going to leave you two guys to get on with it as I've a family due soon for a photograph and need to set up. I know Kim asked earlier which common vegetables we should use that would suit all consumers, but for now, if neither of you have any objections, we should sort out the ideas around the three vegetables Kim has brought. Whichever supermarket people choose to shop in nearly everyone buys carrots, broccoli and green beans, right?'

Kim and Alex nodded while Sidney scurried off through the doorway.

Kim looked at Sidney's back and smiled. No one could ruffle or surprise him, and because of his pleasant nature, no one could certainly ever quarrel with him. Sidney was calm to the extent of being laid back. His movements were delicate and precise, which she supposed, was one of the reasons he was such a good photographer.

When Sidney had gone, Kim looked at Alex who wore a quizzical expression of amusement. She could tell he was thinking that Sidney was a fussy nincompoop, which upon first making his acquaintance was an easy mistake to make.

She smiled at Alex, 'He's what some people would call an acquired taste, but his heart is in the right place. And once you get used to his quirky habits and personality, you'll find he is actually okay.'

Alex nodded. 'Yeah, we'll be fine,' he said. 'I don't think we'll ever be best mates, but I'm sure we'll be okay working together.'

'Oh, good,' she said. 'Because I think we're going to have fun working on these ideas and although I'm used to working with Sidney, it's nice to have a fresh voice with different ideas on board.'

Alex grinned. 'Great stuff,' he murmured and stared directly into her eyes. 'However, even though I've no desire to be close friends with Sidney, that doesn't mean I don't want to get to know you a whole lot better. Being close to you wouldn't be any problem whatsoever.'

Kim raised an eyebrow and couldn't help feeling quite giddy and light-hearted at his comments. But

she remembered her earlier embarrassment and
steeled herself.

Pulling a notebook out of her handbag she decided
to keep this meeting on a strictly professional basis.
After all, it was a work contract and Sidney was
paying her a daily rate for her services. There was no
way that these little bits of flirtation should get in the
way of what Sidney would call in his new business
language, the dynamics of the group. She gave Alex a
cautious smile and hoped that would suffice.

'Now then, green beans,' she said and turned her
attention to the vegetables on the table.

Alex muttered, 'Aah, green beans. I was just
thinking about the adverts we talked about. Why
don't we think of some actions or movements that
these vegetables would make because of their shape
and size?'

Kim frowned and pulled on her ear lobe. 'Em, I'm
not quite sure what you mean.'

Alex opened the cellophane packet of green beans
and took one between his large fingers. 'If this bean
were to move at all, what would it look like?'

'Oh, right,' she muttered as suddenly the penny
dropped.

Grinning, she said, 'Could the beans form a type of
matrix or square grid? Or,' she said and picked up a
few beans to criss-cross them. 'Maybe they could
form a ladder?'

Alex whistled in appreciation. 'Fantastic,' he cried.
'That's a great idea. And we could make a bridge out
of them if we trimmed them into smaller identical
lengths.'

She could tell that he was impressed and when she looked up from the table, she caught him staring at her intently. Kim felt an actual shiver run the length of her spine. Apart from being hyped-up and engrossed in the project she was loving every second of being in Alex's company.

When she rattled off ideas that were flying through her mind and he complimented her, she wanted to shout and laugh with joy.

Hardly taking his eyes from hers, Alex began to make a ladder and snapped some of the longer beans to form the centre rungs.

Kim watched his concentration and how he ran the tip of his tongue backwards and forwards over his upper lip. Even though he was the size of a giant bear, this made him look like a small cheeky schoolboy and she couldn't help smiling.

She noticed a spark of recognition in Alex's eyes and thought of how most people would cook the green beans. They would use a pan of boiling water to steam for five to seven minutes. She cried out, 'That's it!'

She hurried to the large cupboard in the back of the room where she knew Sidney kept basic equipment. Returning with a large stainless-steel saucepan, she banged it onto the surface top.

Alex grinned. 'What?' he shouted with excitement. 'What have you thought of now?'

'Well,' she gabbled. 'How about if this ladder could lead up the side of a pan of boiling water and maybe when the beans reach the edge, they throw themselves down into the water?'

'OMG! That is amazing,' Alex cried. 'I love it! I absolutely love it!'

Kim had bought the carrots peeled and cut into both batons and rounds, and getting carried away, she tore open the cellophane bag. Holding two batons in the fingers of her right and left hands she marched the batons across the table. 'Maybe the batons could march to the music of a brass band and the rounds could roll along towards the saucepan as they both pass these purple broccoli stems which would be wafting in a breeze.'

Alex was furiously typing on his tablet as she spoke.

'Of course,' she muttered and waved the broccoli stems in the air, 'I've no idea how we'll create the illusion of movement or breeze in a still shot.'

Alex stopped typing and laid a hand over the top of hers. He squeezed it reassuringly. 'You just leave all of that to me,' he said.

Kim felt as though she was at the funfair, riding a rollercoaster of new ideas and suggestions which ranged from the sublime to the ridiculous. Although Kim knew they'd sift through them all later, she found it difficult to stop her mind from buzzing. But, she thought happily, they had it. They had the basis of the project laid out on the table and she told Alex just that.

With more talks about different vegetables, asparagus, cauliflower, and cabbage leaves, and how they would fit into the development plans, they set an agenda to begin shooting the following day. Kim and Alex left the studio together after calling farewell to Sidney.

***

Kim folded a lengthy shopping list into her handbag and turned to walk away from Alex.

He turned to her and asked, 'Are you going to start shopping now?'

Kim watched him slot a finger through the loop on his jacket and drape it casually over his shoulder. She smiled at his ease. 'Nooo,' she said. 'I'll pick it all up fresh in the morning. It's best to start a shoot with the food as fresh as possible because it's amazing how quickly things can wilt or wane under the lights.'

He nodded. 'Right, well as it's a lovely day and too early to go back and sit in the apartment, I'm thinking of a stroll along the river. I don't suppose,' he grinned. 'Well, do you want to walk with me?'

Kim sighed in pleasure and lifted her face up to the warmth of the sun. There was nothing she'd like more, but she hesitated. Since the embarrassment of the tangerine bra strap earlier she had intended to keep this relationship on a strictly work and professional basis. However, the temptation to spend more time with Alex was excruciating.

She dithered, pulling the strap of her handbag further onto her shoulder. 'Well…'

Alex laughed. 'I haven't asked you to marry me, Kim,' he said. 'It's simply a walk along the riverside.'

She giggled then let her shoulders droop. 'Okay,' she nodded. 'Well, if that's the case, I'd love to.' She moved to his side and walked with him towards the bridge.

Alex began to whistle, and she could see how happy he looked to have her company. It wasn't just Alex who was enjoying himself, because she too recognised an unmistakable spring in her step as they followed each other down the old stone steps to the river.

While they walked, Alex told her how surprised he'd been at arriving in Durham to find it was such a beautiful city. Never having visited Durham before, Alex enthused about the old-world feeling in the marketplace, the narrow lanes, and the cobbled streets. He'd already bought far too many books in the second-hand book shops and had frequented many of the garden cafes and coffee shops.

Kim was delighted to hear his enthusiasm about her hometown and smiled, agreeing that the mixture of old romanticism and the vibrant student atmosphere was a winning combination. They soon reached the bottom of the stone steps.

Kim landed from the last step onto the path and looked down at her new sandals. Feeling quite lightheaded and happy, she wondered if these sandals had been a lucky omen. The river was slow flowing today and she breathed in deeply enjoying the fresh air, and the familiar damp smell of the riverbank.

Alex took her arm and slotted it through his as they walked. She felt quite at ease with him by her side. The short sleeve on her dress meant her skin lay on his bare arm and as they chatted, she could feel the heat radiating from his skin. It was a long time since she'd had any human contact, let alone from an attractive guy.

With Patricia living in London, and her best friend Vicky now living in France, she never had the opportunity to hug family or feel the warmth of someone's embrace. Nevertheless, here she was at only the second meeting with Alex, and already they were linking arms in a comfortable, friendly manner as if they'd been friends for years.

Realising that Alex had asked her how long she'd been food-styling, she replied, 'Oh, for around twenty-five years now, but it's changing all the time. For a long time, food photographs were shot and composed in a manner like the way people were used to seeing and eating their food. It was being laid out on a table and shot from an overhead perspective. We used to arrange the food to appear good from above with the items flat on a plate, clearly separate from each other.'

Alex stopped walking and looked down into her face. 'Really,' he said. 'As a relative newbie to the business I didn't know that.'

She nodded and they carried on walking along the empty footpath. 'Then later we all went through a Vogue type of photography shot with romantic lighting, shallower angles, and we used more props. At the time, you might have heard some photographers calling it food porn...' she paused, watching him raise his heavy eyebrows at the term and giggled then shoved his arm playfully at his teasing insinuation. 'Seriously though, it's not used nowadays,' she continued. 'Now we all concentrate on presenting the food as simple, clean and natural-looking as possible. Sidney will probably advise us to use selective focus, tilting plates, and extreme close ups.'

By now they had reached the frontage of the castle with the cathedral alongside on the hill.

Alex stopped to lift his head and gaze at the scene. 'Marvellous sight,' he said. 'It's a vista I would never tire of looking at.'

Kim nodded, following his gaze. 'You're right there. I have the same view from the other side of the cathedral and even though I look out on it every day, I never tire of it.'

'Yeah, I don't suppose you would,' he said, lowering his gaze into her eyes.

She stared back into his eyes and all her previous warnings and objections seemed to fade away down the river. 'The students with rich parents actually live in the castle now as it's been turned into student accommodation,' she murmured.

Alex nodded, but didn't take his eyes from hers. She felt as though they were boring right inside her and her heart began to thump. Her body filled with desire and longing at the intensity and raw passion she saw in his deep green eyes. She knew he wanted to kiss her as much as she wanted to kiss him. She hesitated slightly praying he would make the first move.

She moved a fraction towards him fighting the urge to throw her arms around his neck and cling to his big solid body. The lingering scent of his aftershave filled her nose as their faces and lips grew nearer and nearer. Only to be abruptly halted by a loud screech of tyre and an urgent cry of warning.

Alex pulled Kim to the side as a boy whizzed past on his racer bike along the inside of the riverside path and yelled the word, 'sorry!' into the air that surged behind him.

She could see Alex's big shoulders relax from the hunched-up position that had been his instant reaction

to imminent danger. His eyes were filled with
concern and he grabbed her hand. 'Are you okay?'

The near miss with the bike had winded her. Or had
it been the closeness to Alex that had caused the
breath to leave her lungs? She gulped and smiled with
relief that it had been nothing more serious.
'Blooming kids,' she muttered.

The moment for kissing had dissolved and she
sensed disappointment around him as he held onto her
hand then raised it slightly against his chest.

This time, it was Kim who felt the close physicality
and she nodded. 'I'm fine,' she reassured him. She
slotted her arm through his again. 'Come on, let's
walk a little further and then we'll turn around.'

He grunted and moved them both to the riverbank
side of the path which Kim knew would be further
away from any more straying bike riders. The sun
shone down upon them between the over-hanging
laurel trees as they continued their comfortable easy
saunter and Kim felt herself tingling with pleasure at
the simple closeness of him.

She let her thoughts wander for a few seconds,
deciding how new it all felt and marvelling at her
need to reach out for him. It felt so incredibly easy.
This was a surprise because her earlier thoughts of
kissing a man who wasn't David, had been daunting.

But earlier, when their faces had moved close to
each other and she'd thought they were going to kiss,
it had been scary but exciting. She had felt so full of
longing that the feelings of desire had dispelled her
anxiety.

David had been the first boy to kiss her in her
second week at university. Before that, when her

sixteen-year-old friends had been experimenting with make-up, kissing boys on dates, and deciding whether they liked cider or larger, she was still reeling from the loss of her parents and clinging to Patricia for normality.

Kim shook her thoughts aside while Alex began to tell her about his twins, Josh, and Jamie.

'Ah, they're great kids,' he sighed. 'But the years after they were born have been difficult in my marriage. I'd tried to cope with what Sally called her post-natal depression, but I had to work long hours to build up my photography business. There were nights when I'd arrive home at seven and find the babies in wet nappies crying for their bottles of milk while she watched TV, saying how it was my turn to do it. I had wanted to scream at her that their needs should come before our petty disagreements and that I was working hard to make money for the family. But instead, I stayed silent, rolled my sleeves up and did the necessary bathing and feeding before cooking our supper. While all the time listening to her irrational accusations that I'd stayed late at work to shag my latest mistress.'

Alex kicked at a stone on the path. 'Sorry, I shouldn't be mouthing off like this when we've only just met,' he said. 'But already, I feel I can talk to you about anything.'

Kim swelled with pleasure at his remarks but noticed the dark shadows under his eyes and his clenched jaw. She could almost feel her heart squeeze in sympathy. 'Nooo, it's fine, Alex, I really don't mind listening.'

Alex smiled his thanks and then grunted. 'Hell, it was laughable really, because even if I'd had a bit on the side, I wouldn't have had the bloody energy to undo my trousers let alone have sex.'

Kim tittered at his sarcasm but could tell how grieved he felt. 'Well, that is grossly unfair,' she said. 'It's not easy being accused of something that you've not, shall we say, had the pleasure of doing.'

Kim wasn't the type of woman to show her feelings easily because in the past all her emotions had been tied into David's. She'd been cocooned in such a solid relationship for most of her adult life that it hadn't been necessary. But now all her senses were full, and she wanted to show Alex how much she cared. She wanted to support and encourage him through this. So, when he looked at her, she smiled and hugged his arm into the side of her body while he talked.

'One night, in a drunken argument Sally admitted that the doctors hadn't diagnosed post-natal depression and that she'd made it all up to keep me at home as much as possible. The tablets she kept in her bedside cabinet were not anti-depressants, just vitamin pills. However, because I was so trusting I'd never had reason to doubt what she told me.'

Kim sighed loudly and stopped on the path. She looked up into his eyes. 'But that's awful.'

'I know, it was,' he sighed miserably. 'That was the night I knew our relationship had deteriorated so much that it became the beginning of the end. I never believed another word she said.'

'Oh, Alex,' Kim soothed. 'What a sorry end to your marriage.'

Alex nodded. 'Thanks for listening,' he murmured and looked down at his feet. 'You're extremely easy to talk to, Kim.'

She loosened her arm from his and rubbed his shoulder. 'That's okay,' she said.

She was extraordinarily pleased at his compliments. She smiled to herself, although she wasn't quite sure how to react to his praise. Praise was something new after being in a long marriage where the need to complement each other wasn't necessary. David had known her, as she knew him, so basic understanding was taken for granted.

Alex took Kim's hand from his shoulder and slotted it through his arm again and they ambled further along the riverside. He brightened as he talked about the boys who were at school now and their achievements. Kim could tell his previous low spirits had lifted back to his amenable self again.

He began to stroke her wrist with his thumb in an upward movement along her bare arm which was linked through his. It was almost as though he was trying to reassure himself that he was doing the right thing and that he needed the comfort of knowing she was still close to him.

Kim felt the hairs along her arm stand up and prickle at his touch. She breathed slowly and deeply trying to understand what was happening to her. How on earth was it possible to feel so close to someone who you'd only just met? And how did her insides feel as if they were melting? He looked so vulnerable, just like a little boy himself.

Alex had such a depth of feeling, which for some reason she would never associate with a big man. Yet at the same time he possessed such gentleness that it nearly took her breath away.

Oh God, I'm definitely falling for him big-time.

Chapter Four

The photographs on the other wall seemed more normal. There were a few shots of Kim's face smiling up into the sunshine and her long bare legs in a white summer dress. She frowned, how had he managed to take those close-up photographs of her legs without her realising?

As Kim struggled through the studio door with three carrier bags in each hand and dropped them to the floor. Sidney popped his head around the door of the camera room.

He'd rang earlier in the morning and told Kim not to come until later as he was looking at the lighting conditions and texture background for the shoot with Alex. They were hoping to have the area ready by eleven to show off the vegetable colours to their best advantage in the light.

Kim stood for a moment resting against the doorframe and heard Alex's low voice while she watched him. This man was the reason why she couldn't sleep last night, she thought dreamily. She smiled because he looked every bit as handsome as when she'd left him at the riverside.

She'd been amazed at how quickly he'd opened-up to her and talked about his marriage and its failings. Most men she had known in David's circle of friends tended to be more restrained and struggled to express their feelings.

However, she reminded herself, Alex was much younger, and she'd read somewhere that modern guys were more forthcoming and easy-going with their feelings nowadays. She smiled, it wouldn't suit his loud gregarious personality to be tight-lipped and reserved. With thoughts of his lips, she stared at his body dressed in black jeans and a white shirt. As he bent over the long wide table with a white backdrop behind, Kim fully appreciated his physic.

She sighed with pleasure and then felt her cheeks flush. Get a grip, you're at work and should know better, she thought. But the longer she stared at him, the stronger the urge to ogle his body became. She listened to the men discussing light source from a soft-box at 60-100cm and knew this was way beyond her knowledge of photography. She decided to make coffee.

When she turned from the door Alex looked up and saw her. His face split into a wide grin. 'Hey, Kim,' he said. 'We're just about ready now. Did you manage to do the shopping?'

'Of course, it's all done,' she said. 'I'm what everyone always calls a resourceful shopper. I got some of the vegetables from the market and others from M&S. The bags are out front. I'll carry them in after I've made the coffee.'

'I'll get them,' Alex declared. He followed her out of the room and hurried over to the six carrier bags on the floor.

Kim smiled and watched him pick up the heavy bags up like weightless balloons after she'd struggled carrying them up from the shops. Quickly, he walked to the corner of the room and stood behind her while she flicked on the switch for the coffee machine.

'I loved our walk yesterday,' he crooned into her ear.

Kim gasped at his presence. She felt his breath on the back of her neck then swallowed hard. 'Y...yes,' she croaked. 'Me, too.'

Kim could feel one of the carrier bags sticking to the back of her leg and then felt the warm glow from his closeness spreading throughout her body. She took a deep breath knowing the understanding they now shared, even though they'd been thwarted from kissing, was clinging around them as if building up into a volcano that was ready to explode.

She heard Sidney's voice calling for Alex from the other room. She shook herself and spooned coffee into the machine while Alex strode back to Sidney.

When Kim carried coffee into the room, they all busied themselves preparing for the shoot. Thankfully, her mind was occupied with preparing the carrots and green beans to look as appealing as possible. Editorial still shots of the vegetables were first taken on a plain black background. Kim arranged six of the Chantenay carrots with their green tops uppermost into an attractive pile all facing in the same direction. She looked at Alex, who smiled and asked her to slice one lengthways and balance it on top of the pile.

'We need to make it look sweet and tender,' he muttered. 'I'm loving the bright orange colour on the black background.'

Alex raised himself up on his toes to take the photographs from above and Kim watched his skill with the camera. She smiled, usually when Sidney lined up overhead shots, he had to stand on a stool but with Alex being so tall that wasn't necessary.

Kim agreed about the colours on the black background and began to pile the green beans with their trimmed ends uppermost in an opposite position to the carrots. She grinned at Alex, as if to say she was on the same wavelength, and one step ahead.

Following this, Kim boiled water in a saucepan and Alex took great pains to shoot the effects of the bubbles. As the afternoon progressed numerous shots were taken, deleted, and re-shot until Alex was satisfied with the images. Kim was amazed at how quickly the time had flown over.

As a food stylist at photo shoots, Kim had long since learned the value of the saying, patience is a virtue. Much of her day was spent waiting around in between shots for the photographers. It was during one of these gaps that Kim had time to think about Alex's work.

She could tell by the way Sidney behaved around Alex that he thought him very clever and excellent at his job. In fact, most of the work that afternoon had been organised and carried out by Alex and her. Sidney had only contributed a small amount to the project.

Hmm, Kim mused, maybe Sidney was doing it this way to test Alex and find out the extent of his capabilities.

At four o'clock Sidney went off for a dental appointment and Kim was left alone with Alex. She carried on arranging the vegetables and Alex continued taking shot after shot to try and translate the appeal of the fresh vegetables into images. By six, with Kim sitting patiently on the stool at the end of the table, Alex looked up from his tablet.

'They're good,' he muttered. 'I think we're done for the day. I'm happy with what we've got so far, but maybe it'll need just a few more tweaks tomorrow.'

Kim straightened her cream pencil skirt and slid down from the stool as elegantly as possible. She rubbed the back of her neck. 'Great, I'm pleased we've got some concrete results from the day's work.'

Kim cleared away the vegetables into black rubbish sacks and rinsed out the saucepan while Alex clicked off his tablet.

'Yeah,' he said, 'I think we've done a brilliant job, Kim. In fact, I think we work well together, and if you'll excuse the pun, we're like two peas in a pod.'

Kim placed the pan in the cupboard and giggled. She closed the door and when she swung around, Alex was standing right in front of her. He caught her hand. 'What are doing this evening,' he asked. 'Have you got plans?'

She gazed up into his eyes and shook her head. 'No, I've nothing arranged. Just a little supper, soak in a long hot bath, and an early night...' she paused then tilted her head to one side. 'Why?'

Alex shuffled from one foot to another and pushed a hand into the pocket of his jeans. 'Oh, I just wondered if you'd like to have dinner with me. We missed lunch and I'm starving.'

Kim smiled. She was still trying to understand how he could transform from a jovial, loud giant when they were in company into a controlled gentle man when they were alone together. She decided that it was a heady combination.

'Well,' Kim hesitated. 'I'm hungry, too. I suppose we both have to eat and it's not much fun eating alone, especially for you on your own in a strange city.'

Alex laughed and placed his hand on her shoulder. 'Okay, I'll repeat what I said yesterday, I haven't asked you to marry me. For once, could you just answer, yes straight away without this charade every time. It's just a meal in a restaurant with a friend, Kim.'

She joined in his laughter. 'I know, it's just that I'm not a very impulsive person. I usually take time to think about things before making decisions.'

'Right,' he said. 'Then I'll make the decision for us both. It's a lovely evening, and I fancy sitting outside at the end of the bridge to eat French food at Cafe Rouge. We can overlook the river as we eat, how about that?'

Kim nodded and pushed an arm through the sleeve of her jacket. She smiled up at him when he lifted the other half of the jacket over her shoulder.

***

After green olives with artisan garlic bread to start, followed by tender Poulet Breton with courgettes, leeks and mushrooms in an herby wine sauce washed down with a bottle of Chardonnay, they both declared themselves fit to burst.

Friendliness and light-hearted laughter mingled throughout their conversation. And when Alex went to the bathroom, Kim decided she was having the most fun she'd had in years.

Alex had told her hilarious stories from his days on the rugby field and afterwards in the pubs, until she had put her hand up and cried, 'Stop! No more, please. My sides are aching with laughing!'

With a gentle evening breeze blowing down the river Kim looked around at other couples sitting by the riverside enjoying their meals together and smiled. She slipped her feet from the cream sling back sandals and wiggled her toes. She felt alive again. And although she would have done absolutely anything for David when he was alive, the misery of recent years had taken its toll. So much so that she'd forgotten how good it felt to laugh out loud and feel upbeat in a man's company.

At one stage, their conversation had reminded her of when she'd first met and fallen for David at university. How their young love and attraction to each other had swept her off her feet. She'd only been eighteen, and was innocent, naïve, and clueless as to how to cope with falling in love.

Now in her late forties, Kim tittered, she should be more worldly-wise, experienced, and know exactly how to cope with meeting a gorgeous new man. But she didn't and felt just as vulnerable as in her youth.

Kim had also seen what she hoped was pleasure in his eyes when she laughed at his reminisces and he continued to entertain her. They both refused dessert and left the restaurant weaving between the tables with his hand on the small of her back. She wanted to hug herself with delight. They walked up through the marketplace arm in arm and before he turned to make his way home, he pulled her into a large jewellery shop's doorway.

Alex glanced from side to side then raised an eyebrow. 'I'm just making sure there's no bike riders this time,' he said and lowered his lips to hers.

The kiss, and she was always to remember that first one of many, was intimate and gentle yet at the same time powerful. She wound her arms around his neck marvelling at the solidness of his body against hers. The taste of garlic and wine mingled while he probed her mouth with his tongue, and she responded greedily with her own.

Gasping for breath, he pulled away and murmured into her hair, 'Oh, Kim, I knew you'd taste good.'

She nibbled his ear lobe and giggled. 'Yeah, we both taste of garlic.'

'Look,' he whispered. 'I have to go home as the boys are ringing at nine and I can't bear to miss their call. I only get to speak to them twice a week and I…' he paused, cupping her face with his huge hands. 'Well, I don't want them to ever think I've no time for them.'

Kim nodded and smiled. 'Of course, you don't. Go talk to them and thanks for dinner, and everything else.'

He gently pecked her on the lips once more. 'Mmm,' he laughed, 'I think I've got the taste of olives now.'

Kim laughed and walked away passing Elvet Bridge in a daze. Once home she stripped off her clothes and pulled on her favourite white cotton pyjamas then wandered from room to room feeling as though she was in a drunken stupor. Although she'd only had two glasses of wine, she felt so deliriously happy it was as though she had drunk two bottles.

Feeling the need to tell someone about what had just happened with Alex, but conscious of the later time in France, she opened her laptop and quickly typed a few lines to her friend, Vicky. Also, Kim thought if she wrote her feelings down in black and white it might help her understand how it had happened so quickly.

Her oldest friend, Vicky had moved to Provence the year before and she still missed her terribly. She'd settled into an old run-down farmhouse with her husband claiming she loved her new life and would never return to Durham. Kim planned to make a three-week trip in September. Vicky had sent beautiful photographs of the market stating that Kim would love the vibrant colours of enormous sunflowers, lavender, and displays of luscious peaches and huge purple aubergines. Kim had practically swooned, imaging herself in the market surrounded by the sights and smells that she had described.

After Kim had explained about Alex and how she felt in the email, she walked into the kitchen to make a mug of hot chocolate. Her hands were trembling, and she split milk across the work surface, but instead of feeling annoyed at her clumsiness she simply grinned and mopped it up. She spooned cocoa powder into a tall glass instead of her china mug and once again giggled because all she could think about was the feel of Alex's body against hers.

Kim decided she might as well go to bed than make more mess in the kitchen, and turning the lights out, she skipped up the stairs to her bedroom. Kim threw the quilt aside, climbed into bed and lay flat on her back staring at the ceiling.

She remembered the kiss and touched her lips where his had been then the passionate desire she'd felt from his tongue exploring her mouth. She remembered the longing that had raged through her and how all her senses had tingled. The considerable size of his body, his sensuous green eyes and what she knew would be firm roving hands, made her squirm around the bed longing for more. After only two days with this hulk of a man, she felt like a teenager again, and hooting loudly she pulled the duvet over her head.

***

The atmosphere between Kim and Alex in the studio was practically on fire. Every time he spoke to her, she read other meaning into his words. When he looked at her, she felt as though he was caressing her body with his eyes. If their hands touched while arranging the vegetables, she felt her insides churn with a strong and powerful longing to be with him. It took every ounce of her professionalism to keep her thoughts and feelings grounded as they worked.

Kim blanched the green beans to keep the green colour bright and they worked out a lattice design, which looked amazing by the time Alex had finished cropping and working his magic on the tablet. This time they used grey slate placemats for the backgrounds to compliment the orange colour and the texture of the carrots. When they'd finished positioning the rounds and batons into a sequence, Kim heard her stomach rumble embarrassingly.

She placed her hand over the waistband of her new white cotton trousers. 'Excuse me,' she giggled. 'I missed breakfast this morning and my body clock is saying feed me. Shall I nip out and bring us some sandwiches?'

Alex raised an eyebrow. 'Yeah, I'm hungry too, but I could do with a break. Let's pop down to Costa and grab a sandwich in the café. The change of scene will help clear my mind.'

They turned and looked towards the door as Sidney appeared nursing his jaw. Kim grabbed her white cardigan and nodded to Alex while she listened patiently to Sidney give a full-blown account of his dentist's handiwork and how he was suffering. Kim told Sidney they were popping out for lunch and offered to bring him soup, at which he pouted, but thanked her for being thoughtful.

***

They hurried out into the sultry heat as a drizzle of rain began and practically ran down the road to the café.

Once inside and waiting at the counter to be served, Alex grumbled. 'I couldn't bear to listen again to that whole sorry saga of the dentist from Sidney. He rang me last night after I left you pretending to ask how the day's work had gone. But I could tell all he wanted was someone to whinge at about his tooth extraction.'

'Hmm, maybe he's going to be your new bosom-buddy after all,' Kim teased.

Alex grimaced and placed their order while she secured a table in the back of the café. At one o'clock the café was busy with lunchtime customers surrounded by their shopping bags cramped under the few tightly spaced tables. Kim could tell it was going to be a close fit for a man as big as Alex.

Just then a tinkle on her mobile alerted a new email. It was from Vicky. Kim skim-read her words, 'I've just read your email from last night. Go for it, girl!'

Kim grinned at her friend's carefree words and looked up to see Alex carrying a tray with tea and cheese salad sandwiches to the table. Kim moved along the bench for him to squeeze in beside her, and while they ate hungrily, Kim watched his every move.

She stared at his full lips, remembering the feel of them on her own last night. Her lips were much thinner than his, but whatever the size or shape they did seem to fit together perfectly. Alex was talking about his best friend at school and how much he'd missed him when he immigrated. And although Kim was still listening to him, she was fighting the urge to run a finger along his bottom lip or kiss him.

Alex stopped eating and grinned. He picked the paper napkin up from his plate and wiped his mouth. 'What, have I slopped something?'

She smiled and felt her cheeks blush. 'Nooo,' she said, trying to cover up for staring at him. 'I was just wondering how you can eat and talk so quickly at the same time.'

He paused then nodded. 'Yeah, I've always been guilty of that. When I was little my dad used to say, hold your horses, there's two prizes. Which I think was his way of telling me to eat slower or to shut up.'

Kim giggled. 'I can just imagine you as a little boy. I bet you were a right handful.'

Alex grinned. 'Well, the word little never really came into my childhood. From the day I started school I was bigger than every other boy in the class. And my size was more of a burden to me…' Alex paused and twirled the napkin between his fingers. 'When I was a teenager, two of what we used to call 'bad boys' befriended me. At first, I was amazed and flattered that they'd chosen me from the class to be in their gang. But then I realised I'd only been chosen for my size so they could use me as a bargaining tool to threaten the smaller boys to get what they wanted.'

Kim sighed and gave him an understanding nod. 'Not good,' she murmured.

'I know,' Alex said and shrugged his big shoulders. 'I'd been hurt and confused, but I knew even then that bullying wasn't for me. And I also knew how disappointed my dad would be. So, I left the gang and did my best to make it up to the few quieter boys that I'd obviously scared. I began to hate being big and could only see it as a major disadvantage in life until Dad threw me into the rugby club where I learned to use it to my advantage and didn't feel so out of place.'

Alex sucked his cheeks in and shook his head as though shaking the memories from his mind. 'So, come on,' he said, 'that's enough about me. I want to know all about you and your home life.'

It was warm in the café and Kim could feel her white cotton shirt sticking to her back. His body was close to hers and when he sat back then half turned towards her, she shuffled on her seat.

'Well, there's not that much to tell really,' she smiled.

His right thigh pressed against hers and although the material of her cotton trousers wasn't thin, she could feel his warmth penetrating through his jeans and onto her leg. She moved an inch away, but Alex wormed his way closer to her.

He tilted his head slightly, as if to say, you're not getting away from me that easily. It was as though he could read her mind through the slightest of actions. The raise of an eyebrow, that cheeky wink he often gave her, and the smile that seemed to penetrate her deep inside.

Alex sighed playfully. 'Surely after last night you're not still shy about talking to me?'

Kim felt a little lost at their closeness and was struggling to cope, whereas Alex seemed to be perfectly at ease. She took a deep steadying breath. 'No, of course I'm n…not,' she stuttered then tried to push her feelings aside and make normal conversation.

He scrunched the empty sandwich packet and smiled. 'I'm not asking about David, which I know is understandably still hard for you to talk about. I was wondering about your life before him.'

A waitress approached the table to clear the debris away. Kim began to tell him about her childhood and how her parents had been killed in a car accident when she was sixteen and Patricia was eighteen.

Alex squeezed her hand in his. The waitress thumped a tray onto the table and clinked the empty mugs when she picked them up. He interrupted Kim, 'Come on,' he said. 'I'm feeling claustrophobic in here. Let's walk back up slowly and you can tell me the rest.'

Kim was pleased to follow him out of the café because it had stopped drizzling and she welcomed the fresh air after the oppressive atmosphere in the café. He took her hand again and happily swung it backwards and forwards while they walked up the road.

'Well, there's not much else to say really,' she said, getting into her stride. 'Patricia looked after us both in our family home in Sherbourne, which is just outside Durham. She finished her degree in psychology at the university and then I started at Durham technical college doing A Level in Domestic Science before going on to university and the Home Economics course. Neither of us have had any children so there is just the two of us. She's all the family I have.'

'Okay, and does she still live in Sherbourne?'

Kim shook her head. 'Oh no, she married years ago and moved to London just after I got engaged to David. But she gave up her job and her husband five years ago. Now she writes crime novels.'

They had reached the studio doors and Alex whistled through his teeth. 'Wow, that's impressive.'

Kim turned the door handle and Alex placed his hand over the top of hers. 'I don't feel as if there's been enough time for us to get to know each other because I really want to find out all about you, Kim. I want to know every detail as soon as possible,' he said, squeezing her hand as he pushed open the door. 'But it will have to wait until later because we now have the illustrious Sidney to deal with.'

'Oh no!' Kim cried. 'I've forgotten the blooming soup!'

The afternoon progressed and just as Kim felt that if she had to arrange another cabbage leaf into position she would scream, Sidney called a halt.

Sidney had bookings for passport photographs and other minor commitments up until six and needed to clear the camera room. It was just after four when Kim and Alex left the studio.

***

Kim turned right and called goodbye. Alex turned left doing the same. Inside she felt heavy with disappointment because she'd hoped he would ask her out for dinner again. Maybe he has other plans, she thought and tried to remain cheerful. But at the same time, she felt such a sense of discontent that it shocked her.

She remembered their lunch and how she'd shuffled away from him on the bench. Kim knew that she could often give the impression of being indifferent and somewhat cold towards people without meaning to do this. She took a few steps up the road and kicked at a stone thinking about her indifference. In the past, on a couple of occasions when she'd had unwelcome attention from men, one look or the raise of her shoulders had been enough to let them know she wasn't interested.

Of course, she hadn't meant that with Alex, she'd simply been trying to pull herself together with the intimate feelings that were overwhelming her. She hoped he didn't think that she wasn't attracted to him now. Although it hadn't seemed to deter him, in fact, all it had done was to make him more determined as he'd moved in even closer.

Wanting to have one more look at him, she turned around and watched him walk with his head bent down the side path.

At the same time, he stopped and turned back to look at her.

She lifted her hand to wave, and he took a quick step forward.

Was he coming back to her?

She smiled and took a step forward towards him.

Suddenly he was grinning and hurrying back up the path to her.

Oh, thank you, God, she breathed and quickly scurried back down the path.

Alex weaved between people on the cobbles as did she, until they reached each other then throwing all caution aside she flung her arms around his neck and clung to him.

'I didn't want to leave you,' he muttered into her hair. 'It seemed forever until tomorrow morning when I'd see you again.'

She breathed in the scent of his body in her arms. He felt so solid and so incredibly sexy that there wasn't a doubt left in her mind. She had to be with him. She curled her fingers through his hair and clung to him feeling his urge press against her stomach.

'Oh, Alex,' she murmured. 'I can't stop thinking about you.'

He stood back and held her hands in his. 'Me, too,' he moaned. 'Come home with me, please?'

She nodded then laughed as he grabbed her hand and practically ran down the path and up to his flat as though the devil himself was behind them.

Giggling and breathing hard they ran into the hallway to his apartment. She caught her breath and was about to offer comments on the neutral décor when he placed an arm under her knees and another around her waist and swooped her up into the air.

'This is the only way to take a beautiful lady to my bed,' he declared.

She began to laugh and mildly protest but when she saw the raging passion burn in his eyes, she too was overcome with the same longing. The laughter left her lips as she stared up at him when he placed her gently on the bed and towered above her.

He looked down at her and sighed. 'Beautiful. Elegant. Sophisticated, in fact,' he said opening the buttons on her shirt. 'Everything I could ever wish for in a woman.'

'Alex, it's a long time since I've...' but her words were halted when he covered her mouth with his and totally swept all logical thought from her mind.

Chapter Five

*Saying goodbye as one door closes, and another
door opens to new beginnings*

'Oh, David,' Kim breathed softly. She was huddled
up in her husband's red leather armchair wearing her
pyjamas and his old herringbone dressing gown with
her knees tucked under her chin. The chair was in the
bay window where David had loved to sit looking out
over the castle and cathedral. She ran her hand along
the arm stroking the old leather and thinking about
him. They'd never tired of the view, as she'd already
told Alex, and it was the main reason they'd bought
the house when they were first married.

She had been in the same position for over an hour
after leaving Alex in his apartment and insisting on
returning to her own house. He'd begged her to stay
the night, but she had refused, claiming she needed
clean clothes for the early start in the studio next
morning. This excuse was true, but the main reason
was to say goodbye to David.

Before David died, they'd had the same
conversation that most couples would have when they
knew one of them was leaving the marriage. He'd
wanted her to be happy with someone else. Choked
with grief, Kim had obstinately shaken her head,
refusing to agree to his request. She'd thought at the
time, and since, that she would never again have
feelings for another man. That was until three days
ago when her life had been turned upside down by
Alex.

Patricia had once said. 'I hope you meet a nice, older, guy-next-door type, and in years to come re-marry.'

Kim had agreed with her sister, that in time that scenario might be a possibility, but never in her wildest dreams had she thought she'd meet and be swept away by a younger man like Alex.

Kim sighed, knowing that she would never miss David again with that deep dull ache, as though some part of her had been wrenched away. Now she felt like a whole woman again. Nevertheless, in a strange way David seemed nearer to her now than he had ever been. She shivered and felt tears pricking her eyes. She knew her late husband would be happy for her and tried to find solace in this.

A few months after the funeral Sidney had stressed that David would have hated to see his wife so stricken with grief. And in a state of mind that she'd seemed on the point of losing the will to live. At the time, although Kim agreed with Sidney, she had struggled to drag herself out of the quagmire because of her guilt.

From the day the consultant had asked David how long he'd had his symptoms and her husband had confessed that it was just before Kim went to see the gynaecologist, she'd been stunned. First, that David hadn't told her about the blood in his urine, and second, that being a medical man himself he'd done nothing about it. His excuse had been that he'd been so concerned about her results, before and after the hysterectomy, that he hadn't wanted her to worry until she got the all-clear for cancer cells. This statement had tortured her until the day he died.

Patricia had tried to console her during this time, 'But, Kim, the guilt is not yours to carry around! David was an educated man, and you were not responsible for his actions. And, furthermore, I think he was selfish to shift the culpability onto you.'

Nevertheless, it hadn't really helped Kim when she'd struggled with the knowledge that David had loved her so much, he'd put her wellbeing before his own illness. And she'd felt this way until a few days before David died.

In his most vulnerable state when he knew the end was near, he'd admitted his symptoms had started a full year before her treatment. He'd grabbed her fingers between his own trembling hands and with tears in his eyes had admitted to being too scared to seek help. David had chosen to bury his head in the sand. They had wept together at this confession and Kim had felt relief at finally knowing the truth.

Her thoughts and feelings in the months after the funeral had been troubled. Kim had always thought they were a close couple who had no secrets from each other, but she sighed now, she'd been proven wrong in this belief.

It still bothered her that if she'd known about his symptoms from the start, she might have been able to persuade him to act. When she mentioned this to Sidney, who had known David as long as she had, he'd disagreed and shook his head. 'But David had been his own man and would only have done what he wanted, Kim.'

She wiped the tears from her face with the sleeve of his old dressing gown and glanced down at the wedding ring on her finger. She used her thumb to

roll the ring around which was a habit she'd started
after David's death. It always reminded her of their
happy wedding day and honeymoon.

Kim walked over to the mantelpiece and picked up
his framed photograph. 'It's time, David,' she
whispered. 'It's time to let go.'

She saw the happiness and zest for life shining in his
eyes and felt as if he was saying, go for it, Kim. She
decided that the ability to love life and everything it
possessed had been her dead husband's gift to her.

A feeling of peace washed over her. She had the
overwhelming sense that David was close to her. That
he was standing behind her with his hand on her
shoulder making her feel she was doing the right
thing. She held up her hand and removed the wedding
ring from her finger to keep in her jewellery box.
Switching out the lights, she mounted the stairs
knowing that tomorrow she would throw out all
David's belongings. She would cancel the magazine
and ditch his old chair.

***

The next morning, when Kim stepped out of the
shower, a text tinkled on her mobile. It was from Alex
to say he would call in thirty minutes to have
breakfast together before going to work.

In a complete scramble, she dressed in seconds,
blow-dried her hair, and hurried into the kitchen.
Thoughts of the previous night flooded her mind as
she lifted eggs, milk and butter out of the fridge.

The act of making love itself had been amazing and
she knew it would be a memory she would treasure.
They'd torn the clothes from each other in a frenzy as

though they were stopping each other from joining together in the most natural way possible.

Kim had been right about his confident roving hands and powerful body. She'd clung to this throughout her passionate drive to reach blessed release. She had dug her fingers into his thick shoulders and cried with relief at the intense climax and all the fantastic feelings associated with it.

Afterwards, she had lain sated in his arms and looked at their naked bodies entwined. She'd briefly felt self-conscious about the hysterectomy scar across her abdomen. But Alex had listened carefully while she told him about the necessary operation and how David had been so worried that he'd ignored his own symptoms. Which had turned out to be prostate cancer.

Alex had run his big hand along her scar and soothed her troubled thoughts. 'But it's just like the operation scar on my ankle, except yours is on your belly.'

The sound of the front doorbell startled her now and she hurried along the hall to greet him. Before she opened the door, she caught sight of the cricketing journal and quickly covered it with her food magazine before opening the door.

Alex bounded over the front step and threw his arms around her, practically lifting her off the carpet. He was wearing a pale green polo shirt and black jeans. She swooned against his chest nuzzling her face into his shoulder. He looks gorgeous, she thought and instantly felt desire build up inside.

Carefully he set her feet back down onto the carpet. 'What a lovely sight you are. Freshly scrubbed and minty toothpaste breath,' he murmured hovering his lips over her mouth without actually kissing her. 'I missed you last night.'

She clung to him with her arms still around his neck and tried to be as candid as he was being. 'And you look gorgeous in that green shirt,' she whispered.

She felt his warm breath over her lips and wanted to kiss him so badly that it gave her an ache way down in the pit of her stomach. She inhaled deeply and noticed the black stubble on his chin. He hadn't shaved. 'The only thing missing is your aftershave?'

Alex pulled back and nodded. 'Well last night you said you'd never kissed a man with a beard. And because I get sick of shaving, I thought I'd grow a beard to see if you like it.'

'Hm, that's nice...' Kim paused then grinned. She was pleased he'd remembered her saying this and that he wanted to grow the beard just for her.

His eyes sparkled while he stared into hers. 'Oh, Kim, I want you to experience new and exciting things all the time you're with me,' he murmured, burying his face in her hair. 'And, although I'm longing to throw you back onto these stairs and make love to you again, I'm restraining myself because I am a guest in your home.'

Kim giggled and stood back remembering her own manners. 'Yes, of course you are, and I'm keeping you out here in the hallway,' she said then waved her arm in a dramatic swoop. 'I'll give you the guided tour.'

She took his arm and walked him slowly along the hall. 'Maybe I should pretend to be an estate agent when I show you round,' she laughed.

Alex raised an eyebrow. 'You can pretend to be anyone you like, Kim. I'm always up for a bit of play-acting. Anytime you want to dress up. . .' he paused and teased her with a knowing look, 'you just feel free.'

Kim lowered her eyes. She didn't want to stare back at him because she knew that he'd make love to her there and then.

Her stomach fluttered with excitement, but she struggled to retain a modicum of sobriety then wondered if she was always going to feel like this in his company. She cleared the rasp from her throat and continued, 'So, Alex, this is the large entrance with burgundy carpet, original cornices and high skirting boards. As you will see, the wealth of original features continues throughout the house.'

Alex began to walk towards the lounge door with her and they entered the large double aspect room. She heard him catch his breath in awe when they walked in and light flooded through both windows. Kim's natural pride in her home took over while she described the mosaic tiled fireplace, the furniture and colour scheme David had chosen. She explained how her husband had been determined to make the most of the light in the room.

Alex walked to the window and stood behind David's chair to look at the view of the cathedral while she continued to describe the antique pieces of furniture David had bought in auction rooms.

She turned and walked through a door into the far corner which was now her study but had been David's. She talked about the antique desk, the huge picture he'd chosen to hang over the fireplace and the classic sage-green colour scheme. As she passed the old desk, she stubbed her toe on the oak leg which jutted out and cursed softly under her breath.

She lifted her foot and slipped off the sandal to rub her toe. 'I don't know how many times I've done that over the years,' she said. 'You'd think my poor little brain would be used to its position by now.'

Alex was beside her in an instant full of concern. His eyes roamed over her foot. 'Have you hurt yourself?'

She smiled. 'Nooo, I'm fine. I've just stubbed my toe.'

'Well, if you moved the desk round into the other corner of the room it wouldn't stick out,' he suggested. 'I could move it for you.'

Kim felt a moment of panic at the thought of changing anything in the room, and although she knew she was being ridiculous, and it was a good suggestion, she chewed the inside of her cheek. 'I'm n...not quite sure,' she stuttered. 'David always liked it there.'

She could hear the pathetic whine in her voice. Her sister and Vicky would shake their heads and roll their eyes with exasperation at her resistance to any type of change. But this was Alex, Kim reminded herself and last night she had decided it was time to start again and let go.

Alex took her hand and squeezed it firmly. 'I can see that this is where David liked the desk, Kim. But where would you like it to stand?'

Kim took a deep breath and nodded. He took hold of the desk and pulled it easily across to the other side of the room. She watched his muscles flex under his shirt and the power in his arms as he manoeuvred the desk into position. She realised that Alex possessed the strength of two men.

Kim looked at the dents in the carpet where the legs of the desk had stood for years and felt a tremor of apprehension spread up her back making her shiver.

She watched Alex straighten up and turn towards her. 'In fact,' he said. 'All I've heard since we started walking around the house is what David liked, what he wanted, and how he chose everything...' he paused then crossed the room to join her. 'But what do you like, Kim? Do you like this heavy old furniture? Are these the colours you would choose in the house, given a blank canvas.?'

Alex's words pulled her up short and thoughts whirled around in her head. She remembered when they first moved in and how they'd planned the rooms and the renovation. She tried to remember if any of the ideas they had decided upon had been hers, or were they all David's? Had she always gone along with her husband, agreeing to everything that he'd wanted?

Alex rubbed her arm and she nodded which brought her mind back to the present and to him.

'Well, maybe without knowing it, I did allow David carte blanche in the house. But I did like all his ideas at the time. However, times change,' she mused. 'As does décor and fashion, but I can see what you're saying.'

Alex cupped his big hands around her cheeks and grinned. 'I hope I haven't upset you by saying that. It's just that when I see you at work with food and watch you shape and develop groups of colours and sizes together, I'm amazed at your ability to think outside the box with new ideas,' he said. 'But here in this house, I can't see you anywhere. I can't see your vision or your ideas in any of these rooms.'

Kim gulped as his words began to sink in. He was right and she had to agree with him. There was none of her flair and creativity anywhere in the décor or soft furnishings. She had been so intent on keeping her life with David sacred and untouched that she hadn't given any thought to her own preferences.

A thought came to her mind and she smiled up into Alex's face. 'Ah, well come this way because there is one room which is totally my domain, the kitchen. David had no input there at all.'

They sauntered into the kitchen while she described the mixture of old Victorian characteristics combined with contemporary design with the island in the centre of the room and the breakfast bar with high stools. Black granite work surfaces gleamed, and the large American-style fridge-freezer stood proudly in the far corner.

'Now that's more like it,' Alex breathed in her ear. 'This is you. I can picture you here cooking and working with your usual style and aptitude.'

Kim sighed with relief. They were back on track and she felt her spirits lift. In a way, Alex was only saying what Vicky and Patricia had said to her over the last fourteen months. She sighed and shook herself, park up your feelings until later, she thought and feed the man his breakfast.

Over scrambled eggs on toast and freshly brewed coffee, they chatted about the house and Alex enthused about the views over the cathedral. He loved the size and grandeur of the large airy rooms. Kim admitted to being initially shocked at his words earlier but agreed with everything he'd said and promised that she would make plans for home improvements to include her taste and preferences. She felt more relaxed and reassured when they talked things over, because more than anything else Alex understood how grief had muddled her judgement.

Kim explained how she loved to cook and try new recipes when David was alive and how she would host dinner parties for their friends. They had mainly been couples and over the months since his death those friends had drifted away. Now she hardly heard from them at all.

'I suppose being the grieving widow didn't quite work with odd numbers around the dining table. David's chair was obviously empty, which for some reason caused an awkward atmosphere,' she explained. 'A couple of the women actually looked embarrassed for me and, after the last dinner I cooked, my guests made hasty exits with feeble excuses, I decided it would be the last.'

Alex frowned and shook his head in dismay. 'Well, they can't have been such good friends, or they would have supported you no matter what,' he said and gave her a hug.

After breakfast they left the kitchen and Kim glanced into the study, noticing the space by the window where the desk had always stood. This was the first change. Although there would be many more to come, she knew it wouldn't feel half as daunting with Alex by her side.

Chapter Six

Once in the studio it was agreed they would steadily work their way through the vegetable section of editorial shots before starting a new product. Every time Kim had a few moments to herself she hugged herself with happiness.

It was an odd feeling, not new of course, because she'd had many happy years married to David, but she knew her feelings for Alex were growing by the hour, if not the minute. She would sometimes catch him staring at her, or when he was absorbed with a shot, she would take time simply to watch him.

Sidney, having recovered from the dental surgery, was also more active with the project that morning. He stood beside Kim chatting while she trimmed cauliflower florets, huddling the pristine white clusters together for the overhead shot. They discussed mutual friends and he enquired after Patricia, saying he hoped she would soon be coming for a visit. Kim told him there were no definite plans while she arranged the purple sprouting broccoli onto the grey slate placemats.

'I'm not keen on these colours together,' Kim told Sidney and Alex. 'The stems have more of a purple hue than green, which doesn't look as vivid against the grey background as the green and orange colours.'

Both men came to the table where she was working and agreed.

'How about switching it to green broccoli?' Alex suggested.

Kim readily agreed and gave him a winning smile, to which he placed his hand on her shoulder and squeezed gently. Out of the corner of her eye she saw

Sidney staring at them and she swallowed hard. Had he noticed their closeness? She supposed it must be obvious by now and made a mental note to talk to him about Alex later that day.

Just as she offered to go out to the shops to buy green broccoli, Sidney pulled on his jacket and headed towards the door.

'I need to get some more milk,' he muttered. 'So, I'll get the broccoli while I'm out.'

Kim nodded and turned her attention back to the cabbages in front of her. As she began to strip the outer leaves and rub off the soil residue from the inner leaves, Alex startled her by wrapping his arms around her waist. She could feel him behind her, pushing into the small of her back. He began to nuzzle her ear lobe.

'Alex!' she protested, 'Not here at work. I know Sidney's gone out, but anyone could walk into the studio.'

He groaned. 'We'd see them come into reception, darling. Anyway, I can't help it. Its torment being so close to you and not being able to touch you. I keep thinking about last night and how we made love. I can't wait to be with you again.'

Kim let herself go and swooned against his chest for a moment, feeling his strong body and wanting the same. While he nibbled her ear lobe and drew his lips down the back of her neck, feelings of desire flooded through her at an alarming rate. She threw her head back to rest against his chest. 'Oh, God,' she moaned with pleasure.

His hands roved over her stomach and her mind was soaring. She was caught up and away with the feelings raging inside her until she felt quite light-headed. His breath was hot on her neck and his lips were firm as he kissed her skin. Was she back in his bed last night or just remembering it? She thought of how he'd made love to her with such passion and intensity. The smell of their bodies writhing together and his devouring mouth which had relentlessly covered her whole body until she'd practically cried out for mercy.

Now, the same powerful cravings were begging to be released again and her knees trembled against him. She felt her whole-body weaken and knew he was holding her firmly against him for fear she would slump to her knees.

'Look,' he breathed into her ear. 'I've an appointment at the solicitors' at four this afternoon, so I'll be leaving early, but please come to mine later so we can be together.'

The studio door opened, and Alex stepped back, but waited until she had grabbed the table edge to steady herself. Startled at the state of her usually composed body, she leant forward and took slow, deep breaths, willing her trembling legs to steady again.

It took a few minutes for her to regain her balance and she sighed with relief then hurriedly began arranging the cabbage leaves on the placemat just as Sidney came back into the room.

Kim saw Alex wink at her and found it impossible not to grin at his cocky self-assurance. She couldn't believe how her body had reacted. How every inch of her usual dependable self-control had disintegrated at the mere touch of his hands to such an extent that she'd been left in a quivering heap.

Staring at his back while he talked to Sidney, Kim decided, there was an infectious energy in his demeanour which at times, Kim had to admit she found overwhelming. He was quite simply, irresistible.

When Alex left for his appointment with the solicitor, Sidney brought two mugs of coffee to the table and insisted she join him. She had hoped to leave soon after Alex because she wanted to go home and prepare herself for tonight. But she knew it was only right to give her old friend an explanation about what was happening, and although she was technically self-employed, for this assignment Sidney was her boss.

She slipped onto the chair and crossed her legs. The room seemed too quiet since larger- than-life Alex had left and she felt awkwardness in the silence which seemed to wrap itself around her and Sidney. Picking up her coffee, she sipped then wrapped her long fingers around the mug as though hoping to draw comfort from it.

'I can see how well you and Alex are getting along together,' Sidney began cheerfully. 'I'm really pleased because at first I did have my concerns. For years now it's been just you and me working together and I wasn't sure how an extra body would fit into our little partnership.'

Kim smiled thinking of Alex's body which was having such an effect on her. She wondered if he were a nine-stone weakling would she still find him so attractive? She started as Sidney said her name loudly, and realised she'd been lost in thought again.

'Oh, sorry,' she muttered, dragging her mind back to Sidney. Get a grip, she remonstrated, you're making a fool of yourself.

'Yes, Sidney,' she agreed. 'We are getting along very well. I find him easy to work with and we seem to think along the same lines, especially when it comes to the photography. And I should add a personal note too because in a different way to me, he has suffered his own personal tragedy. Which I can well relate to and we seem to be on the same wavelength.'

She watched Sidney fiddle with the pink cravat at his neck and looked at him properly for the first time in days. He looked as if he had lost weight and there were dark circles under his beady grey eyes. The cream linen jacket he always wore in summer was badly creased as though it hadn't been ironed for months. Although in the past he'd often resembled a dapper, well-groomed professor, now his image looked more down and out. How long had he looked like this and why hadn't she noticed? Or maybe it was the case these changes had happened so gradually that she simply hadn't noted the exact time when his appearance had begun to deteriorate.

'Well,' he said, sipping at the coffee, 'I can see that Kim. Nonetheless, I think you should take care. You are, might I suggest, still in a vulnerable position as a new widow.'

Kim raised an eyebrow at the antiquated words, but knew this was just Sidney being Sidney, and the way he was. Although he was an old friend, she didn't want to tell him about the intimate side of her relationship with Alex, or indeed, how they had become close in many ways. Not yet at least.

She took a deep breath. 'Sidney, it's fourteen months since I lost David, and you, along with everyone else for that matter, have done nothing but push at me to start a new life. So, that's all I'm doing by making new friends. And, by the way, at this stage that's all Alex is, a good friend.'

Sidney licked the wet coffee from the bottom of his coarse moustache. 'True. I want to see you make new friends too. But there's…' Sidney paused and ran his hands down the side of his brown corduroy trousers. He avoided her eyes and stared at the tripod in the corner of the room. 'Well, there's something not quite right about Alex.'

At her obvious protest, he held a hand up in warning. 'Just let me finish, Kim. I can't quite put my finger on it, but there is definitely something amiss with him.'

Kim felt herself bristle with indignation at first because Sidney dared to say derogatory things about Alex, and then with trepidation in case he was going to tell her something dreadful about the big man she'd fallen for so quickly.

She nodded. 'So,' she whispered, trying to calm the anxious feelings prickling up her spine. 'Have you any facts or proof to substantiate this feeling?'

Sidney hedged. 'No, as I said, it's just a feeling I've got.'

Kim breathed a big sigh of relief and sat back in the chair dropping her shoulders. She looked to the side of the table and down at the brown Jesus sandals that Sidney wore and how one of his brown socks had a hole in the toe. He's definitely not himself, she thought, and knew out of respect for his longstanding friendship with David she should be concerned.

She asked, 'Has it anything to do with the fact that Alex is separated from his wife and has left his family in Scunthorpe?'

Kim asked the question because she thought Sidney might have heard something more than Alex had told them and it could be his marital status that was making him wary. Or in Sidney's old-fashioned strait-laced world where he lived, this separation could be construed as desertion of two small boys who need their father.

Sidney tutted and laid a hand over hers on the table. 'No, Kim, it's nothing to do with that. I can't explain it, but you know I'm generally good at judging people's characters, and on this occasion, something is making me cagey,' he said. 'Be watchful, that's all I ask.'

Kim nodded but at the same time she wanted to tut with indignation. The stickiness of his palm on hers made her stomach heave and she withdrew her hand quickly then made her excuses to leave.

Chapter Seven

Alex breezed his way down the street towards the solicitor's office. He'd made the appointment a few days ago for an update on the status of his separation and divorce proceedings. Previously, all dealings with the solicitors had filled him with wary trepidation and flattened his spirits, but today he didn't think anything could do that.

After being with Kim the night before and with anticipation of more to follow this evening, he felt buoyant and upbeat. Kim was certainly a surprise, he thought crossing the bridge and meeting someone like her was a dream come true.

At first, he'd been delighted to get the job with Sidney because photography-based roles were scarce in Scunthorpe and he needed the permanency of a monthly salary to start his life anew. His long-term ambition was to have his own studio and be in a similar position as Sidney with loyal clients and a good reputation as a photographer.

Alex thought about the shots he'd taken earlier and smiled; this new area of food photography had all his senses on alert and ideas filled his mind constantly. Although this shoot was for specific vegetables, while he'd worked, he imagined broccoli positioned and shaped into trees, courgettes shelled-out into boat shapes and mushrooms made to look much bigger than they were and in a dark eerie forest. The possibilities in this new area of work were endless and he whistled as he walked, feeling happier than he had in months.

Meeting Kim so soon after moving to the new city was a bonus. He smiled and hoped she was not only going to be a partner who he would enjoy spending time with, but also a worthwhile contact for future photography assignments. Walking up the incline towards the solicitor's office he thought of her and grinned. She was clever, attractive, and could tell by the way she handled Sidney's somewhat bizarre personality that she was also very kind-hearted.

Stopping outside the office doorway, he remembered his surprise at her reactions last night in bed. He had known from the minute they'd met that she was attracted to him and he'd felt the same too, but during the first few days they'd spent in each other's company, he was expecting her to be timid and reticent when making love.

Kim had mentioned her age and the fact that she was eleven years older than him a few times. He could tell it was preying on her mind, but he'd assured her that age didn't matter to him one iota. Not only did she have the body of a thirty-year-old, but she also had such a young outlook in life that he never noticed the age difference.

Alex also knew how difficult it must have been for her to make love to another man after the death of her husband, and he'd tried his hardest to make it easier for her. However, once she had relaxed, she'd thrown herself at him with enormous gusto and during their second slower session she had been amazing.

Alex felt himself stiffen with the thought of her long lean body and her skinny legs that wrapped around his back in a vice-like clamp. He remembered her flushed happy face after she'd climaxed then just now after their little close-up in the studio, and he grinned. He figured she was eager for more tonight. Shaking the thoughts from his mind he entered the solicitor's office and took a seat in reception to await his appointment.

The busy young receptionist was typing quickly, and Alex glanced round at the bland décor in the small room. He wondered if his solicitor had a reply from Sally's lawyers. And if so, he prayed it was good news because he was desperate to have his visitation with the boys finally sorted out. When it was then he could set dates in his calendar and arrange to do special things with them.

From the day they arrived in the world he'd felt what everyone called unconditional love which often overwhelmed him at times. It was just as powerful today as it had always been. When they'd been born, he'd felt such a rush of love that it had practically taken his breath away. As tiny babies, they had seemed so fragile and vulnerable that his protective instincts swelled through his body wanting nothing and nobody to ever hurt them in any way. He'd cuddled them carefully in each crook of his big arms, worried at first that he would hurt them in some way with his huge, sometimes clumsy hands, but after a few seconds he had bent forward and kissed them gently on their sweet-smelling heads.

His mind had been full of high hopes and dreams for them and he determined that as they grew up their happiness in life would always be his priority. Josh had been born first, followed a couple of minutes later by Jamie. Even though they were identical, and friends and family couldn't tell them apart, he'd always been able to recognise Josh from Jamie.

Sally had left the tiny hospital bracelets on their ankles for the first few weeks. With being tired and breast feeding, she'd sometimes get confused as to whether she had fed Jamie first or Josh. But he didn't need the bracelets because he'd never once mixed them up. In his eyes they were poles part, not to look at maybe, but they felt and smelt different.

Their personalities were also complex. Where James didn't mind if Josh had his nappy changed first, if Josh wasn't fed first, he'd howl and turn red in the face with temper. When they were toddlers, James was the most independent and would play on his own for hours with toys in front of him. But Josh would constantly crave attention especially from Sally.

Not that it mattered to Alex because he loved them both equally. When people thought Josh was harder to handle, all Alex could see in his little crying face was his vulnerability and he gave him more attention than he probably should have. One of James's front teeth was ever so slightly crooked, and most people used this as a guide to which boy was which, but Alex knew that even if he'd been blindfolded, he would still have been able to tell them apart.

To help teachers and other children at the nursery, Sally had never dressed them the same, making sure they had their own clothes and identity, which had helped. However, the boys developed their own sense of humour about their likeness and sometimes swapped T-shirts and pyjamas just to confuse people. They especially teased their granddad and as the old man would say their names then look from one to another scratching his bald head in confusion, Josh and Jamie would collapse into hoots of laughter. Alex sighed with longing to see them.

When the solicitor came to the doorway, he got up and followed him into his office.

Chapter Eight

This must be what they call trick photography, she thought, peering closely at a close-up shot of her small cleavage in a V-neck T-shirt. The way he had enlarged the size of her breasts was rather flattering, of course, but it was a little creepy how he had made her into something she wasn't.

Kim stood in front of her full-length mirror wearing the orange bra and panties. She turned from side to side scrutinising herself and quivering with excitement. Did they look okay? Was she too old to carry off something so young and frivolous? Although Alex seemed oblivious to the fact that she was eleven years older than him and had said it wasn't an issue, she knew it was there. The age gap was not going to go away however much she wished it would. She was always going to be older and she doubted that she'd ever feel it was irrelevant. She could almost hear people asking if Alex was her toy-boy.

Kim took a deep breath hoping to instil herself with more confidence. She turned around trying to see her back view in the mirror. Remembering the night before, Kim knew that he liked her body because he'd said so numerous times when he had ravished her from head to toe. He hadn't been bothered about her abdominal scar. Which, Kim had to admit, didn't seem to stand out as much as she'd always thought it did. Maybe the orange colour was so bright that it drew the eye away from the scar.

With her decision made, she dressed in white jeans and T-Shirt and dropped her makeup bag, more underwear, toothbrush, and a clean shirt into an overnight holdall. This time, unless Alex asked her to leave, she was determined to stay overnight. Nothing would drag her from his bed.

***

Alex was at the doorway to his flat when she hurried up the footpath under a light drizzle. He was handing over money to a delivery boy and waved as she approached. Carrying the take-away brown paper bag in one hand he threw his other arm along her shoulder and pulled her though the door.

'I'm starving,' he said. 'And I was hoping you would be too.'

Kim dropped her holdall by the front door and hugged his big bicep then grinned. 'I am. I'm so pleased you ordered Indian food – it's my favourite.'

She followed him into the kitchen where he set out the cartons on the workbench and she opened cupboards and grabbed two plates.

He pulled the rings on two cans of lager and handed her one. 'I ordered a selection of dishes as I wasn't sure how hot you like it.'

She raised an eyebrow teasingly and he threw his head back giving out a huge belly laugh.

'I meant the curry,' he said. 'I do know how hot you like the other!'

Kim giggled and followed him through to the lounge where they sat at the small glass table in front of the French doors which led out onto a small, decked area. After two trips back and forth to the kitchen, Alex finally sat down and they worked in unison, spooning rice, Bombay potatoes, and two different chicken dishes onto each other's plates. Sniffing the air, full of aromatic spices, Kim tucked into the hot food hungrily while Alex tore off large chunks of naan bread.

Kim glanced around the room as they ate and noticed the coffee table in the centre was loaded with big glossy photography books. There were a few names she recognised, Annie Liebovitz, and Brian Duffy, but most books were from photographers she didn't know. The bookcase behind him was also full of textbooks on the same subject. Kim could tell how fanatical he was about his camera and how he loved his photography.

In between mouthfuls, Kim sighed. 'Oooh, there's nothing quite like the flavours in Indian food,' she said. 'When I'm really hungry other take-outs come an extremely poor second.'

Alex grinned. 'They certainly do. But there's one more thing about this that is making me even happier,' he said. 'I'm hoping...' he paused, looking towards the hall and raising an eyebrow, 'that the holdall is saying you won't run off again and leave me tonight.'

Kim filled with joy and relaxed her shoulders. She tilted her head to one side. 'Yes, it does. It means that, if you don't throw me out later, I'm here for the night. And I'm glad that makes you happy too.'

He pursed his lips. 'There's not much chance of me throwing you out, Kim. But don't expect an easy night,' he warned. 'Now I'm tanked up with food I can go forever.'

She giggled and mentioned their close-up session previously in the studio and wondered if the thought of being caught out by Sidney had made it more thrilling for them.

'Could be, but I think he has a soft spot for you,' Alex teased. 'And I thought I'd better check that there's no history between you two, is there?'

Kim nearly choked on a piece of naan bread. She gulped a mouthful of lager. 'What! Me and Sidney? You've got to be joking,' she said. 'I told you that he went to University with David and over the years, well, we've only ever been good friends.'

She looked into Alex's eyes and saw them dancing with amusement and could tell there were no jealous connotations in his question.

'So,' Alex murmured, swallowing a large mouthful of lager. 'He's not your type then?'

Kim giggled. 'To be perfectly honest I don't know what my type is anymore. Until I met you, the thought of different types of men hadn't entered my mind. It's a subject that didn't exist on my radar.'

Alex nodded, placed his fork across his empty plate and grinned. 'Hmm, well, I'm hoping that big men now figure on that radar of yours, because tall sassy ladies are certainly at the top of my list.'

Kim blushed at the word sassy, and pushed her plate away, declaring herself full. They folded the lids back onto the cartons and discussed the merits of keeping some food back for a midnight feast. Kim's stomach began to churn, not with curry, but with excitement when she saw the fervent look in Alex's eyes.

While Alex carried the containers and plates into the kitchen, Kim settled back in the cream block-leather settee and slipped the sandals from her feet. The oak floor was cool on her toes and she stared around the walls at the neutral colour, wondering if the same colour scheme would lighten her old rooms.

'I'm just thinking about this light and relaxing colour scheme and if I could work something like this into my house,' she said when Alex flopped back down next to her.

'Yeah…' he wavered. 'Colours can be deceptive. Not all colours suit every ambience and setting. But I do prefer these light tones as opposed to darker colours.'

She nodded and smiled. He turned to her and then slotted an arm around her waist. 'You see, these white jeans don't look so good on this cream-coloured leather. If they'd been blue, they'd be more vibrant.'

'Hmm,' she muttered as his face closed in nearer to hers and she parted her lips ready for his kiss.

He sat further forward and opened the top button on her jeans. 'In fact, I think it would look better if they were taken off altogether.'

Kim gasped at his cool fingers on her skin when he eased the white T-Shirt out of the waistband of her jeans. She suddenly remembered her orange underwear and decided to play the sassy lady he obviously thought she was. 'Well, there are two items underneath that aren't white and may blend in better with this colour scheme. In fact, they may well be too bright.'

Alex stared at her and hunched his shoulders in puzzlement. He furrowed his eyebrows. 'May I,' he asked formally, and she dissolved into a fit of the giggles.

'Be my guest,' she teased and playfully ran a hand through his thick hair. Her heart began to beat fast while desire built up inside her and he lifted the edge of the T-shirt then quickly pulled it up over her head.

Alex gasped at the sight of the orange bra. 'Oh, my God,' he moaned. 'It's the bra that I saw inside your carrier bag.'

She could feel him stiffen against her leg and smiled with pleasure. He obviously liked the bra and found it a turn-on. She was so pleased that she had been brave enough to wear the underwear. The one thing she hadn't thought about was how much he would appreciate the gesture.

'And maybe,' he said, undoing the zip on her jeans, 'there's something matching down here.'

'Only one way to find out, Alex,' she breathed hard then wriggled out of the jeans.

'Oh, my God! You look fantastic. I can't believe you've worn these for me, Kim,' he cried and threw himself on top of her while she prayed the settee was strong enough to hold their weight.

Chapter Nine

The sound from Alex's alarm clock on the bedside table woke him with a jolt. At first, he couldn't understand what the noise was, but when he looked around the bedroom and felt Kim's warm body in his arms, memories from the night before loomed large. His arm was draped across her and he stretched further over her shoulder to reach the clock and silence the noise. Alex groaned and fell back onto the pillows.

Kim smiled up at him. 'Thick head?'

'A little, maybe the last can of lager wasn't such a great idea. But it seemed like it at the time.'

She looked beautiful this morning with her blonde hair spread out on the pillow and her soft hazel eyes staring up at him. He could feel her small breasts against his chest and a long leg draped across his hip. He sighed with pleasure.

She was so different from his wife, Sally, which made him like her even more. Where Sally was noisy and common, Kim was quiet and cultured. He could tell that Kim was often self-conscious about her body, mainly because she was older, very tall, and thin. However, he saw her as elegant and loved her slim lines and slightly olive-coloured skin which made her look tanned and healthy.

He stroked the length of her leg and decided it was up to him now to make her feel better about herself and try to build up her confidence.

Kim sighed happily and traced a finger down the thickened stubble on his cheek. 'I do like the designer stubble,' she murmured. 'It really suits you.'

He'd asked her twice last night if it was scratching her skin when they were kissing but she'd reassured him that it just tickled, and she was growing used to the feel of it. Memories of their love making swept through his mind, and how after a few cans of lager she had totally relaxed then became so much more adventurous. At one stage, she'd wrapped her legs around his back and cried aloud, 'Oh God, I do like sex.'

He'd hand-punched the air in delight because he was pleasing her so much.

Kim began to ease her legs away, but he grabbed her closer. 'Where do you think you're going?'

'I need the loo, Alex,' she said. 'And if we don't make a move we're going to be late getting to the studio.'

Alex released her and waved his hand in the air. 'Aah, there's no rush, it'll be an easier day today. Then tomorrow morning at least we can have a lie-in.'

Alex watched Kim sit up on the edge of the bed and look around the room for her clothes. Idly he traced a finger down the length of her long slim back and moaned with pleasure. This was an image he would love to recreate and knew any artist would appreciate the sheer beauty of her spine and slim shoulder blades.

The orange bra and panties were on the floor where he'd removed them last night. He smiled, remembering how amazing she looked in them. On the back of a chair near her side of the bed lay his black T-shirt and she turned to him with an eyebrow raised.

He knew she was asking his permission to wear it and he grinned his answer. Kim grabbed the shirt and pulled it over her head then slid from the bed and walked through to the bathroom just as his mobile began to ring.

Kim pulled the bathroom door behind her but didn't fully close it and he could see her rummage in her holdall then start to clean her teeth.

'Hey, great news,' he shouted.

She walked to the bedroom door with the toothbrush lodged in the side of her mouth. 'So,' he said. 'That was Sidney. Apparently, the studio and the whole street are in darkness. There has been a power cut. He figures I'm not to rush in and will ring me back in an hour. If the electricity is still not on, we might as well give today a miss and start afresh Monday. He said he's going to ring you next to tell you the same.'

Alex stretched out in the large brown sleigh bed and grinned at her then felt his insides melt with longing. He ran a hand through his tousled hair and patted the empty side of the bed. 'I reckon you should get yourself straight back in here so we can make the most of the extra hour.'

Kim left the toothbrush and walked across to the bed. 'Well, maybe I should go home because Sidney will have left a message on my answering machine.'

But as soon as she was within his reach, he pulled her back onto the bed. He wrapped the quilt around her then slid out of the other end. 'Do not move an inch,' he instructed. 'I'm just going to do the same, use the loo and get rid of the dog breath then I'll be back.'

His muscles were still aching after making love three times during the night, but he still wanted her again. And again, and again, he thought, striding into the bathroom.

Alex saw her gazing at him in what he hoped was approval as he stood at the hand basin brushing his teeth.

'You're so easy with your own nakedness compared to how I feel about mine,' she said. 'Maybe it's because you're much younger that you seem to have more self-confidence than I do.'

Alex flung himself back into the room and picked up the bra and panties as he neared her side. He remembered her underneath him on the settee wearing them and how delighted he'd felt that she had made a special effort. He knew this side of their relationship still wasn't easy for her and determined to make her feel more comfortable with him. 'I think you should put these on again,' he grinned and dropped them onto the quilt.

Kim looked aghast. 'I couldn't do that! Oh no, Alex, not in the cold light of day,' she said, shaking her head. 'It took all my courage to wear them last night and strip off in front of you, but I, well, no, Alex, I just can't.'

Alex sat on the side of the bed, fingering the lace on the bra. 'They're fantastic,' he cooed and raised an eyebrow, 'but there're even more fantastic when you're inside them.'

Kim shook her head determinedly. 'No, Alex. I'm not like you. I can't parade around the room with no clothes on. I'm a lot older than you are. I know you're going to say nudity is perfectly natural because you are so free and easy with your body, but…' she paused and lowered her eyes to look at the delicate bra lying in his big hands. 'That's just not how I am.'

Alex laid the bra down on the quilt. Kim's body image was still poor, and he chewed his bottom lip. In the past, he'd done a fair amount of photography with clothes designers and models who had no inhibitions about their bodies whatsoever. But when they were tired, he'd learned how to flatter and get the best out of the women. This usually lifted their flagging spirits and he decided to try it now.

'Well,' he hedged. 'I really can't see what difference our ages have to do with this. I don't think of you as being older than me because you do not look it. Your body is amazing. But I can accept we are different in some respects,' he said. 'I think I became used to walking around naked in my rugby-playing days when we thought nothing of being together in the big steam hot tub after a game. I suppose I lost my inhibitions about nakedness way back in my teens.'

Alex lay flat on the bed next to Kim and noticed the concern in her gentle eyes. He prayed he hadn't over-stepped the mark because his feelings for her were growing stronger. Not day by day, he thought, but hour by hour and he didn't want to say anything to upset her.

He tried again. 'It's just that I love looking at your body and I think you should be proud of it. For a woman in her mid-forties, you're tall and slim and refined in such a way that it makes me shiver with excitement. In my eyes, Kim, you are beautiful. There's nothing wrong with that, is there?'

Kim gasped at his words and he saw her swallow hard then her eyes moisten.

Alex could tell she wasn't used to flattery and for a moment he was annoyed at her late husband. Obviously, he had been a man of few words and he could tell David hadn't taken the time to tell her how beautiful she really was.

Kim whispered, 'I can't quite believe what you've just said. It's such a long time since I've had compliments from a man, other than David of course,' she said. 'A...and what you've just said is lovely. Of course, there's nothing wrong with saying that.'

Alex placed a finger gently under her chin, forcing her to look up at him and gave her the most genuine, honest smile he could. He wished he could reach inside her to make her realise how sincere he was. 'I mean every word, Kim. I know you keep harping on about our age difference, but honestly the years between us simply don't mean a thing to me.'

Rolling into him, she wrapped a leg over his hip and laid her face on his hairy chest. He wrapped his arms around her and rubbed the stubble on his chin against her soft hair.

She sighed, 'It's just that this is all so very new to me and it's taking me a while to get used to it. Well, not you, but us being together, that's all.'

Alex grinned with pleasure when he felt her run her fingers through the hairs on his chest and knew by her touch that she was with him again. 'Shush, we'll be fine,' he murmured into her hair.

She looked up and grinned. 'I'll definitely try to be a little more laid back like you are,' she said.

He cradled her body further into him, feeling
happiness surge through him once more and knew he
was getting through to her. It was going to take a
while, but he loved a challenge and knew that
eventually he could make her feel good about herself.

wanting to let her know that he understood, he said,
'And I will try and tone it down a bit.'

'Nooo,' she moaned. 'Don't do that. I love the way
you are. Please, Alex, don't change a thing.'

He could feel her desire as she wrapped her leg
further up his hip and smiled when she rolled over
onto him completely then pressed herself flat on top
of his body. He could feel the delicate thinness of her
ribcage against him and wanted her so badly that he
felt an actual ache in his loins.

'Like I said before, Kim, I know we're different in
some respects, but in this area when our bodies are
together, I think we're the same.' He looked into her
eyes, wide with longing and devoured her mouth with
his lips then heard her almost sob with passion.

Chapter Ten

An hour later, Kim practically skipped down the
road to the studio wearing a clean green T-shirt with
her white jeans. Alex had remained in the flat to await
Sidney's call, but Kim wanted to help Sidney out.

She explained to Alex that the fridge and freezer
would need emptying of all the vegetables because
even if the electricity burst back into action straight
away, the condition of the vegetables wouldn't be
good enough for further shots. They'd need to buy it
all fresh again for Monday. She'd cheekily told him
that making sure photographers always had a supply
of food at its optimum state was part of her food-
styling role.

Alex had thrown his head back and hooted with
laughter. Letting go of her, he'd whistled under his
breath when she headed into the shower.

Hurrying through the marketplace Kim marvelled at
the difference in herself in such a short time with
Alex. After they'd talked this morning, she felt so
much easier and relaxed in his company. She
replayed their lovemaking in her mind. Kim knew
him well enough by now to know the difference
between his teasing, joking face and the sincere look
in his eyes when he was genuine. When he'd told her
that the age gap didn't matter to him, she'd finally
believed him.

She'd felt humbled and wanted to try and put him at
ease again as the last thing she wanted was to offend
him, especially after she had refused to wear the
underwear. She had realised this morning that when
she did share the things that pleased him it made her

feel good about herself too. And that, she decided, could only be a good thing.

Heading up the street, she remembered his parting words when she left the apartment. 'Why not leave your holdall in the bedroom because it'll save you going home for more things and we can have the whole weekend to ourselves.'

The Whole Weekend To Ourselves, she repeated his words slowly as she entered the studio grinning with happiness.

Sidney told her that the electricity had just been turned back on when she dropped her handbag on to a chair. She offered to make him coffee and clear out the fridges plus some unwanted items he had stored in his small freezer. He thanked her.

When she switched the percolator on, she noticed how nervous and agitated he appeared flapping around the camera room looking at equipment and plugs. She knew that for Sidney this studio was his whole life and that he had conducted his working life in the same pattern every day for years. She also understood that the upheaval of a power cut, although a small incident in many people's minds, wasn't easy for a person so set in his ways, and Sidney needed balance and symmetry in his work area. She poured hot coffee from the pot into two mugs and took them into the camera room.

'Coffee,' she said cheerfully and set his mug on the table.

Watching him fiddle with a pile of cables behind the clear backscreen, Kim could tell that he hadn't coped very well with the unexpected trauma and felt sorry for him.

'Sidney.' she called again. 'Come and have this hot drink, it'll make you feel better.'

Sidney nodded and hurried towards her. He picked up the mug and sipped the coffee then began to tell her about his traumatic morning when he'd arrived and how the other shop keepers had all rallied round.

'Of course, I rang you first, but your landline went straight to answer and then I rang Alex,' he said, peering furtively over his mug.

Kim's heart began to thump. The last thing she wanted was for Sidney to know she'd spent the night at Alex's flat. 'Oh, yes,' she said. 'I was in the shower when you rang and rather than ring you back, I thought I'd grab my breakfast and get here as quickly as I could to help out.'

Sidney seemed satisfied with this explanation and she breathed a sigh of relief. After their conversation about Alex yesterday she didn't want to mention him again today and gave Sidney a big reassuring smile, 'We'll soon get things back to normal.'

***

'Alex!' Kim called his name when she neared the doorway to Café Rouge and he swung around to face her, grinning. They had arranged to meet for lunch, and he was sitting at the same table where they'd first had dinner together. They both commented on how quickly they had got to know each other.

'I can't believe what a difference you've made to me already,' Kim told him. 'I'd forgotten what it was like to wake up in the morning and feel happy and to have a purpose for living again.'

Alex took her hand across the table and squeezed it tenderly. 'It must have been dreadful for you to lose

David like that…' he paused and looked into her eyes. 'Is it okay for me to call him David?'

Kim pushed her plate to the side with the remains of the sea bass and salad she had eaten. 'Of course, it is,' she said. 'You know, Alex, I think you two would have got along well together. Although he was the total opposite of you, quiet and a little withdrawn at times, he did love to be surrounded by boisterous jovial people. I know he would have liked you or at least loved your energy and zest for life. Just as I do.'

Alex grinned. 'It's okay. You can call me loud and mouthy if you want to. You won't be the first.'

They were interrupted by Kim's mobile ringing and she stood up to take the call. She wandered towards the empty tables at the end of the seating area where it was quieter. Alex indicated that he was using the men's room and she concentrated hard on the conversation with her friend.

When Alex returned Kim was thoughtfully digesting the news from her telephone call. She explained how, during The Olympic Games, she had gone on holiday for three weeks to see Patricia in London while her house was lucratively rented to two families of oarsmen who were guests at the rowing club.

'It's a good way of earning more money for little effort,' she said. 'Especially as it's such a large house it means two lots of rent. And afterwards, the club paid for my house to be cleaned.'

Alex leant forwards over the table and slotted his fingers together into a steeple to listen while she continued.

'So, they're asking if I could do the same next week for the Durham regatta. He's apologised for such short notice, but someone who was booked to take in a family from Oxford has let them down at the last minute.'

Alex smiled. 'Sounds like a good idea. If you want to do it, I'd say go for it. Although I don't think I can bear the thought of you being down in London and miles away …' he frowned looking out across the river.

Kim saw his bushy eyebrows draw together and the cloud that passed through his eyes. It was the cloud she usually saw when he talked about his boys.

She swallowed hard. 'Nooo,' she said quietly across the table. 'I can't accept the offer now and go to London. I couldn't let Sidney down when he's booked me to work on the project. I must see it through for the duration however long that takes. It's such a shame the regatta is next week. If it were at the end of the month it wouldn't be a problem.'

Alex knotted his eyebrows and she saw the relief in his eyes. 'So, in essence,' he said, 'it means you need somewhere local to stay while your house is being rented out, allowing you to cash in on the extra money. Is that right?'

Kim put her head on one side. She could almost see the cogs in his mind turning while he thought the problem through. This was great, she thought, after the last year of making decisions and puzzling her way through issues alone, she now had someone to talk things over with.

'That's it!' he yelled. Kim almost knocked over her wine glass she was so startled at his loud voice.

'You can come and stay with me in the apartment. That way I get to have you to myself for a whole week, and you can cash in on rent.'

Kim's hand flew to her throat. Her mind was in a total whirl. 'B...but I can't do that.' she floundered. 'I can't just move in with you.'

'Why not, there's plenty of room. But,' he grinned lecherously, 'I will expect to be served breakfast in bed every morning.'

Kim was astounded at his generosity and forethought. This big-hearted man was generously offering her a place to stay. 'A...are you sure?'

Alex grinned. 'Of course, I'm sure. I wouldn't have invited you if I wasn't. It'll be great fun and give us time to really get to know each other. I'll be able to go to sleep and know that you aren't going to run off home in the middle of the night,' he said raising an eyebrow. 'Plus, I'll have you parading around that flat in your orange bra and panties before you know it!'

A woman squeezed past their table and tutted loudly. Obviously, she had heard Alex use the words bra and panties and taken offence. It was on the tip of Kim's tongue to shush Alex, but she decided, what the hell and burst into giggly laughter. He was her big noisy man and already she loved him for being who he was.

Chapter Eleven

The images on the second wall, where she was
dressed in elegant clothes, were more recent, but had
been drawn over with a marker pen. One close-up
shot of her bottom in a tight-fitting white skirt now
had a red thong drawn on it. Kim gasped and felt her
stomach knot with tension.

By Sunday night, with help from Alex, Kim was
settled in his riverside apartment and her house was
ready for rental. Alex had helped clean the house
from the top landing, five bedrooms, bathroom, to the
lounge, study, and kitchen. The beds all had fresh
linen and he had climbed into the loft, piling things
away in cardboard boxes. He'd retrieved his Audi
from the garage, and upon her instruction, had taken
David's red chair to the rubbish tip. She explained
that her decision had been made after the first night
she spent with him and although he protested that
maybe she should hold on to it a while longer, she'd
insisted that it went.

Now they were together in his apartment lying on
the settee watching an old movie. She lay beside him
dressed in a grey fluffy onesie and he had stripped
down to an old pair of tracksuit bottoms. Glasses of
wine poured earlier sat on the coffee table practically
untouched because they'd been engrossed in the film.

As the credits rolled Kim took a few minutes to
recap the last couple of days and the huge turnaround
in her life. She'd agreed to Alex's suggestion without
a great deal of thought, which looking back now, was

a surprise. Normally big decisions, and this was a huge change of circumstance, took her days of deliberation. In some situations, she even wrote a 'pros and cons' list before coming to a decision.

Vicky had simply told her, if it feels right – go for it, which had helped her decision because that was exactly how it did feel with Alex, exactly right. She also comforted herself with the fact that it was all part of being close to him and in an intimate relationship. She smiled, imaging Patricia saying, 'Well my dear, it'll either make or break you.'

Kim felt Alex sigh behind her and pull her further into his arms. 'Oh, Alex,' she murmured, 'this is so cosy. I feel totally unwound and relaxed.'

'Me too. I love you being here with me. It's more than I could ever have dreamt,' he muttered into her ear and stroked her hair.

Her heart soared at his words. He always said lovely things to her when they were making love, of which there had been plenty during the weekend, but now when they were sharing everyday things together his words meant even more. 'Hmm,' she sighed taking his hand and holding it tightly against her chest.

'I suppose...' he said, then paused.

Kim heard a note of caution in his voice and swivelled around to face him while he clicked the DVD box off with the remote control. Wariness clouded his eyes, and she felt a tremor of alarm run down her back. 'What?'

'Well,' he said, 'it's been great holed up here all weekend, but we should plan how we're going to do things from tomorrow.'

She thought of work and Sidney then nodded.

Alex smiled and laid the palm of his hand on her cheek. 'Really all I ask, Kim, is that we don't go shouting from the rooftops that you are here with me and that, dare I say, we are now an item.'

An item, she mused, this was more of the trendy speak that she wasn't used to, or even knew what it meant. She supposed that in her younger, pre-David years, they had said, we are going out with each other, or we are dating. She smiled, deciding that she quite liked being part of an item. It made her feel as though she belonged somewhere with somebody after her grieving time alone.

'I'm fine with that, Alex,' she grinned. 'An item we are then. It's probably for the best if we keep the next week under wraps with Sidney.'

Alex frowned and wrapped his fingers into strands of her hair. 'True, but I was thinking more of my situation in Scunthorpe. My solicitor reckons that, because Sally is trying to stop me from seeing the boys, I've got to be squeaky clean. In his words, no affairs, and no wild nights out which would give the wrong impression. In other words, we're not to give her solicitors any ammunition to fire at me.'

Kim raised herself onto her elbow to be level with him. She nodded. 'Ooh, right. I understand,' she said. 'Well, the only person I've told is Vicky, my friend in France. But she doesn't keep in touch with anyone in Durham, other than me of course, and I know our secret will be safe with her. But now I know, I won't tell another soul.'

They decided it would be best to arrive at the studio separately in the morning and they'd try to leave at different times of the day. They also agreed, that although Kim hardly used social media, that there would be no mention of their togetherness on Facebook or Twitter, just to be on the safe side. She could see Alex relax his eyebrows and shoulders as she cuddled into his big chest.

***

There was a definite shift in the atmosphere when they worked together the next day. Kim noticed the difference and decided it was like a settled togetherness because there were no more doubts in their minds that they were, as Alex had said, an item.

She felt a concrete assuredness about them in a partnership which filled her with comfort and a pleasant type of security that she loved. She liked watching him work and unlike the last few days, she didn't have to wonder when she would be able to touch him again because she knew it would be as soon as they reached the apartment.

They had decided to start with new still shots for the fruit selection and to replicate the concept they'd used for the vegetables. Following Alex and Sidney's instructions, she'd been out to the market to buy a selection of whole fruits and square wooden placemats. They'd decided these would work better with the colours of the fruit rather than the grey slate and black backdrops. She chose dark oak for the pineapple, cantaloupe melon, grapes, and kiwi fruits, and a lighter oak for the bananas, pears, and red apples.

While cutting a couple of kiwi fruits in halves, Sidney began to explain what was written in the retailer's brief.

'The customer wants to call the fruit, naked fruit,'
Sidney said, tilting his head slightly. 'Therefore,
maybe we should peel all the skin from the kiwi,
apples, and melon. Then, I suppose these fruits would
be as if they were naked?'

Kim heard a soft chortle from Alex and Sidney
swung around to glare at him.

Sidney raised an eyebrow in warning, 'Excuse me,
there are ladies present. I won't have any smuttiness
in here!'

Alex didn't comment but merely shrugged his
shoulders and looked at the fruits on the table.

Hmm, Kim thought. As well as there being a shift in
atmosphere between Alex and her this morning, there
was also a definite change in Sidney's behaviour
towards Alex. She hoped that whatever it was Sidney
didn't like about Alex it wasn't going to cause any
awkwardness between them because she knew how
much Alex was enjoying his new job.

Kim sliced large Jaffa oranges and bright Sicilian
lemons while Alex made the images look like big
cartwheels bursting with droplets of fresh juice. He's
such a clever guy, she thought, picking up a kiwi
fruit. She began to peel one-half of a kiwi fruit and
left the long length of brown outer skin curled and
hanging from the fruit.

'If this was a moving shot,' Kim said. 'It would look
as if the kiwi was spinning around like an old-
fashioned top.'

'Hey,' Alex said, 'that's given me another idea. We
could put the small fruit into clear round globes and
make them look as though they're hurtling through
Space around the sun.'

Kim giggled. 'Oh, yes, but what could we use for the sun?' She paused and glanced at the large pineapple.

Alex followed her gaze and then they both looked at each other and smiled. 'We really are on the same wavelength today.'

Kim grinned then nodded. 'It's not exactly a complete round shape, but by the time I've peeled and cored the centre, it might resemble the glowing sun.'

Alex danced a little jig from one of his big loafers to another. 'God, I love it when a plan comes together so well.'

Kim laughed at the sight of his huge feet skipping lightly, at which he exaggerated the movement and laughed too.

Alex said, 'Contrary to popular belief, you have to be light on your feet to play rugby and I still miss playing. But I content myself with watching it on TV or at local matches when I'm down in Scunthorpe.'

Kim saw the light and happiness shine in his green eyes as he looked into hers and felt her cheeks flush with the same pleasure. She placed her hands on her warm cheeks and stared at him. It wasn't a sexual intensity that she saw. It was more of a oneness, a togetherness, a deeper understanding between them as a couple. She wondered, is this love? Are we what people call soul mates and that's how we think on the same wavelength? Whatever it was she felt buoyant, full of inner peace and true happiness that she had found this with such a wonderful man.

Alex returned her stare and put his head to one side. He took her hand in his and squeezed it tightly.

While Alex worked quickly with the images on his tablet, Kim cleared the work surface lost in thought.

The feelings she had for him as a man and a partner were totally different from her appreciation of him as a master of his craft.

As she glanced over his shoulder while he whirled the cartwheels of fruit into position, she let out a breath of sheer admiration. Not only was she falling for this man because of his amazing body and bubbling, generous personality, but she was also astonished at his creativity. He'd told her that much of his previous photography work had been with commercials and models. Now she knew he had certainly found his forte and the perfect area in which to showcase his talent. His genius with scenes and motions around the fruit and vegetables were staggering.

Kim grinned and clapped him on the shoulder. 'They're fabulous, Alex. It's amazing what you can do. I absolutely love it!'

'How about you, Sidney?' Kim asked, but she turned around to see Sidney amble away out into reception.

Kim shrugged at Alex and tutted. 'Maybe he's just having an off day.'

Alex raised an eyebrow. 'He's been strange all morning. And that last comment was uncalled for,' he snorted, moving closer to her. 'What does he think I am? I would never embarrass anyone with smutty comments about being naked. Not unless I was thinking of you, of course.'

Kim glanced towards the door to make sure Sidney was out of earshot and saw Alex practically stripping her naked with his eyes. She giggled conspiratorially and felt her insides melt under his gaze.

'Come on,' Alex said, 'let's get cracking. The sooner we get done today and outside for some fresh air the better.'

Holding back on Alex's ideas until they could find some props to make the round globes, they concentrated on the still shots. The black backdrop was spread over the table and Alex placed three apples together. Kim frowned as the image looked quite boring and uninspiring compared to the rest of the project work.

Touching his arm lightly, Kim removed the three apples. 'How about if we make long rows of the apples and pears side by side?'

She placed seven apples all with their stalks facing upwards, and then seven pears on their sides with their stalks all lying to the left.

She looked to Alex who grinned and nodded as she repeated the order twice more so that there were six rows of fruit.

'Fab,' he said. 'But maybe in that third row the apples could be cut in half to show the white crispness inside?'

'What a marvellous team we are,' Kim cried.

She cut each apple precisely down the centre, making sure all of them had the same number of pips in each then added them to the display. 'Shall we do the same in row five with the pears cut lengthwise?'

Alex agreed and did another little dance around the table, shouting in excitement and Kim howled with laughter.

Kim could hear Sidney making tutting noises from the adjoining room and sighed. She put her finger to her lips and motioned Alex to keep it down. 'Maybe it's best not to wind him up today,' she said.

Kim began peeling the outer skin from the melon. She explained to Alex how it was best to leave on some of the outer skin so that when it was sliced the contrast between the soft orange inside and outer bright green made good images. Carefully she arranged the pieces on the wooden placemats with perfectly sliced apple and titbits of cheese. She placed a dip bowl with sweet chilli sauce on the end of the placemat to show the 'ingredient buffet' concept that the retailer had asked for.

The grapes had been washed and Alex moved to help her dry them with a paper towel, but she put her hand on his arm. 'No, Alex,' she said. 'We'll leave them a little wet as it gives them a shine under the lights and makes them look fresher.'

Alex nodded and whispered. 'Not just a pretty face, then. But more of a very clever lady, methinks.'

'Just doing my job,' Kim said. 'But thanks for the compliment. However, it's nothing any other food stylist wouldn't do.'

Alex smiled. 'Aah, but you're my food stylist and nobody else comes close.'

Kim glowed, placing a small bunch of the grapes in the centre and then two separate grapes on the side as though they had strayed away from the rest of the pack.

Alex began taking shots with the camera and they worked together in harmony until after five when Sidney re-appeared. He thanked them warmly for a good day's work when he looked at the still shots and genuinely seemed pleased.

***

During the rest of the week, they fell into a pattern of working in the studio intermittently between other photography work that Alex and Sidney had planned. After this they'd hurry back to the apartment to cook supper and enjoy each other's company. Kim learned that Alex liked to cook. She taught him useful tips as he prepared and cooked different meals. He insisted on shopping to buy the ingredients and they drove out of Durham to other supermarkets so they wouldn't be seen together.

Alex had stressed on more than one occasion that his child visitation should be sorted out soon and then they would not have to look over their shoulders, but Kim wasn't unduly perturbed. 'I'm a patient woman,' she told him. 'And I happen to think you are well worth waiting for.'

They also discovered a mutual love of old films and took turns in selecting DVD's. Alex loved Doris Day and Clark Gable and told Kim a little about his mum before she died. And how in the afternoons, she would watch old films with him.

'Because she was so ill, she didn't have much appetite,' he said and smiled. 'But she never lost her love of Galaxy chocolate and we'd gorge ourselves while watching the movies.'

Kim told him how she loved Bette Davis films and the next night her choice had been to watch one of her classic films. They settled down on the settee with a throw snuggled around them and a carton of popcorn to share.

When the film finished, she said, 'That was great. But my favourite film of all time is, 'All About Eve' where Bette Davis plays Margo Channing and she says the famous line, fasten your seatbelts it's going to be a bumpy night. I just love Bette's raw energy when she's acting. She was the first famous actress to stand up to the big moviemakers in Hollywood and sometimes I wish I had more of her courage.'

Alex hugged her close. 'But, Kim, I think you do. You just show yours in a different way. I mean, it can't have been easy nursing someone you love when they're dying. I bet you did a great job of caring for David and you must have been very brave to look after him at home as you did,' he said and kissed her. 'I can also see your energy at work, especially when you're styling food.'

Kim gulped with emotion and felt tears were not far away. He always seemed to know exactly the right thing to say at the right time, especially when her confidence was low. She knew that she was far more forthcoming and open with Alex than she'd ever been with David.

Although at first Kim had struggled with Alex being very touchy-feely, she had gradually become so used to his loving attention and compliments that she now showered him with the same. By the end of the week Kim had noticed that she often touched him first and loved to caress his body in much the same way as he did hers. But now she did it without being prompted.

Shopping in Newcastle the following day had been an experience she would not forget. Kim felt desperately in need of new clothes as her social life gathered speed. The few classic items she possessed were not enough to last a week, and while in the shops, Alex encouraged her to be more daring with colours and adventurous with stylish, more fashionable clothes.

He persuaded her to wear a shorter length skirt, stressing that she had the legs of a model and should make the most of them at every opportunity. She cringed at the twenty-two-inch mini-skirts, knowing that they wouldn't suit a woman of her age, but agreed to a twenty-seven-inch length, which, with opaque tights and flat loafers, looked sensational on her long legs.

Kim could tell Alex was proud of her. She could see it in his eyes or when he gave her a low whistle when she modelled an outfit for him. This made her feel more assured in the decisions she made when buying the clothes. She also indulged herself, and him, in a few more sets of silky underwear.

'I love that black lace set,' Alex said, touching the silk. 'You'd look sensational in that and it will feel gorgeous on your skin.'

Kim tried it on and agreed. It was expensive but good quality and she emerged from the changing rooms grinning. 'You're right, it's fabulous,' she said and walked back to the rails of lingerie. She bought the same set in white and red. With his continued encouragement and support Kim learned to feel much more confident in herself and her feelings.

On Sunday evening, Alex talked to his sons on the telephone. Kim liked to give him time on his own and lay soaking in a warm bubble bath. It was the last night that the tenants were staying in her house and she closed her eyes to recap over the last week.

Alex hadn't asked her to leave and return to the house. In fact, the subject had not arisen, and she supposed that if she didn't mention the end of the tenancy, they might never talk about it. She was very tempted to play dumb and stay in the apartment with him because she was having such an amazing time.

Kim smiled and felt the warm water swish around her body. She thought of their past conversations where the most he had said, was how much he loved having her with him and how he never wanted their closeness to end. She hoped, therefore, that he felt the same way she did, and he didn't want her to leave.

Kim laid her head back and remembered Alex's comments the first time he'd come to her house about David's influence. She thought more intensely about the years of her marriage and their lifestyle.

When they were first married and David had started at the local hospital as a trainee radiographer, it had been her wage that they'd spent on renovating the house. Even in those days she'd been able to make more money in a week that he did in a month. Every penny spent had been on David's choices, in fact she could see now that all the decisions during their marriage had been his. And because he worked in the radiology department all his career, David loved peace and quiet at holiday times. He loved being away from the hustle and bustle of the hospital. Often, he'd tell people, 'Oh, we don't like towns and cities. We'd rather go walking in the Yorkshire Dales and stay in basic, rural cottages.'

And she'd gone along with this, telling herself that she loved it too. But now she questioned this.

Since David died, she'd been to London twice to stay with Patricia and had loved the noise, shops, pubs, and restaurants. She had felt alive and full of energy wandering the streets, looking at the architecture, walking through parks, visiting museums, and imagining how other people lived their lives.

She was planning a trip to Provence to see Vicky and already had flight details, which made her bubble with excitement. And last month, an old-school friend had flown into Glasgow and Kim had joined her for a spa weekend in a luxurious hotel where they'd spent their money on great food, wine, and pampering. She knew David would have classed this as an abdominal waste of money, but she'd loved every minute.

David had had a fear of flying, hence they'd never holidayed abroad, and she'd never been on an aeroplane. So, yesterday when Alex had told her Rome was his favourite city, she had excitedly suggested going for a long weekend. The thought of experiencing true Italian culture and food thrilled her to the point of giddiness. And Kim knew she was coming out of her shell.

She lifted a foot out of the water and circled the tap with her toes while remembering when she'd first met David and how overawed she had been then willing to please him on all levels. She sighed. Had she gone along with everything David wanted because she adored him and had forgotten about herself? And dare she even use the word domineering where David was concerned? Well, if that was true, she decided, then she was as much at fault for letting him domineer her as he was for doing it.

She remembered reading somewhere that if a couple spent all their lives together, they morphed into each other, and she wondered now if this was what she had done. Had her own personality been swallowed up and moulded into a facsimile of his?

She was quietly reserved, loyal with thoughtful honest beliefs and values, which summed up the characteristics of her personality. And these had been identical to David's. But, she wondered, if she'd spent twenty years married to a different man, like Alex, would her personality have changed?

Kim shrugged and thought back to that dreadful day when she had lost both her parents and Patricia had stepped into the role of mother as well as sister. She sighed and remembered feeling as though the pain of missing them both would never leave her. She'd clung to Patricia, and as the months passed, life had taken over and she had left school to start at college. As a teenager, she'd needed someone to take care of her, and then as a young adult, she had met David who had stepped into Patricia's shoes.

So, she decided, this was the first time in her life that she was making all her own decisions and taking responsibility for herself. It was a good feeling and Kim relished the exciting changes to come.

She sat up and reached for the sponge on the corner of the bath. The major thing she'd discovered about herself was that she liked to have fun. She loved being more spontaneous and wearing new styles of clothes which made her feel younger. She wanted to have a beach holiday and walk with her feet in the sand. She wanted to feel the sun on her shoulders wearing a bikini. Which, she smiled, would make a lovely change from looking at sheep in a field when huddled in a waterproof jacket.

Therefore, if meeting Alex has done nothing else, she decided, it had awakened her mind and made her question her lifestyle, and how she wanted to live the rest of her life.

Lathering the sponge with soap, Kim began to move it over her stomach. She knew if she wanted some assistance all she would have to do was call Alex because on previous occasions he had washed her from head to toe. However, just for these few moments she was enjoying the luxury of the bath alone with her intimate thoughts.

Her sexual experiences with David, and she cringed because not for one minute was she comparing the two men, but merely thinking how she had behaved with them. Which was so quite different. All she could ever remember about making love with David was that it had been in the missionary position, sweet and soft, and her climaxes had been a pleasant experience. And very, very, quiet.

With Alex, however, it was completely the opposite. It wasn't always gentle although he never hurt her, but often it was the sheer power of his big body that made it like this. Her climaxes were rarely sweet and mild. They were explosive and tore through her body until she cried and shook. He loved her to sit on top of him and she too loved to be there.

But the biggest difference with Alex was that she was never quiet. He wanted her to make a noise. 'Tell me how you're feeling,' he would demand, and she would tell him. 'Louder,' he would yell. 'Tell me if it feels good like this? Talk to me, I need to know you're still with me.'

And she did. She would shout, cry, laugh, and scream her way through making love, which for someone as reserved as she'd always thought she was, it was mind-blowingly out of character. But she loved every second.

Chapter Twelve

Alex went into the studio ahead of her the next
morning and just as she picked up her denim jacket to
go shopping to the market, she forgot which fruit they
needed for the day's work. Were they doing bananas
or pineapple? She sighed with disbelief at how poor
her memory was lately and opened her laptop to find
the folder that Sidney had created for all three of them
to access.

This was the first time she'd used the folder and she
knew most of it would be full of photography shots,
but there should also be notes about preparation and
their ideas list. She entered the password and opened
the list, which told her that it was the banana section
for today's shots.

It was just as she went to log out that she spotted a
separate file marked, Alex only.

She frowned and hesitated. Why would he have his
own documents in this file? The work folder was for
them all to access when they thought it necessary. So
why the segregation?

Kim felt light beads of perspiration settle on her
forehead while she fought with herself for a few
seconds knowing that if he had named the file for
himself, she shouldn't look inside. Nevertheless, she
paused. He wouldn't have personal stuff in there,
would he? Surely not when he knew that she and
Sidney could see it. No, she decided, Alex wouldn't
allow Sidney to see his stuff. She clicked on the icon
to open the file.

Kim gasped in abject horror at the screen in front of
her. 'Oh, my God,' she cried aloud and stared at
photographs of naked women with enormous breasts.

The woman in the first shot had her hands in front of her with black handcuffs around her wrists and a doleful expression, as though she was begging to be released. A black leather whip hung next to a younger girl in the second image, whose arms had been pulled high above her head with her wrists tied together by a thick rope. This position made her breasts look even bigger, but her head was slumped forward as though she was in pain.

The sweat on Kim's forehead now intensified and she swiped it away with the back of her hand. Nausea rose through her gullet and her legs trembled. She couldn't stop staring at the photographs.

How could he? She raged. How could he even want to look at photographs like this? She scrolled down the page where one woman after another in erotic positions appeared on the screen. All with huge breasts staring morosely into the camera.

Kim reached behind her and grabbed hold of a dining chair to steady herself and then swung it around and slumped on to it. She didn't think her legs could hold her up and she took slow deep breaths, trying to rationalise her thoughts.

Stay calm, she thought, breathing hard and focusing once more on the women. They were not all older women. Some looked as if they were eighteen or early twenties, but nearly all had huge breasts which she decided had been exaggerated by the camera. For a second she glanced down at her own small chest, which seemed to be flatter than ever in a tight shirt and gulped. Her eyes seemed glued to the screen as she stared at the women's huge, engorged nipples as if they were poking fun at her. Panic flooded through her mind and she wanted to howl with shock at what she'd found. With shaking hands, she slowly closed the folder and logged out.

Why? She moaned, why are the images even there? Why on earth would he want to look at stuff like that? Although she knew that in some men's eyes it was only a little harmless fun, but she couldn't believe this of Alex. Was it because he liked large breasts? And if so, she cried, what was he doing with her? She felt sickened at the thought that she was comparing herself with these women on the screen and shivered with disgust.

Her mind raced with different scenarios. Had Alex positioned the women and taken the images? Or had he downloaded them from another source? She struggled to remember what he had told her about the work he'd done previously in Scunthorpe with different models, but only recalled his stories about commercials for hand cream and the like. Kim fumed. What bloody difference does it make whether he took them or not? He's still looking at them and obviously wants to see them or they wouldn't be in his folder.

Kim laid her head on her forearms and began to sob. She thought of all she knew about him and how she'd thought him a decent honourable man. In her eyes, he'd been like a hero on a galloping horse thundering into the studio that day, as though he was on a mission to save her from a life of misery.

However, this knowledge about him and his dirty little secret wiped the word hero straight from her mind. He certainly didn't warrant the label anymore, because he wasn't the man, she'd thought he was. Kim felt crushed by an overwhelming sense of disappointment. She wrapped her arms around her chest and cried. The hurt was just too much, she thought, simply too much to bear.

A text tinkled on her mobile and she glanced down to read how Alex and Sidney were waiting for the bananas to start shooting. She sat back in the chair, wiping the tears from her cheeks. It was a work commitment, and she knew that somehow, she would have to push this nightmare aside and get on with the contract. Pulling on her jacket, Kim strode to the mirror in the hall. With a quick brush of concealer under her eyes and a coat of pink lipstick, she took three long, slow deep breaths until she felt capable of leaving the apartment.

***

Kim stood in the market with a selection of bananas. She tried to smile at the young man who served her. He was making wisecracks about monkeys and the number of bananas she was buying. Ordinarily she would have responded to his light-hearted banter, but today all she could muster was a half-hearted smile. The whole of her insides felt deflated as though the excitement and build-up of the last week had evaporated in seconds and now her limbs felt too heavy to move. All she wanted to do was go back to her house and curl up in her bed, where she could try to sort herself out.

Kim walked out of the covered area of the market and into the daylight again. She stopped and sat on the bench outside the church with the carrier bags of bananas beside her. A tiny voice of reason in the back of her mind queried her previous thoughts. Did looking at images of naked women make him an indecent man? After all, there must be thousands of men who looked at this type of thing behind their women's backs. They couldn't all be indecent, could they?

It wasn't illegal and if women like that turned them on, they could buy newspapers and ogle the women on page three if need be. Therefore, she concluded, maybe she was making judgements about Alex based on her own opinions and what she thought of as dirty magazines, when she didn't know anything about this subject.

However, Kim winced. It was the handcuffs, rope and whips that made this scenario a hundred times worse. The girls in the newspaper looked happy and proud to be showing off their lovely young bodies, but in Alex's images those pieces of equipment, if that was the correct term to use, made the women look uneasy, degraded, and certainly not happy to be photographed.

She had seen TV reports about how young girls were tricked into making porn movies and images, thinking it was the start of a glittering modelling career when it was the total opposite and the start of a downhill slope.

Kim twisted the handle of the carrier bags through her fingers and sighed. Was she exaggerating those images out of proportion because of the sheltered life she'd led and her own lack of experience with men? Kim knew, other than her husband, she had no other experiences to compare Alex's behaviour with. She'd only ever kissed David and lost her virginity to him on their wedding night. So, this old-fashioned, limited experience didn't help when it came to the subject of men's sexual preferences and habits. Kim tried to recall all the boyfriends Vicky had in their younger days but couldn't remember her complaining that they looked at photographs of naked women.

At the sound of another text on her mobile she knew the guys were waiting for the bananas and she picked up the bags. She walked through the marketplace and decided not to say anything about the photographs to Alex in the studio. At least not until she'd had time to think the situation through properly. She hoped in the meantime that Sidney didn't stumble across the folder as she had.

Oh God, she thought, remembering their talk on the afternoon that Alex had left early. What had Sidney said? Queasiness rose in her stomach when she remembered Sidney's words about Alex; there was something not quite right about him.

Chapter Thirteen

The images were becoming more sinister now. On a photograph of her sitting on a chair with her legs crossed she was wearing black fishnet stockings. Kim paused to remember if, and when she had ever worn these stockings. She squeezed her eyes tight shut with fear. She knew the answer was no. Obviously, he had drawn over the photograph with a black marker pen, but it was the jagged black leather whip hanging from the side of the chair which really scared her. Sexual paraphernalia was another thing altogether.

Where was she? Alex worried as he strode around the camera room. It was over an hour since he'd left the apartment and Kim was supposed to be following in ten minutes. Sidney had the area all ready for the shots and was moaning because they didn't have the fresh bananas, but she hadn't answered either of the texts he'd sent.

Maybe he should try ringing her mobile or the apartment, he thought, when in a whirlwind, Kim hurried through the reception carrying two bags. He could tell immediately that something had happened by the forced, false cheeriness in her voice. She apologised to Sidney and relayed a garbled excuse about the busy market and how the bananas in M&S were not what she was looking for. She emptied the bag and explained the different qualities from under-ripe and over-ripe and how they would have plenty of colour variations to choose from. He wanted to go to her and wrap his arms around her to soothe whatever it was that was troubling her.

When she excused herself and went into the toilet and Sidney began to make ready the wood placemats, a tremor of apprehension filtered up Alex's spine, making all his nerve endings tingle. He knew her well enough now to know there was something badly amiss.

When she came back into the camera room carrying a tray with three mugs of coffee, she looked up at him and he felt his insides tear as they often did when he thought about the boys or heard their quiet little voices on the telephone.

She looked terrible and he knew, although he'd never actually seen her cry, that she had been in tears over something. Her soft eyes looked puffy and there was a thick layer of make-up covering the area as though she had purposely tried to conceal redness. Her usually bright, shiny eyes looked dull and lifeless as though they'd had all the life drained out of them. What was wrong with her? What had happened?

Alex tried to catch her eye as she slithered on to the stool at the table and sipped her coffee, but her face was turned deliberately towards Sidney, who chattered animatedly about someone he had seen from university times with David.

Was that it? Was it something about David that had upset her? He supposed it could be an anniversary of his death, or a birthday, or wedding anniversary, but surely if it had been, she would have said something about it this morning.

Kim didn't answer Sidney, she simply nodded and smiled at him as he continued to prattle in his usual inane manner. Which Alex knew wasn't like her. She was always polite and good mannered around him.

After all, he remembered her often saying, he was paying her wage.

Alex took his camera and began to shoot the bananas in their skins and Kim busied herself with peeling back the skins of two bananas and then slicing them lengthways.

Finally, when Sidney ambled into the reception to answer the telephone, Alex immediately went to her and put his hand on the small of her back. 'What's wrong, darling?'

Alex wasn't sure who got the biggest shock at the way she jumped away. It was as if he had burnt her with a red-hot iron. She stood away from him looking down at the floor and then lifted her eyes to stare at the doorway as though willing Sidney to return.

'Nothing, there's nothing wrong. I'm perfectly fine,' she almost hissed.

But he could see her bottom lip trembling as if she were going to cry.

He started to say, 'But you're not...' then paused when Sidney re-entered the room and the moment was lost. Sidney set the wood blocks out in front of the backdrop and the work continued throughout the next few hours.

There was a strained atmosphere between them all and Alex felt he was walking on broken glass around Kim. Whereas in the past they'd been stuck to each other like glue and Sidney had been the outsider in the team, now it appeared to be the opposite.

Sidney was bright and breezy. He was much more involved in the shoot and accentuating the old camaraderie between him and Kim. Alex now grimaced at his conclusion. There was a wide gulf running between him and the woman he adored, and he didn't know what to do about it.

Alex didn't give up, however, and at every opportunity he tried to catch her eye and smile reassuringly. He wanted to say whatever it is we'll sort it out, but all he received was a cold blank look that he'd never seen before. When they broke for lunch, she refused a sandwich and sat on the stool drinking tea and looking everywhere around the room than at him.

Alex felt his stomach tie in knots as he tried to swallow mouthfuls of tuna and bread while looking at her dressed in a clean white shirt and black jeans. Her long slim legs were crossed at the ankles with the cream sling back sandals demurely resting on the bar of the stool. He loved those sandals. She was wearing them the first day they'd walked along the riverbank together. Sensual yet elegant, which just about summed her up. He sighed; she's a sexy, mature woman who could set his pulse racing with a mere nod of her head or catch of his eye. But not now, he exhaled loudly. For God's sake, what had gone wrong?

Alex didn't usually suffer from paranoiac tendencies, but he was now convinced that it was something connected to him. It couldn't be something that had happened outside their relationship because they were so close and he knew if she were upset, she would look to him for comfort and support. But she wasn't. And, although he was not Albert Einstein, this hadn't been hard to figure out, because now she was behaving as though he didn't exist. Throwing the sandwich into the bin near the table, he looked at her one last time and sighed as she turned her head to the wall.

During the time they'd been together he'd got used to having her eyes follow him around the room when they worked and their secret body language. Now he missed it dreadfully and couldn't help feeling forlorn, as though he'd lost his best friend.

Adjusting the camera tripod and downloading the last few photographs, he realised with a pang, that's just what she had become. His best friend. More so than Sally had ever tried to be over the years they were married. Alex felt his mind was as one with Kim and when her amazing body was joined to his making love, he knew they were inseparable. An item he had called them because that was exactly how she made him feel.

The work with Sidney seemed to drag on interminably as Kim arranged the bananas time and time again for each shot. Sidney began a lengthy discussion about coloured filters for the bananas and how the green filter wouldn't work well to show off the banana's yellow colour tone as the light didn't reach the film.

Alex ground his teeth at the irritating tone of Sidney's voice harping on about filters and light. He had to swallow his rising temper and try to look mildly interested when all he wanted to do was yell, I couldn't give a toss, because the woman he thought the world of was sitting on a stool in absolute misery. He had to find out why.

At three, Kim told them she had a crashing headache and asked to leave early. Sidney readily agreed and Alex could see the older man's eyes fill with concern.

Maybe that's it, Alex thought, maybe she's ill? As
she pulled on her jacket, he tried to catch her eye, but
she left the camera room without a backward glance.
Could it be hormones and PMT like Sally used to get?
But Kim had finished with all of that after the
hysterectomy, or so she had told him. So, what the
hell was it?

He cast his mind back to that morning, racking his
brains to remember if he had said something to upset
her, but as far as he could recall they had been
normal. In fact, she'd surprised him by sauntering
into the shower cubicle, and tenderly washing him
before making love as if their lives depended upon it.

During the last week, his intention had been to help
her loosen up more and relax with him. He'd hoped
this would build up her self-confidence. And this had
worked sooner than he had thought. She'd flourished
and blossomed into a self-assured woman who knew
just how to please and excite him. Far more than any
other woman had before.

Within days of living in the apartment she'd begun
to walk about the bedroom stark naked. Just as naked
as this bloody pineapple, he thought looking down at
the fruit on the table. The extra sets of underwear
she'd bought told him that she wanted to please him,
because it pleased her just as much to wear them. He
sighed in bewilderment.

Finally, an hour later, Sidney suggested they finish
for the day and Alex hurriedly gathered his things
together and flew out the door. He practically ran
back to the apartment, his mind racing all the way, in
sheer desperation to see her. When he opened the

door, the first thing he saw out of the corner of his eye was her suitcases in the hallway.

'Kim,' he called, rushing into the lounge and saw her sitting at the table scribbling on a piece of paper. Was she writing a Dear John note? His stomach heaved in agitation. She was leaving and hadn't even intended to tell him face to face. His mouth and throat were dry, and he ran his tongue over his top lip. 'Y…you're not going, are you? What's wrong? What's happened?'

Kim stood up slowly. 'I…I'm sorry, Alex. But I have to leave.'

His heart began to race and thump inside his chest at an alarming rate. This couldn't be happening, he thought. His mind was scrambling facts together but none of it made sense. It was more than he could bear to think of her leaving when he wanted her so much. 'But why?' he pleaded. 'Talk to me, Kim, please.'

She shuffled her sandals on the wood floor, which made a squeaky sound in the deafening silence between them. 'I'm sorry. I just can't do it,' she whimpered, folding her arms across her chest. 'I'm just not ready to commit to another man. It's not your fault. It's all mine. I shouldn't have come to stay and let it go on this long.'

Alex took a step towards her and held out his arms. 'Okay, we can take it slower and easier. It doesn't have to end altogether,' he begged. 'We can tone it down and maybe see each other once a week for the time being.'

She shook her head and took a step back.

He couldn't believe he was going to lose her and felt bereft and terrified that she was breaking off their relationship completely. Alex dropped his arms by his sides and could hear the emotion choking his voice when he spoke again. 'I don't want us to end like this. I'll do anything for you not to go. Just tell me what I've done wrong and I can fix it.'

He saw her hands tremble and her eyes were wide, blinking with fear.

To try and calm her down, he breathed quietly, 'I'm here for you, Kim. It's just you and me.'

He took hold of her hand, but she brusquely pulled it from his and recoiled rubbing at her hand where he'd touched it.

She looks panic-stricken, Alex thought, as though she was facing a cruel monster. He clenched his jaw, wondering what the hell was going on.

'No, Alex, it's over,' she cried and flew past him into the hallway.

He turned quickly and strode after her.

She bent to pick up both the cases at the doorway and stumbled slightly.

He grabbed her arm. 'Don't go, Kim,' he pleaded. 'Look, at least let me carry your cases.'

'Noooo,' she cried, burst into tears then shook her arm free. She practically ran out of the door and down the footpath.

All he could do was stare after her.

Chapter Fourteen

Kim ran through her own front door, lugged both suitcases into the hallway, and slammed the door shut behind her. She leant against it taking deep breaths. Her legs were still shaking. Not only with fright at the scene with Alex, but also with pulling two heavy suitcases from his apartment over Elvet Bridge and up the road. She wiped the sweat from her brow and allowed the tears to course down her cheeks as she prised herself away from the front door and plonked herself down on the bottom step of the stairs.

Her hands were trembling, and she clasped them tight together between her knees to try and steady herself. She looked around the hallway and upwards at the high ceiling, relishing the old familiar smells and sights of her house. This was where she felt safe, here with the comfort of David and her memories. This was where she belonged. Her heart rate calmed, and she laid her head against the rosewood balustrade.

Kim pulled the sleeve of her shirt up her arm and stared at the red mark where Alex had roughly grabbed her to make her stay. She tenderly stroked the area, knowing there would be a bruise the next morning, and sobbed.

The menacing image of his face with the black stubble came into her mind and how there'd been wild panic in his eyes as his jaw clenched. She had never seen him look like that before and her whole body, not for the first time that day had filled with panic and alarm.

In the studio, when she'd seen him grimace and even heard him grind his teeth at one stage, it had disturbed her, but she had felt reasonably safe with Sidney present. However, once Alex arrived at the apartment and she had been alone with him, she'd been terrified that he was going to hurt her and stop her from leaving.

She got up from the stair and wandered into the kitchen, searching for paracetamol as her head was beginning to pound. She knew it was probably stress and coupled with the fact that she hadn't eaten since breakfast. Finding a crumpet in the freezer, she dropped it into the toaster and made herself black coffee because there was no milk left after the tenants. She sat on a stool at the breakfast bar and couldn't help recapping over the whole day since she'd discovered the images.

The hours in the studio from arriving that morning until three o'clock had seemed never-ending. At first, she'd thought she might be able to talk to Alex about the grotesque images, but within minutes of being in his company she had felt so disgusted she couldn't even look at him. Let alone speak to him.

She'd tried to think rationally about what she had found while ignoring him because she didn't know the extent of his input at taking those types of images and who the women were. Maybe he'd only taken a few. Or maybe he had taken them daily for years and was so used to seeing naked women that all bodies seemed the same to him. Which could be one of the reasons why he was so free and easy with his own.

Then, as Sidney had prattled on with his absurd conversation, she had looked down at Alex's big hands holding the bananas and foolishly imagined them fondling the big breasts in the images. She'd felt physically sick. She knew then that she would never be able to touch him again or allow him to touch her. Kim sighed and wondered if all she had meant to him was another body to paw.

Kim buttered the crumpet and thought how other women might think she was over-reacting, but she couldn't stop herself. It was simply how she felt. With these thoughts in mind, she wearily climbed the stairs to immerse herself in a hot bath. She wanted to scrub every trace of him from her body.

While she lay in the water she began to cry; huge racking sobs that hurt her ribs. Kim knew she had no one to blame but herself for racing headlong into a relationship when she hardly knew anything about the man, other than the fact that he had an amazing body. She rubbed a flannel over her eyes, deciding that Sidney had been right to tell her to be cautious, but she'd had her head turned by Alex's compliments and words of encouragement. Sadly, she hadn't taken the time to find out anything about his background, or more importantly, what had happened in his marriage.

She had listened to his account of Sally, who he reckoned had turned into a she-devil after the twins were born, but was this true? Maybe the poor woman had cause to behave that way if she'd been treated badly. And what if Sally had found him looking at naked women locked in handcuffs? In her delicate state after giving birth, it could have been more than she could take. Kim remembered Alex's version of her post-natal depression and how he had tried to support and care for her and the twins. And, had Sally really lied to him about the drugs which he'd discovered were vitamin tablets.

Kim frowned. Sally may well have lived with his liking of those naked women in photographs for years. Could this be one of the reasons why Sally thought it wasn't safe for him to be around? Kim remembered how his black mood would descend whenever he talked about his wife, and she gulped.

One night when Kim had been in the apartment with him, Sally had rung, and not wanting to listen to his conversation, she had meandered casually into the bathroom and stared into the mirror. It was his wife, she'd thought, and had immediately disliked the sound of the sentence. She had re-phrased it and consoled herself with the fact that she was soon to be his ex-wife and had smiled. She felt the words, ex-wife sounded so much better.

Now Kim sighed at her naivety. Were there more secrets behind Alex's loud and bubbly personality that she didn't know about? She lay back in the warm water and tried to soothe the tension out of her body. Kim supposed there was no genuine reason to believe that he had been lying to her, but that was the problem with trust once it was broken the niggling doubts would never go away.

Her thoughts were interrupted by her mobile ringing and she reached over to the bathroom chair then retrieved it from her trouser pocket. His name came up on the screen and she cursed under her breath. Not wanting to answer, she let the messaging service take the call and then played it back. Kim listened to Alex's voice begging for the chance to talk and saying how he wanted to come around and see her. It was the last thing she wanted and decided to ignore the message. She hauled herself out of the bath and pulled on her robe.

Once downstairs, Kim sent a text to Vicky hoping to ring her and talk through the situation. Vicky replied saying they were in Avignon for a couple of days and would ring back when they returned. She frowned with disappointment at having no one to discuss the problem with and felt incredibly lonely.

By ten that night Alex had sent three text messages full of love and concern then pleading to be given a second chance. Ignoring them all, Kim re-made the bed and crawled under the quilt. As she closed her eyes and tried to sleep Kim had a feeling this wasn't going to be the last she would hear from Alex and that he was not going to be an easy man to shake off.

***

As soon as Kim opened her eyes the next morning, she rang Sidney at home and asked if she could talk to him in the studio before Alex arrived for work. They arranged to meet at seven.

In the hallway she picked up the post from the mat and looked at the cricketing magazine then sighed at the lovely man her husband had been. He would never have looked at naked women. All he was ever interested in was his cricket. 'Oh, David,' she whimpered aloud, 'I've been such a bloody fool.'

She passed the office and looked once more at the grooves in the carpet where the desk had stood. She humped and puffed, pulled, and tugged until she managed to move the desk back into the position where it had always been before Alex had entered her home.

Chapter Fifteen

*Her heart began to race, and she dived behind the
curtains, praying he hadn't seen her at the window.
Sinking to her knees she whined, what is he doing out
there? Sweat formed under her armpits as she began
to tremble, crouched under the windowsill. Her phone
tinkled again, and she almost screamed with fright.
She imagined his menacing look and his clenched jaw
and began to shake. Was this what everyone called
stalking?*

Kim had intended to keep her conversation with
Sidney short and to the point without explaining too
much about what she'd found. Although her work
was nearly finished for the project, she didn't want to
put Alex in a position where his job could be in
jeopardy. However, after a fretful night's sleep and
Alex's text messages, when she saw Sidney's familiar
friendly face she burst into tears and blurted out the
whole story. Sidney was appalled.

After a strong cup of coffee sitting at the table in the
quiet studio, and the loan of Sidney's clean white
handkerchief to dry her eyes, she managed to pull
herself together. She told him how she'd been staying
with Alex while renting her house to the rowing club.

'Oh, my dear,' he commiserated. 'What an awful
thing to happen. At the risk of repeating myself, and
hopefully not sounding too patronising, I knew there
was something not quite right about him. And now
I've been proven right.'

Kim lifted her shoulders and looked at him. He was
being patronising and in any other situation she would

have bristled at the comment, but Kim decided that she was in no position to retaliate. She had to accept the fact that he had indeed been right after all.

She looked past his shoulder and let her mind re-visit the happy times she'd had with Alex in the studio and sighed with misery that it had all ended in such an unpleasant way.

In the meantime, Sidney began to boot up the computer. Kim stared at the back of his head and noticed how his hair was sticking upright. He had obviously rushed into the studio to meet her and hadn't had time to do his usual gelled style which slicked all his hair down and swept across his forehead.

'Thanks for coming in early this morning, Sidney,' she murmured while he typed the password into the keyboard. She also noticed how thin his arms were. They seemed to stick out from the short sleeves of a cream un-ironed shirt. Or maybe they weren't any thinner than normal, and because she'd got so used to Alex's huge biceps from now on all men's arms were going to look thin.

She was startled out of her thoughts by Sydney's loud gasp and instantly snapped her attention to the screen. There they were again, the images of the naked women.

'My God!' Sidney snorted. 'They're disgusting. No wonder you got a shock.'

He snapped the folder shut with a click. 'A lady like you should never be exposed to such trash as that.'

Kim couldn't help but smile at his old-fashioned words and attitude, which after the last two days seemed sweet and endearing. 'Well,' she said, 'I think it probably seems worse because I've led a very sheltered life with David and have never seen anything like it before.'

Sidney placed his hand on her arm. 'Of course, you haven't, and neither should you. I can only apologise that you've seen something so grotesque in my studio. If I'd known for one minute...' he paused and tilted his head to one side, staring at her. 'Well, I would never have employed him in the first instance. In fact, I'm going to finish him right now.'

'No!' Kim almost shouted. 'Please don't do that, Sidney. I need to walk away from this with my head held high and a guilt-free conscience. If I think I've been the cause of him losing his job it will make me feel even worse.'

Sidney tutted. 'You've nothing to reproach yourself with, Kim. As usual you've behaved just like a lady should in this unfortunate matter,' he furrowed his thin eyebrows. 'However, as much as I'd like to see the back of him, I do need him to finish this project and some other work he's doing for the retailers. It's such a shame because, as you've said on many occasions, he is excellent at his job.'

Kim smiled and then placed a hand on his shoulder. She squeezed it reassuringly. 'Thanks, Sidney, if you just keep him long enough to do that, and then afterwards if you are still not happy it's up to you what you do.'

Kim glanced at the clock and stood up. 'Maybe you could tell him that I'm ill and having a couple of days at home. We'll see what happens in the meantime,' she said, pulling on her navy jacket. 'I need to slip off now before he comes into work.'

She made her way to the door and Sidney mentioned a photographer in Northumberland who had just managed to secure a big autumn contract with a retailer. He told Kim that he was looking for a food stylist in August. Kim thanked him and agreed to ring the photographer the next day.

Sidney walked behind her to the door and patted her arm. 'Don't worry,' he said conspiratorially. 'We'll sort this matter out with Alex. Once again, I'm so sorry this has happened.'

***

Walking down to cross the bridge, Kim thought what a nice person Sidney was and how grateful she should be to have him as a friend. She'd been unfair to pass over his attentions in the past because of the way he looked and behaved, and she determined to be kinder and more receptive towards him in future.

Within an hour of leaving the studio and reaching home the text messages from Alex started once more. Kim received one nearly every hour until late afternoon with each message begging for another chance.

She began to feel troubled and agitated. After cleaning the house and unpacking her clothes she found it difficult to settle. The TV held no interest and everything she tried to do seemed to have some connection to the last week with Alex. The late afternoon sunshine shone through the patio doors while she cleaned the kitchen. Although she longed for a good walk, she didn't want to leave the house fearful that if he was anywhere in the city, she might bump into him. She shivered at the thought of another confrontation.

Kim found it hard to switch her mind from the loving, excited state she had been in with Alex to being alone and sad again. Although she knew the relationship was over, the memories of how happy she'd been made her tearful.

While she loaded the washing machine with the linen from the bedrooms the tenants had vacated, her mobile rang and she jumped. His name came up on the screen and she took a deep breath. Should she talk to him once more to try and make him understand that it was over between them? As she dithered, the voicemail picked up once more and she listened to him pleading to come and talk. His voice was low and choked with emotion and she could tell he was suffering just as much as she was.

She did miss him. She wavered for a few seconds, but then caught herself. No, it was the man she'd thought he was that she missed and not this new Alex who enjoyed looking at degraded naked women. Determined to keep this thought uppermost in her mind, she resolved to stop thinking about him as he had been and concentrate on what she now knew about him.

Following supper, which she'd made but pushed around her plate because appetite eluded her, she picked up a book and wandered through to the lounge. With David's old comfort chair gone she settled herself into the leather fireside chair and turned the first page of her novel. She froze as her mobile began to ring again. The screen read Alex, but this time she held no qualms about not answering the call.

While she listened to the message, she could tell by the sound of his voice that he'd been drinking. Her heart began to beat a little faster. Why couldn't he just accept that she didn't want to see him anymore? It wasn't as though she'd made up a feeble excuse; she had told him outright that it was her fault and that it was over, but still he persisted. She decided this was now bordering on harassment. She prayed that tomorrow he would accept what had happened and leave her alone.

Trying to read the same page repeatedly in a novel she'd been enjoying, she gave up because she couldn't concentrate. Kim laid the book aside and wandered over to the window. She gasped in shock when she looked out on to the pavement. Alex was standing on the other side of the street, staring at the house.

Now her heart did begin to race, and she dived behind the curtains, praying he hadn't seen her. Sinking to her knees she whimpered, Oh, God, what is he doing out there?

What did he mean by coming around when she hadn't answered his phone calls - wasn't it blatantly obvious she didn't want to see him? Sweat formed in her armpits as she began to tremble while crouched under the windowsill. Knowing that there was the small oblong of grass between the window and the roadside railings Kim thought it was unlikely that he had seen her, but still she felt threatened and didn't know what to do.

Her phone tinkled again, and she almost screamed with fright. She imagined Alex's menacing look and clenched jaw then began to shake. She crawled along the carpet towards the chair where her mobile lay and sat cross-legged looking at his name on the screen again and read,

I know you are home, Kim. Please let me in so we can talk, darling. I need you. I just want to talk, please...

Kim clicked off the text and burst into tears. What should she do? He was drunk and might be argumentative. She was scared of him. If she ignored him would he get fed up and leave? But what if he didn't? Who could she call for help?

She breathed in and out deeply, dreading the sound of the front doorbell or his knocking and demanding to see her. Should she ring the police and tell them he was harassing her? But what if they asked if Alex was violent? She couldn't very well say: well not yet, but he did grab my arm and look menacingly at me. She could hear the ridiculous thoughts in her mind and knew she was being over-dramatic but could not stop herself.

She trembled, maybe he would get sick of hanging around and go home, then she'd feel an idiot later for wasting police time.

Kim made an instant decision and rang the one person who she didn't mind making a fool of herself with and that was her sister.

'Now, Kim, if you don't calm down and stop crying, I won't be able to help you,' Patricia remonstrated.

Trying to stay out of view of the window, Kim had slithered out of the lounge and used the landline on the hall table to ring her sister. Luckily, Patricia was home.

She sat on the bottom step and gulped down her sobs at the sound of Patricia's calm and reassuring voice. Slowly at first, sniffling into the sleeve of her sweater, she told Patricia about Alex and what had happened. Her mobile rang again, but she didn't even look at the screen, just ignored it and kept on relating the story.

Patricia asked, 'Is he still outside now?'

Kim dropped her shoulders and took a deep breath. 'I don't know. I'm in the hall sitting on the stairs,' she whispered. 'He keeps ringing and I'm not answering his calls.'

She heard her sister sigh in exasperation. 'Well, I suggest you stay on the cordless line with me and look.'

Kim stood up and found some strength returning to her cramped legs. She tested a few steps as though she was a child learning to walk and slowly moved back into the lounge.

She listened to Patricia's tirade. 'But, Kim, why didn't you tell me about meeting Alex in the first place? And how long have you been seeing him?'

She was such a comfort, Kim thought, crossing the room to beside the curtain. Never again would she pull faces behind Patricia's back as she usually did when she was on the end of one of her sister's scathing attacks. Patricia was her sister and she loved her, and for probably the first time in her life, she loved her for being who she was.

Kim reached the curtain and peered out. Alex was gone. Oh, halleluiah, she thought, he had finally gone. She stood up against the windowsill and looked as far up and down the street as she could – there was no sign of him.

Tears gathered in the back of her throat again, but this time with relief when she told Patricia the news. At Patricia's insistence, she walked around the house checking that doors were locked and bolted, and all the windows were securely closed. They both agreed that if he did ring again, she wouldn't answer his calls and certainly would not open the door to him.

'I'll be up in the morning to see you, Kim. Although I'm writing the last chapter of my new novel I can work on the train,' Patricia said. 'We'll get this mess sorted out.'

Kim sighed with relief, knowing that however cantankerous Patricia would be, she'd be glad to see her sister.

Chapter Sixteen

Pulling the jacket's hood over her hair when a light rain began to fall, Kim walked briskly up the steep bank to Durham train station. She'd taken the long route around the city, hoping to avoid any sightings of Alex. Although she knew he should be inside the studio, she didn't want to chance an impromptu encounter, especially after last night.

After Kim had ended the conversation with Patricia, Alex had rung another five times and during each voice message he'd sounded more and more inebriated as the night progressed. In between those calls were text messages with smiley icons where he proclaimed his love for her. They were all signed: from your best friend. Kim ignored them but had hardly slept and had lain with the quilt tucked under her chin quivering for most of the night.

Now, as she reached the northbound side of the station platform entrance she yawned and stretched her stiff shoulders. Patricia's train was due in ten minutes and she was longing to see her.

Kim knew Patricia wasn't the easiest person to get along with and Vicky had once asked, 'So, why do you tolerate Patricia's abrupt, sarcastic comments without retaliation?'

Kim had sighed and replied, 'Look, you don't know how it feels to be orphaned at such a young age, and I worked out years ago that whatever I had to put up with from Patricia would always be better than being completely alone in my life.'

When their parents died Kim had heard an old aunt comment, 'If it wasn't for Patricia, poor little Kim would have to be taken into a children's home!'

At sixteen this image had filled her with dread. She didn't know what was meant by being taken into care, but it had sounded scary and alien. She had clung to Patricia for months, not wanting to lose sight of her. Then the horrendous nightmares had begun. Kim would wake through the night crying and confused, having dreamt that Patricia had left her, and she was all alone. Patricia would sit on the edge of the bed stroking her and repeating the same words, 'I'm here, I'm here. I'm not going to leave you.'

This would settle and calm her down again until she'd drift back to sleep, often with Patricia's hand clutched firmly to her chest.

Kim shook the memories from her mind and stood to the side of the ticket gate leaning on the railing, looking up and down the platform. Kim knew that as soon as Patricia stepped from the train, she would feel relieved and comforted. And that she wouldn't be alone to face whatever the rest of the day brought. David had often maintained that Patricia was a force to be reckoned with and Kim knew she would feel so much safer with her in the house.

Even though she felt wretched at having not slept, with red sore eyes, she remembered previous occasions when she'd come here with David to collect Patricia. Kim couldn't help but smile at the memory of David's affectionate words.

He'd often said that Patricia was like Mary Poppins, arriving in a flurry with her carpetbag and long bone-handled umbrella. He would recite the words from the film in a ghoulish voice, 'The wind is in the East, there's a mist coming in…'

A young mother with two small children hurried onto the platform. The little girl dropped her dolly and Kim bent down to retrieve it for her. The girl looked up with tears in her eyes when Kim handed it to her then smiled.

Kim thought she looked like David's niece when she was little and remembered how they used to baby-sit. She'd loved her niece's company during those weekends and on Sunday evenings, when his sister arrived to collect her, David always pronounced he was glad, but Kim had been wistful and had wanted her to stay longer. However, her sister-in-law had emigrated to Australia five years ago and after his funeral, apart from a Christmas and birthday card, Kim had not heard from them anymore.

Kim sighed with pleasure at the sight of the little family and thought back to when they'd tried to conceive a baby. It had been after two years of marriage but had been without success. David had always said he didn't mind if they had children or not. And after tests on them both had proved inconclusive as to why they were not conceiving, she'd begun to think along the same lines.

She'd never had what other women called maternal pangs to be pregnant, but on a few occasions, when her period had been late, she had known a brief delight at the thought of expecting a child. However, this had always been short lived.

Kim began to pace up and down the platform deep in thought. Dressed in her jeans and denim hoody jacket that she'd bought in town with Alex, her thoughts turned to their discussion about her not having any children. And how he'd gushed, 'But Kim, I think you would have made a lovely mum.'

She'd shrugged her shoulders, 'Maybe, but I figured it was something that wasn't meant to be, but I do love to be with youngsters,' she had told him. 'So, if I do get a chance to meet your boys in the future, although I know little about rugby and football, ten pin bowling sounds fun and I'd love to join you all.'

She sighed knowing there wasn't much chance of that happening now as the East Coast train from Kings Cross thundered into the long platform. Kim shook away her miserable thoughts and turned her attention to the last four carriages because she knew Patricia would be travelling in first class at the end of the train.

Kim heard her sister's querulous voice talking to the guard standing on the platform before she actually saw her alight down the steps. The guard's shoulders were slumped as though he had done battle and was magnanimous in his defeat when he lifted Patricia's holdall down to the platform. Kim called her sister's name and waved when Patricia looked along towards the ticket gate.

Patricia Wood was as different to Kim as any woman could possibly be. As sisters, they were total opposites in both appearance and personality. Patricia took after their mother's side of the family and was only five-foot two, a matronly size eighteen, with one of the widest bottoms Kim had ever seen. She always wore flat brown shoes and Harris Tweed jackets winter and summer alike, which Kim thought made her look sixty-four, not fifty-four. With her laptop case slung over one shoulder and carrying a large leather holdall, Patricia strode towards Kim.

'Oh, thank goodness you're here,' Kim cried and flung her arms around the roundness of her sister's body.

She could feel Patricia stiffen in her embrace and knew this greeting wasn't the norm for either of them, as a brief kiss on the cheek was the usual welcome. Nevertheless, Kim was so relieved and happy to see her that she didn't care if she was being melodramatic. She let go of her sister and stood back smiling at her.

A flush swept across Patricia's cheeks and she cleared her throat. 'All right, Kim,' she said brusquely. 'There's no need for all this drama.'

Kim picked up her holdall and they walked through the station café and stood outside in the queue for a taxi. Even if Patricia didn't have a bag to carry Kim knew her sister would not want to walk. She classed walking, or any other form of exercise, as an unnecessary waste of time and energy that she could put to good use elsewhere. Settled in the taxi as it wove through the streets of the city, Patricia sat in the front seat chatting to the driver about The Regatta and the much-needed money it always brought into in the city.

With their voices in the distance Kim reminisced to the years after their parent's accident and at the time how an old family friend had stated that Patricia was going to have to take on the role of both sister and mother to her. While she gazed out of the taxi window, she decided that Patricia had been just that.

Although they'd always remained close as sisters when David died, Patricia had once more stepped into the mothering routine. Up until now this had aggravated Kim, and many times during the last year she'd had to bite her tongue, not wanting to cause animosity between them. But now, wearily resting her head back on the seat, she glad to have Patricia close.

Settled in the kitchen with a pot of tea and biscuits, the two women sat on stools with the patio doors wide open enjoying the fresh air although the sun was hidden by huge billowing clouds. Patricia had taken off her jacket and slipped the shoes from her feet, while Kim pulled off her denim jacket and draped it over the back of the stool.

Patricia frowned. 'So, is this Alex the reason you're now dressing like a teenager?'

Kim sighed at her sarcasm but was determined not to back-answer the comment as it would end up in an argument.

'Well,' she said. 'I don't think denim jackets are strictly for teenagers, and yes, I have had a bit of a wardrobe re-vamp. I have some nice pieces that I'm sure you'll like?'

Patricia waved her hand nonchalantly and sat back on the stool with her short legs swinging aimlessly backwards and forwards. 'Okay,' she said. 'Take me through it all again from the beginning, and slowly this time. I couldn't understand much of what you said last night.'

Kim relayed the whole story again, starting with the nuisance calls and text messages she'd had received the night before, and how she hadn't been able to sleep. She opened a few of the texts on her mobile and Patricia read them. Her sister listened carefully and asked a few relevant questions while Kim told her all about Alex from meeting him in the studio.

Patricia had completed a degree in psychology before she became an author and was forever dissecting people's personalities. David had once said it was annoying that everyone had to be given a label or diagnosis for the way they behaved and that in Patricia's eyes it could never be that some people were simply a little bit different.

However, Kim thought, sipping her tea, and munching a digestive biscuit, her sister certainly had a steadiness and sensible outlook to people and their lives. Which, after the last couple of days, she welcomed.

Patricia sighed. 'Well, I don't think photographs of naked women or girly magazines, as we once knew them, are illegal. If he is an artist, he might class the naked body as pure art in its simplest form,' she said, dunking a biscuit. 'Although, I believe there are lots of men who do look at them, I agree with you that whatever form nakedness takes it can be a little unsavoury, especially where sexual paraphernalia is involved...' she tilted her head to one side. 'Like the handcuffs and whips. However, there are many couples nowadays that buy into these games; especially those who've read Fifty Shades of Grey.'

Kim gaped at her sister wondering exactly how much she knew about this area. Then she shook her head more at her own naivety than anything else. She wondered if she was the only woman in the country that hadn't read the famous book.

Even after all the years she'd been married to David they'd never been adventurous when it came to sex. They had basically known how to please each other in what she thought of as an ordinary way and had both been satisfied. Her experiences with Alex, of course, had been much more liberating and different, but those too, she thought, were simple positions that all couples used – weren't they?

Kim felt exhausted with all the worry and information cascading through her mind. Her eyelids drooped and she stifled a yawn. 'I feel so stupid now and can't believe I went headlong into a relationship knowing so little about him.'

Patricia tutted. 'Look, you're exhausted, and I can't see any merit in torturing yourself over silly mistakes you've made in the past. Get yourself up to bed for an hour and sleep then then you'll feel better.'

'But I can't go to bed when you've just arrived,' Kim cried. 'I should make us some food.'

Patricia snorted. 'Rubbish, I had lunch on the train and I'm not hungry. While you sleep, I'll go and sit in the office with my laptop and write. Then you can cook us a meal. And, Kim,' she suggested, 'leave your mobile down here then you won't be disturbed.'

Feeling too tired to object, Kim nodded and slid from the stool then walked around to the back of her sister. She put a hand on her chubby arm and squeezed it. 'Thanks for being here, Patricia,' she mumbled, heading for the stairs.

***

'Oh, no! Not again,' Kim moaned and looked at another text that had tinkled onto her mobile from Alex. They were in the middle of eating a late supper

in the dining room and Kim read the message then
handed the mobile to Patricia. Alex apologised for the
bombardment of calls and texts the previous day,
when by his own admission, he'd had too much to
drink, but he still confessed how much he missed her
and wanted to talk.

'Well, Kim. You've certainly made an impression
on him in a short space of time. And he does seem
enamoured with you. Reading between the lines I
think he seems very fond of you and his feelings do
appear to be quite genuine.'

Kim looked at Patricia and nodded miserably. She
finished eating and laid her knife and fork across the
plate. 'I know. We did get along so well, and I felt the
same as him right up until I found the images. But I
just can't get my head round it...' she paused and
took a sip of the red wine. 'I suppose if I wasn't the
type of woman who was offended by this, we could
still be happily together.'

'Hmm,' Patricia nodded. 'While you were sleeping,
I thought about his reactions to you leaving and have
to admit that yesterday they were quite erratic. His
feelings had been fuelled by the fact you'd not
answered him, and of course, the alcohol. Is he the
type of man who's used to getting what he wants?'

With a clear head after hours of uninterrupted deep
sleep, Kim had woken feeling refreshed and more
optimistic. She listened to her sister's opinion and
advice. Simply knowing she wasn't alone rambling
around in the big house made a huge difference to her
state of mind. She decided she felt almost normal
again.

Kim thought about Alex and knew Patricia was right. He certainly seemed used to getting what he wanted in life and didn't like to be refused anything. She answered, 'Well, yes, he is quite a forceful, boisterous character and I know he is ambitious. He told me about his plans and his intention to work hard until he achieves them. I also remember his drive and inspiration when we were working, and how when he first asked me out for a walk, he teased me until I agreed…' Kim paused and smiled at the memories. 'I know if I'd refused dinner that night, not that I wanted to of course, he would have kept on asking until I said yes.'

Patricia finished eating and took a mouthful of wine. She sat back and folded her arms across her chest. 'However,' she said raising her eyebrows. 'There is a difference between being driven and forceful in our wishes, to being aggressive and threatening. I don't like to think that he was dangerous enough to hurt you.'

Kim could tell Patricia had on her motherly hat, and in the past, this was the look that had made the hairs on her neck bristle. But now she could see it was because Patricia wanted to help her put things right.

Automatically, Kim rolled up the sleeve on her T-shirt and showed Patricia the slight bruise. 'He did seem aggressive when he grabbed my arm to try and make me stay, and I did feel threatened when he loomed above me, begging me not to leave.'

She watched Patricia chew the inside of her cheek and Kim knew this meant she was thinking things over. She knew her sister well. And although Patricia loved her and wanted to protect her, Kim also knew she could expect an honest answer.

'I suppose if the man is well over six foot, he's bound to loom over you, or anyone else for that matter,' she hedged. 'But at the same time, I do think you need to take care if you are in his company again. As for the root of the problem, the images, I can see how this would put you off him. I'd probably feel the same myself.'

They took their glasses of wine into the lounge and settled themselves in comfortable chairs. Kim drew the heavy brocade curtains and Patricia tucked her short stumpy legs under her bottom on the sofa then sighed with contentment. 'Maybe you should answer this text he's sent simply to reiterate the fact that you don't want to see him again.'

Kim worried that answering his text may set off another onslaught. She was just recovering from the night before, and even though Patricia was there, it was the last thing she wanted. 'But what if it starts him off again?' she whined. 'Oooh, I just wish it would all go away. I wish to God; I'd never met him.'

Patricia drank the last of her wine and gave a lopsided grin. 'Now that, I think, would have been a great shame because I can see a huge difference in you,' she said. 'I think having this affair has done you the world of good. It's certainly shaken you out of moping around after David and back into the land of the living.'

Kim was aghast that she could even mention Alex and David in the same sentence and told her so. 'It's appalling to think that Alex could ever be half the man that David was.'

Patricia pouted. 'Oh, Kim, that's rubbish and you know it! You're only thinking that because you want to remember all the good stuff about David and not the irritating things that drove you crazy when he was alive.'

Kim gasped at her sister's words. The old battle cry and war of words between them was threatening to rear its head again and Kim decided to back down before it started. The last thing she needed now was an argument because all she wanted for the rest of the evening was peace and quiet. Just as she was going to tell Patricia this, her mobile tinkled again with another message from Alex.

Patricia sighed. 'I do think, however, that you are going to have to take some type of action tomorrow, Kim. Whatever form it takes, via text, or if you want me to come with you to see him, I don't mind, but you will need to do something as this man is not going to give up.'

Kim paled at the thought of another confrontation with Alex whether Patricia was there or not. But as they went upstairs to bed, Kim agreed that once she'd had a good night's sleep, she would think seriously about answering his text to try and draw a line under it once and for all.

***

After breakfast, and as Patricia settled herself at the desk in the office to write, Kim rang Sidney. This was the third day she had missed going to the studio and not only did she want to know if they'd finished the project, but she also wanted to know if Alex had mentioned anything about her absence to Sidney.

Sidney told her the project was nearly finished and that Alex had accepted the news that she was ill without comment. Kim arranged with Sidney to call at six the next day. He was staying late at the studio to do another family photo shoot, and she would also collect her wages.

Pleased that the work in the studio was finished, she sat at the breakfast bar and sipped her coffee while opening the last text from Alex. She re-read the last few from the evening before and remembered Patricia's words; he's not going to give up easily. She hit the reply button and typed slowly whilst carefully choosing her words.

Hi, Alex, I'm replying to this text simply to reiterate that our relationship is over and that I do not want to see you again. I'm sorry to have caused you upset, but I would be grateful if you could stop sending texts and ringing this number. Thanks, Kim.

Before sending the text, she hurried through to the office and held it in front of Patricia's face. Patricia pushed her glasses up onto the bridge of her nose and read the text. 'Great,' she said, 'It's polite, apologetic, although you didn't need to be, and straight to the point.'

Kim nodded and walked back through to the kitchen and pressed send. She crossed her fingers that this would put an end to the affair and Alex would finally accept her wishes to be left alone then move on.

The rest of the morning passed uneventfully, and Kim took Patricia out for lunch at The Palace Green café which was in front of the cathedral. It was one of her sister's favourite places in the city and she wanted to repay her in some small way for all her support.

The sun shone and the city was still busy with people who had lingered following the close of the regatta while both women enjoyed their lunch looking over the green.

The grassy area in front of the huge stone cathedral had always been a peaceful place with an almost reverential atmosphere that everyone in the city respected. When they looked to the left, the imposing castle walls seemed to envelope them in a comforting embrace. This was their city. The cathedral was a place they had been coming to since they were small children, and it was where Kim felt safe with her familiar memories. Although her sister had never said so, she knew Patricia felt the same.

Wandering back to the house Kim stopped to buy a leg of lamb and ingredients to cook a special dinner that evening. Kim was conscious that Patricia was on a deadline to finish her novel and appreciated the fact that she had made time in her busy schedule to drop everything and come to help. When the two women mounted the stairs to bed that night, Kim breathed a sigh of relief since her mobile had remained silent all day.

However, just as Kim slid under the quilt, her mobile tinkled and she jumped to grab it form the bedside table. It had to be him, she fretted, no one else would text at eleven o'clock at night. She gasped in alarm as she read his text.

Kim, I'm outside, please come and talk to me, sweetheart. I need you.

Kim scrambled out of bed and eased open the slats on the shutter. She swallowed hard and her heart began to thump. Alex was standing outside on the street, looking up at her bedroom window. Oh, God, not again, she thought. For a fleeting moment, she forgot she wasn't alone. Memories of the previous night's upset and how frightened she'd been flooded her mind and she gave a small cry of dismay.

The noise of the bathroom door closing brought Kim to her senses and she remembered Patricia in the bedroom next door. Quickly, she grabbed her robe and pulled it on as she flew out on to the landing.

Patricia was just closing her bedroom door and Kim grabbed her arm. 'It's Alex,' she gasped. 'He's outside again. What are we going to do?'

Patricia took Kim's arm and held it against her side firmly. 'We are going to sort this out, Kim. Now take a deep breath and calm down.'

Wearing her chunky brown dressing gown tied around her waist with a thick, multi-coloured cord, Patricia started down the staircase. She had a cream band around the front of her short brown hair holding two foam rollers in her fringe and she stopped abruptly before opening the door. Taking each end of the cord, Patricia tugged it tighter around her waist and pulled her shoulders back.

Kim hurried behind her sister and paused in the hallway while she opened the front door. Patricia instructed her to stay inside but to keep the door open before she strode across the street towards Alex.

Kim's hands were clammy, and her heartbeat pounded in her ears as she cowered beside the front door. Even at a distance, standing under the streetlight, Kim could see the ashen look of shock on Alex's face when Patricia stood in front of him with her hands on her hips and her tartan slippers planted wide.

Kim couldn't hear the exact words Patricia used at first, but when her sister raised her voice and threatened him with the police if he didn't leave them alone, she cringed. She watched him look down and then over Patricia's shoulder towards her while he held up the palms of his hands as though begging Kim to call off the troops and go to him. Kim's stomach rolled and her mouth dried. Alex looked quite pathetic now he was faced with someone who could shout louder and intimidate him.

Patricia swung back around towards her and the open door then held up her hand in a stop signal. Kim trembled with indecision. Should she go and help her sister? It wasn't fair to expect Patricia to fight her battle and took a step forward.

Alex called, 'I love you, Kim. Please, just let me talk to you.'

At the sound of his voice and his declaration of love, she sobbed and began to shake uncontrollably. This was the first time he had said those words and she felt overwhelmed.

Suddenly Alex lowered his arms, shoved both hands into his jacket pockets and turned away. He walked back down the incline of the street with his huge shoulders slumped. Kim felt wretched with guilt and sadness.

Patricia scuttled back to the front door, hurried through, and slammed it shut. Kim could smell and feel the cold air clinging around her sister and instantly put her arm along Patricia's shoulder as they walked slowly back along the hall to the kitchen. Patricia relayed the conversation she'd had with Alex.

Kim offered to make hot chocolate and felt her chin quiver. She fought back tears as she switched on the kettle and reached for two mugs from the cupboard. 'I…I'm so sorry you had to do that, Patricia,' she said, lowering her gaze. 'This whole thing is all my fault. I've really hurt him and made a terrible mess of everything.'

Patricia slid onto a stool at the breakfast bar and handed her a piece of kitchen roll. Kim took it gratefully and wiped her nose.

Kim spooned chocolate granules into two mugs and muttered tearfully, 'I thought when I told him it was over that would be it. I never dreamt he'd behave like this and take it so badly.'

She stirred hot water into the mugs, slid one towards Patricia and lifted the lid from the biscuit barrel. Sighing heavily, Kim apologised again.

Patricia took a custard cream and dunked it into her hot chocolate. 'Don't be too hard on yourself. It's always difficult when you're the one who is cast aside in a relationship as Alex is now. When it happened to me, I'm afraid I didn't behave very well either.'

Kim stared. 'What do mean? When did it happen to you?

Crunching on the biscuit, Patricia shrugged her shoulders as if to say, what the hell. 'Well, I had an affair with a married man and when he ended it, I didn't cope very well and pestered him with emails and telephone calls for a few weeks.'

Kim shook her head as if she were hearing things. She couldn't believe her sensible, no-nonsense sister

was capable of that. She shuffled on her stool and
gaped at her. 'You had an affair? But when?'

'Oh, it was a couple of years ago, and I didn't tell
you at the time because David had just been
diagnosed with cancer and you had enough to worry
about. But I wallowed in self-pity for months
afterwards,' she said. 'You, see, although we were
only together for three months, he was the love of my
life and I worshiped him. Even now, if he walked
through that door, I'd be off with him.'

Kim couldn't take it in. Instantly she did maths in
her head and wondered if this was why Patricia had
divorced her husband. But no, she reckoned, their
marriage had broken up well before then.

Kim had never heard or seen her sister like this.
Tears glistened in the corner of Patricia's eyes and
Kim could tell she was thinking about him. She
thought for one awful moment that Patricia was going
to cry. In any other situation with a friend, she would
put an arm around them, but Patricia had her arms
defensively folded across her chest and Kim knew her
action wouldn't be welcomed. Instead, she leant
across the breakfast bar and stroked her arm.

Patricia pouted and pulled back her shoulders,
dislodging Kim's hand. 'I know it sounds
unbelievable to you, but I'm not the cold fish that
everyone thinks. And at the time when he ended it, I
thought I'd die of a broken heart...' she paused and
looked down at the hot chocolate. 'Though I must
admit I didn't go to his house and stalk him. That's an
invasion of someone's privacy; Alex has no right to
come here like that.'

Kim sat back on her stool feeling dreadful. Not so much that her sister had been hurt this way, because that was bad enough, but how she hadn't known anything about it and had been so absorbed in her own life she'd done nothing to help.

'Oh, Patricia, I wish you'd told me about him. I could...' she paused as Patricia waved her hand indifferently and slid off the stool.

'Come on,' Patricia said. 'We've had enough for one night. I'm tired and need my bed.'

Kim placed the two mugs in the sink and followed her out of the kitchen, switching lights off as they climbed the stairs. As Kim wished Patricia goodnight again, she sighed, not knowing which had been the biggest shock of the night. Alex turning up outside again or finding out her sister had had an affair with a married man.

Chapter Seventeen

*Kim knew having naked images and sexual
paraphernalia were not a criminal offence, but she
wondered if the police should be informed. Was there
a possibility that he was downloading hard porn?
Kim gasped with abhorrence. No! He couldn't be –
could he?*

Kim slipped quietly through the studio door at six
the following night, just as Sidney was ushering a
couple out of the camera room and back into
reception. She made mugs of tea for them both while
she waited. When Patricia had been in the office
writing nearly all day, she'd had time to talk things
over with Vicky on her mobile.

At first Vicky had been appalled and immediately
told her to book a flight over to Provence. However,
when Kim explained the full story and how she
needed to tie things up with the project first, Vicky
had agreed that running off at this stage wasn't the
best idea. But Kim had been reassured with Vicky's
advice and support. Although Vicky, as Patricia so
poetically put it, had kissed many frogs before she
found her prince, even she was disgusted with the
images and Alex's behaviour.

She'd answered Kim honestly. 'None of the men
I've been out with ever liked looking at images of
naked women.'

This statement had been a comfort to Kim because
she'd faltered a few times as to whether she was
doing the right thing or not. Vicky reassured her that
she was doing exactly what she would do in the same

position. She had also stressed that however many times Alex apologised and promised that he'd never look at them again, Kim would never be able to trust him. They'd finished their conversation with much love and Kim promising to try and re-jig her work schedule to visit before September.

As Kim drank her tea, she recalled their conversation hoping to relax the tension in her shoulders. She imagined herself sitting in the garden at Vicky's house surrounded by peaceful, fragrant lavender as she sipped homemade lemonade.

In her younger days she'd been quite good at sketching with a pad and pencil. When Vicky had told her that the marketplace in Provence was often full of artists with their easels, and she hoped to join them. Vicky had also described the famous Paul Cezanne museum and she longed to see his renowned paintings while she was there.

Kim now heard Sidney pottering in the camera room and she turned her head to look at the door. No matter how hard she tried, she couldn't help but think about the days she'd spent in there working with Alex.

The happenings of the night before made her gulp and swallow hard. In particular, the three little words Alex had said across the road, I love you. She frowned with confusion and thought about his behaviour since the day she'd fled from his apartment. Before that he'd signed his texts, your best friend, which she found annoying. She would never behave towards a best friend as he had. She would never intimidate or harass a friend until they crouched behind a curtain at night shivering with fear, so, how could he?

When they'd been together, he'd told her that he loved being with her, or often said he loved her company in the apartment, but had never once said the words, I love you. So why now? Not that it made any difference, because the naked images were now imprinted in her mind and it was far too late. But she did wonder why. If he did love her, why had he decided to tell her now when their relationship was over? Maybe it was a case of the old saying; absence makes the heart grow fonder, and he hadn't realised until she'd gone. Or, had his declaration of love simply been a ploy, hoping that she would run back into his arms?

Whatever his reasoning she knew she couldn't believe his words now as she struggled to find any respect for him. She would have thought more of him as a man, if he had walked away and honoured her wishes, rather than making a nuisance of himself and embarrassing her. Nevertheless, as she had no intention of talking to him again, there was little chance of learning the answers to these questions.

Sidney joined her at the table and gulped his tea. Kim smiled at her friend, feeling genuinely glad to see him. He looked more like his old dapper self today with his hair trimmed and a newly pressed linen jacket. His eyes were brighter, and he fussed around her, obviously delighted that she had come to see him.

Sidney took an envelope from the inside pocket of his jacket and gave it to her. 'Wages for a job well done,' he said. 'As usual, Kim, I'm delighted with the work you've done for me, and I'm only sorry for the upset that Alex has caused.'

Kim folded the envelope and popped it into her clutch bag that lay at the side of the table. 'There's no need for you to apologise, Sidney. It's not your fault,' she smiled. 'I went wading into a relationship without thinking it through properly and have suffered the consequences. So, it's all my own fault.'

Sidney drew his eyebrows together and licked his moustache. 'Maybe,' he said. 'But I was the one who introduced you and can't help feeling responsible in a small way for what he did.'

Kim didn't particularly want to talk about Alex with him again. She certainly didn't want to admit that Alex was still pestering her. Maybe it was because she felt a modicum of regret and embarrassment following the last time she had been in the studio, in tears. 'Whatever,' she said dismissively, 'but it's over and done with now and behind me.'

Remembering that day, she reached into her clutch bag and placed the freshly laundered handkerchief on the table. 'Thanks for that, Sidney,' she said. 'It was a bad day, and you were good to me.'

Sidney simpered and beamed almost coyly at her, making her smile. He is rather sweet, she thought, feeling herself warm to his reliable and innocent personality. Kim told him that Patricia was visiting, and he went into raptures about her well-being and offered to take them out to dinner.

Kim always felt Sidney's regard for her sister a little strange, because on the few occasions Patricia had been in his company, she had made it blatantly obvious that she didn't like him. Kim remembered her once saying to David that Sidney was an odious little creep and her husband had howled with laughter.

Sidney turned and lifted a large portfolio onto the table. He spread open the first two pages, showing the collage of the vegetable shots they'd worked on.

Kim gasped in awe at the work. 'Oh my,' she exhaled softly, 'they look amazing!'

Sidney pulled his shoulders back and Kim watched him preen like a peacock. She smiled. Kim knew most of his actions so well now that he would probably take credit for the portfolio as if the ideas and work were all his own.

Looking at the photographs Kim felt her heart sink with sadness because she could see Alex in the shots. She could see his clever ingenuity with colours and lights. The angles and design of the images were all his, as though he had breathed life into the plain vegetables and fruit. He'd captured and magnified a drop of juice running from the edge of a pear which glistened so invitingly it made her want to bite into the fruit and savour the juiciness. Kim propped her cheek in the palm of her hand gazing at each page as Sidney turned them over one by one, knowing this was truly exceptional work.

Memories of the way she'd felt with Alex on the days the shots were taken flooded through her and she felt a huge ball of emotion gather in her throat. She remembered the instant attraction that had overwhelmed her to the extent that she hadn't been able to think about anything else. She remembered how he had pursued her, but also how she had been glad to be pursued because at the time she'd been just as keen to be with him. She remembered how he had talked to her by the river about his family life, exposing his true vulnerability, and how she had felt her insides melt.

The next page held the shot that they had taken before leaving the studio and going their separate ways on the street outside. She remembered the misery she'd felt at leaving him and how they had turned around and run to each other, and of course, back at the apartment, making love for the first time.

She had trusted him with all her thoughts and innermost feelings and had folded away her grief with David's mementoes. In effect, she had started to live again. After all of this, he'd let her down by looking at pathetic images of naked women. There was a large part of her that hated him for destroying what they'd had together. She felt the first stirrings of anger in her stomach. Hopefully, now she could start to get over their relationship.

Realising that the last page held the banana shots, Kim shivered with those awful memories of the last day she had seen Alex.

Sidney's eyes were full of concern. 'Are you cold?'

Kim smiled. 'Nooo,' she croaked, 'I was just thinking about the happy days we had shooting them.'

Sidney began to turn the pages back, moving towards the front of the portfolio while she murmured appreciative noises at each design. Although upset at the feelings the shots had provoked, Kim did feel enormously proud to have taken part in the project.

'The retailer is going to love these,' she said as Sidney closed the portfolio. 'Are you satisfied with them?'

Sidney nodded enthusiastically, 'Of courses, my dear, and I know you had a great deal of input into this project, so there's a little something extra in that envelope,' he smirked.

Kim didn't want to open the envelope in front of him but smiled with gratitude. 'You're too kind to me,' she said. 'And you always have been.'

Sidney got up from the table to remove the portfolio and manoeuvred his chair further round next to hers. 'I'm worried about you, Kim. You look pale and thin as though you're not eating. Those eyes of yours are too sad for my liking,' Sidney said.

Kim relaxed and smiled. 'I'm fine, really. I didn't have much of an appetite until Patricia came but I've been cooking for us both now.'

Sidney nodded and set his small jaw. 'All the same, and although in between this project Alex has done some other good photography work for me,' he said pointing to glossy posters in the reception area. 'After much deliberation, I've made my decision. Even though the naked images we found are not a criminal offence, I think I should inform the police. You never know what things like this can lead to. I mean, this could be the tip of an iceberg and he could be involved with downloading real porn.'

Kim gasped with abhorrence at his suggestion. 'No! He couldn't be – could he?'

Without thinking she grabbed hold of the lapel of Sidney's linen jacket and felt tears prick her eyes. What if Alex was mixed up with hard-core pornography? She swallowed hard, remembering all their love making sessions. Tears flooded her eyes and she felt panic-stricken remembering an article she'd read in a newspaper about a man who had hidden cameras in his bedrooms. She sobbed, 'Oh, Sidney, if he has involved me in all of this - what am I going to do?'

Sidney wrapped his arms around her as she clung to his chest and cried.

Sidney declared, 'Well if he is, I'm not having him downloading that rubbish in my studio.'

Sidney cuddled her close and Kim thought he felt like David, an older and more dependable type of man. She could feel him rubbing her back and it soothed her until she stifled her sobs in his shirt. Kim knew now that Sidney really did care about her and, she pondered, maybe a gentle, caring type of love at her age was more important than hot-blooded passion. Perhaps she chose the wrong man that day in the studio and should have picked reliable honest-to-goodness, Sidney instead of big untrustworthy Alex.

Her friend Sidney, a man who had been under her nose for years and who she had never really seen before.

Sidney began to rock her gently backwards and forwards. He murmured into her hair, 'I'm going to sack Alex now because I don't want him in my studio any longer. I knew there was something not quite right about him.'

*

Sidney buried his face in her long hair and breathed in deeply. She smelt clean and fresh – exactly how he thought she would. The skin on her arm felt velvety soft, and he could feel the slight heave of her small breasts against his shirt. He was in seventh heaven. Sidney had waited for this moment for over twenty years, but he cautioned himself against frightening her. His lovely Kim was still fragile and needed his support and reassurance. He knew he would have to take things slowly.

Nevertheless, now that Alex was off the scene, she would come to him like a tulip slowly opening its petals in the springtime. He sighed, it had taken a lot longer than he had wanted after the clown David had died, but finally Kim would belong to him.

Chapter Eighteen

The largest poster in the centre of the wall was of her wearing a blue dress that somehow, he'd managed to overprint with a red leather cat suit. The front of the cat suit was open, revealing small pert breasts with blown up images of huge purple nipples. Lower down the suit had an open crotch showing a wave of blonde hair.

When Kim left the studio, Sidney switched on the alarms, locked the doors, and hurried up the road towards his home. He wasn't used to working late and usually left at five on the dot. Sidney liked routine, although this evening he had made an exception for Kim. It was a small price to pay, he thought, cutting across the road behind the bus station because soon she would be his. With a quick stop at the fish and chip shop, Sidney continued to what everyone in Durham knew as the Viaduct area.

Mistletoe Street was a terrace of old houses where he'd lived all his life. Two up and two down, his mother used to call them, and his house was towards the end of the terrace. A walkway, which led into the terrace behind and was aptly named Holly Street, was at the end of the terrace with railings and trees behind it.

Years ago, the walkway had not been a problem, but now teenagers hung out there at night, and kids played amongst the scattered debris of litter throughout the day. The younger children often tormented him when he was at home, and with the light summer evenings they were sometimes there

well into the night. The teenagers didn't torment him
but would often call him, weirdo, when he scurried
through his front door.

In his younger days, he'd gone out to shout at them,
or march around to their parents to complain and
threaten them with the police. However, as his actions
never improved the situation, as he grew older and
tired of the situation, he had long since decided it was
futile as neither the children nor their parents took
any notice of him.

Sidney hurried into the house with a plastic carrier
bag dangling from his wrist. It was dusk now and he
slammed the old wooden door which had white paint
peeling from both the inside and out. He sighed,
knowing it was another job on his list of chores in the
old property that seemed never ending. With the
mortice lock secured he reached up and slid a big bolt
into place along the top of the door. Then he bent
down and slid an even bigger bolt along the bottom of
the door. Nodding his head with concentration he
licked his lips and then slid a rusty old chain across
the door. Sidney liked to feel secure.

In one final check he ran his fingers over both bolts,
pushing at the mortice lock to make sure it was safely
in place. He did this three times and with his routine
complete, he scuttled along the hall to the kitchen to
turn on the oven. He removed his fish supper wrapped
in plain thick paper and placed it onto a dirty plate
from the overhead rack then popped it into the oven.

He could hear his mother chanting: 'No cold plates,
Sidney, I like to eat my fish and chips from a warmed
plate'.

He grimaced at the thought of his mother while he removed his jacket and hung it on a peg on the back door. She didn't even know who he was now. Still alive at the age of eighty-eight, his mother had Alzheimer's disease, or so they now called it, but in his mind, she had been weird since the day his father died had.

When he was a little boy Sidney had once asked his father why he had no brothers or sisters. His father had said, 'Your mam was too fragile after you were born and won't be able to bear another child.'

Sidney sighed now, remembering his last visit to see her in St. Margaret's hospital five years ago when she no longer recognised him. He had tried prompting her to make conversation about their lives together, but it had been fruitless. Sidney had thought at the time that she was like a lifeless dummy. This had filled him with dread. If Alzheimer's disease were hereditary, he could end up the same way and had scurried from the hospital vowing never to return.

Sidney stood at the sink now and ran the hot tap then picked up a bar of coal tar soap. He lathered his hands and using a nailbrush scrubbed his fingernails and the backs of his hands vigorously. The water was scalding hot, but still he persisted making small, ooh and aah sounds, while he whipped his hands in and out of the stream of water. Drying his hands on a stripy towel, he looked at his red stinging skin and nodded in satisfaction. Clean enough to eat now, he thought.

Switching on the kettle, Sidney made tea in a mug that he took from a dirty pile sitting in the washing up bowl in the sink. It all goes down the same way, he grunted ignoring the brown ring on the inside of the mug then sat down at the round melamine table.

Retrieving the plate from the oven he opened the paper and inhaled the enticing aroma from his fillet of battered haddock. He stepped back and reached into the glass-fronted kitchen cabinet to find a small bottle of vinegar and the salt cellar. The door to the cabinet was hanging from its hinges and he shoved it shut with his elbow.

That's another thing on the blooming list, he thought and spooned mushy peas from the carton then sighed. He cast his mind back, trying to remember how long the cabinet had been in the kitchen and decided it had to be from the mid-fifties when his father had bought it, but he'd dropped down dead four days after his wedding to Freda.

Sidney still wished that his father hadn't died so soon from the massive heart attack. He'd hero-worshiped him and ached with grief and loneliness for years afterwards. An academic man, teaching history at Durham University, his father rarely had his nose out of a book and paid Sidney scant attention.

He had been proud to gloat to his pals at school and university that his father was the esteemed Geoffrey Palfry. Unfortunately for Sidney he hadn't inherited his father's brains and natural intellect. He'd had to work hard to scrape through exams with only the necessary to further his education. Sidney had lived in hope of pleasing his father with glowing reports but had never achieved this. Unable to follow in his footsteps he had settled upon a career in photography.

Enjoying a mouthful of the sweet-flavoured haddock, Sidney smiled. He never bought chips to go

with his fish as he hated large amounts of food. He
much preferred to pick at small piles of food on his
plate. He had been intending to ask Kim to join him
in the fish supper but had changed his mind and
decided it would be too much, too soon. His carefully
thought-out plan would stay in place until the next
day when he would offer an invitation that she simply
couldn't resist.

Sidney looked around the kitchen while he ate and
sighed at the mess. He knew that before Kim arrived
for his candlelight supper, he would have to clean up
a little. He tried to see the kitchen through her eyes
and cringed. He imagined the look on Kim's face and
groaned aloud at the amount of work there was to do.
The small room was crammed full of stuff. Sidney
paused and wondered if there another word for it
other than stuff.

'Nope,' he said aloud and shook his head. It was just
all stuff, but most of it could well prove useful or
valuable in the future and he needed to keep it all.

It was a square room with the oven, fridge, and sink
on one side and two old benches on the other wall
alongside the glass cabinet. The floor was littered
with piles of cardboard boxes, carrier bags, full and
empty bottles, cartons, tubs, and water canisters. The
blinds at the single small window were coated with
grease and some of the slats were twisted open and
broken. The windowsill was littered with empty
medicine and herbal pill bottles. Pans were left dirty
standing on top of the cooker and the swing bin was
broken and filthy. Three laundry baskets full of
clothes were balanced haphazardly on top of the piles
of stuff, but the clothes had been there for so long

now that he struggled to remember which were clean and which were dirty. He'd long since given up using the old washing machine and made infrequent trips to the launderette, which he figured was cheaper than buying a new machine.

The only clear space on the floor was in front of the cooker, and sighing, he kicked aside some of the debris with his foot. He had watched a programme one night on TV where homes like his were now being called hoarding. After a few minutes into the programme, he had felt so uncomfortable because he knew he fitted into the same category, he'd had to switch off the TV. Sliding the dirty plate on top of the others in the sink, he decided the clear-up could start the next day and wandered into the lounge.

This larger room was full of even more stuff. The carpet was completely covered with books, magazines, small cardboard boxes, black sacks, and carrier bags that he'd brought home from car boot sales. The space in front of the fireplace and around his upright chair was clear, however, but the fireplace was strewn with old newspapers.

Sidney settled in his chair and drank the rest of his tea while it was still warm. He sighed with pleasure as he planned his treat in the dark room later when he could be alone with his innermost thoughts. His recollections of the lovely Kim and their time together in the studio were now embedded in his mind. And, if there was one thing Sidney prided himself on it was his memory. He was like an elephant and never forgot a thing he didn't want to.

Switching on the TV news, Sidney glanced around the lounge, unable to see the settee under the window for bags and boxes. When had it all got so messy? Five clocks, none of which worked, stood in inches of dust on the mantelpiece and two old standard lamps without bulbs were propped up the corner of the room. There were a couple of big white plastic tubs full of stuff in the corner from when he'd had a tidy-up session before last Christmas, but unfortunately, they'd got no further from where they stood now. How had things slipped into this godawful state?

He shook his head and couldn't remember but comforted himself with thoughts of the future. When Kim moved in and they sold that mansion of a house she owned, they would have plenty of money to do his place up a little.

It was nearly ten years since his wife Freda, had packed her bags and walked out. Sidney remembered at the time how the overwhelming feeling had been one of enormous relief, because he'd hated her with a passion.

From the day they arrived home from honeymoon to find his father at the undertaker's awaiting his funeral and his mother stricken with nervous agitation, Freda had taken charge of the household. Everything had been cleaned and disinfected to within an inch of its life.

'I think your mother should sleep in the small bedroom in your old single bed, Sid,' Freda had said. 'And we'll go into the large front bedroom in the double bed.'

He had been aghast. First, at the thought of sleeping in what had always been his fathers' huge bed, but second, that she'd called him Sid in front of his mother. Freda had started to shorten his name on honeymoon, and he disliked it intensely. No matter how many times he'd asked her not to she ignored him and carried on as if to annoy him even further.

After the traditional glasses of sherry and ham sandwiches were finished at the wake, Freda had set her weekly routines in place. 'Now, Sid, windows will be cleaned on Tuesdays, washing will be done on a Monday then they'll be dried and ironed by Thursdays, while hoovering, with floors mopped, on a Friday.'

Within six months, Freda and what he saw as her flaws, irritated him beyond belief. In those first few years it might have been different if there had been a baby to take her mind of the rigid housework regime, but for some reason the times they made love proved futile. Freda blamed him continually for this and made sarcastic comments about his inability to produce offspring, which at the time had upset him, but in years to come he'd been nothing short of grateful for his lazy, selfish sperm. Sidney knew if they'd had children it wouldn't have been so easy to get rid of her.

A few months after she'd left, Sidney began to feel constantly uneasy, apprehensive. His GP had told him, 'You suffer from a poor work-life balance, Sidney.'

He had been terrified that he'd follow in his mother's footsteps and live the rest of his life demented. However, the doctor had reassured him. 'No, Sidney, this isn't true. I think the untidiness and hoarding is probably a reaction to Freda's dogged cleaning regimes and you'll soon right yourself again.'

Sidney sighed now at the recollections of his failed marriage. But, he supposed, this was totally understandable and was bound to be doomed because he had married the wrong girl. The only reason he'd married Freda was because Kim had bypassed him and been snatched away from under his nose. Although he'd been the first to meet and fall for Kim, it had been David who had whisked her off her feet in a whirlwind romance, leaving him alone to settle for frumpy Freda.

Kim had been the special one from the first day he'd bumped into her in the university canteen and gazed into her warm gentle eyes. Her long blonde hair had mesmerised him with longing to tangle his fingers through it, but the clown, David had beaten him to her.

Another thing Sidney prided himself on was the ability to wear two faces at the same time. He had been very convincing as David's best friend. When in fact he'd been insanely jealous of him and his rich parents. They had paid for their son to sail through university while Sidney had worked in two jobs with only his scholarship to scrape through with. It had been one of the happiest days of his life when David died.

However, that's enough of the past, he thought and placed his mug onto the floor alongside two used cups from the day before. He jumped sprightly up from his chair with excitement rippling through his body as he skipped in a little jig out of the lounge and along the short hallway to the door under the stairs. Taking a large key from a hook on the frame, he opened the old door down to the basement. Sidney carefully made his way down the stone steps and switched on the overhead strip light when he reached the bottom.

The dirty plastered stone and old brickwork on the walls made the area appear darker than it was and the old stone flags on the floor were blackened. In the far left-hand corner, on flattened cardboard boxes spread over the ground, was an old twin-tub washing machine and mangle that his mother had used. Cobwebs and dust hung from the wooden ceiling boards, but to the right of this old dirty area, was his mini studio and darkroom.

Where Sidney's abnormal lifestyle was of hoarding extreme amounts of stuff in other rooms of the house, the basement dark room was minimalistic, precise and in a state of perfection. The constant symmetry and exactness he displayed in his city work studio were here in this basement too, where photographs of Kim, and her alone, were his daily obsession.

Sidney breathed in the familiar damp musky smell he loved, making him feel as if he was truly at home. In the dark. This was his sanctuary, a place where no one else had ever been.

Even when Freda had ruled the roost, she'd refused to descend the stairs. 'I'm not going down there; it'll be crawling with spiders and creepy crawlies.'

Sidney crossed the stone floor into the right-hand corner and grinned at the sight that awaited him. Next to the tiny cupboard that he used as a dark room to develop his photographs, was a small computer table set at an angle facing the corner where the two walls joined. Both walls were covered with photographs of Kim. Eagerly he sat down on the swivel chair and swung it from left to right. Whichever way he turned he could see her face and was surrounded on all sides by her magnificent body.

In the beginning, he had nailed white boards to the area so that he was able to pin the photographs in groups, starting from when he'd first met her until recent shots that were taken only last week. The boards on the left held photos of them aged nineteen, taken with the first camera he'd owned. Many of the photographs held other students, and David of course, but Sidney had snipped off those unnecessary people.

Following these were photographs from her wedding day. He had cut David off and pasted a photograph of himself in the suit he'd worn to his own wedding, standing next to her. Kim had looked so beautiful that day; virginal in her long white dress peeping from under her veil with wide, apprehensive eyes. Then later in her black sequined party dress hanging elegantly on her tall slim body. Sidney had captured her image perfectly as she'd looked into the camera lens with dancing eyes full of excitement and hope for the night to come. Except, Sidney grimaced, none of it had been for him.

Spreading from left to right he had filled these boards with photographs taken over the years when she'd worked for him on different projects. He'd quickly learned the knack of watching her and snapping photographs, so she was unaware that he wasn't shooting the food, but her. These photographs were close-up shots of the side of her neck, her ears with petite pearl earrings, her gentle eyes downcast while she concentrated and the length of her soft blonde hair.

He'd loved her for so many years now that his patience had worn out and he felt he couldn't wait any longer. Years ago, his love for her had been as pure and innocent as she'd been, but now it had taken on a more urgent sexual need for her body.

Sidney knew that Kim thought of him as a kind-hearted, gentle soul with a good character who only cared for her well-being as a close friend and that she was blissfully unaware of his true feelings. He'd cultured this image over the years as a diversionary tactic to gain her trust, and it had worked beautifully. He had taken her out to dinner and remained polite and restrained when all he'd wanted to do was bring her home with him. She had no idea how much he yearned and longed to touch her and have wild passionate sex.

And this was how the boards had remained, right up until this year when he'd begun to change the photographs around and take as many close-up shots as he dared to satisfy his needs. He had made a big close-up image of her lips, which he darkened over the top with a bright red lipstick, a colour that he knew she would never wear.

The lady who had served him in Boots shop, had said, 'Well, your wife's a lucky lady to have her man choosing such a gorgeous present for her!'

Sidney had blushed at her encouraging words and hoped that eventually, when he did get Kim into the basement to join in the fun, she would love it too.

There was a blown-up image of her delicate cleavage in a V-neck sweater. He'd once spent a whole day wondering if she was wearing a push-up padded bra to support the small mounds of her breasts. He imagined his lips on them as they quivered with pleasure at his touch.

The simple, classy shots of her body dressed in elegant demure clothes had now been covered with a marker pen. One shot of her bottom in a tight-fitting white pencil skirt, had a red thong drawn onto it and other photographs included black fishnet stockings, where he had propped a brutal-looking leather whip in the corner of the image.

However, there was one photograph which he could spend hours looking at and dreaming about. It was his firm favourite. Kim was wearing a pale blue linen dress that he'd partially covered with a red leather cat suit. She was standing with her head bowed and her hands together in front with black handcuffs around her wrists. The front of the suit was open, revealing small pert breasts and blown-up images of huge purple nipples. Lower down the cat suit had an open crotch showing a wave of blonde pubic hair.

Sidney wasn't sure if the blonde hair on Kim's head was natural or dyed and he had spent many hours wondering if the image he'd chosen was correct. For all he knew, she could have a mass of dark pubic hair with a mix of grey, because, of course, she was getting older.

Now, he sighed with pleasure at being in his favourite place surrounded by her. He leant back in the chair and folded his hands behind his head allowing his memories of earlier in the studio float back into his mind. When she had rested her head on his chest he had felt like her champion. Finally, after all these years she was intimately close to him and he could have howled with pure joy.

He looked at the photograph of her in the leather cat suit and mixed these thoughts with feelings he relished from the image. He had read somewhere that there was a fine line between love and hate. Now he knew that somehow, probably since Alex had arrived on the scene, he'd crossed the line. The feelings of love he had wallowed in for years were mixed with a strange loathing.

Sidney consoled himself with this reasoning and decided that his mixed feelings about Kim were only because of the way she'd behaved lately. He imagined her soft hair, which at one time he'd wanted to stroke gently in his fingers, but now, because of what she'd done with Alex, he wanted to roughly grasp handfuls and drag her down on her knees before him.

The sweet smell of expensive perfume on her neck enticed him so much that he felt his zip tighten. He imaged the smell of her on his fingers. The skin on her arm when she'd touched his was so soft that instead of a gentle caress, he now wanted to roughen it up and maybe see some coarse marks or even a tattoo.

'Yep,' he said and slid his hand down into his trousers, 'that would be a great idea.'

A deep scar for the rest of her life to show exactly who she belonged to now. Not the stuck-up idiot, David, nor the clumsy oaf, Alex. She was all his now, he thought, beginning to arouse himself. And she would soon know all that it entailed.

Chapter Nineteen
Being the accused was so unfair

Alex trailed his feet walking down to the studio.
He'd never felt so miserable and had forgotten how
awful heartache was. Because that's what it was, he
thought and kicked at a pebble on the path, simple
bloody heartache. He felt so empty inside and
incredibly lonely living his life without Kim that he
wasn't sure he could bear to stay in the city now she
was gone.

When he walked over the bridge, he averted his gaze
to the right. He couldn't bear to look at Café Rouge
where they'd eaten their first meal together because
he'd be engulfed by memories of her. She seemed to
be everywhere around him, along the riverside, in his
apartment and inside the studio, but worst of all, in
his bed at night. Thinking he could still smell her on
the bed linen, he'd changed it twice, and although he
knew this was ridiculous, he had lain alone choking
back tears in the huge bed.

He'd classed himself as bloody lucky to have found
Kim in the first place and should have known nothing
so good would last. Alex swallowed a lump in his
throat knowing he would give anything he owned to
have her back in his life. He stopped at the end of the
old bridge and lowered his head against a lamppost
fighting to gain control of his emotions.

Alex remembered how her eyes lit up when she
laughed and how she would chew her lip when
concentrating, refusing to give up until the job was
perfect. He remembered the look of compassion and
how her eyes had softened when he'd talked about the

boys. It was as though she knew exactly how he felt. He recalled the passion in her eyes when she was turned on and wanted him to make love to her. Or how she'd initiated their love making, stating bluntly that she simply couldn't wait another minute to have him. When that happened, he'd shake his head in disbelief that such an elegant, refined lady like Kim would give a huge clown like him a second look, let alone beg him to get inside her.

The plan he'd devised to build up her confidence had worked by the end of their first week together and the insecurities Kim had felt about her body image had long gone. She had been open and honest making love, often crying, and shouting aloud when she climaxed while he encouraged her. She would parade around the apartment free and easy in her new undies with a smug look on her face. Once she'd even said, 'I've got you now, mate, and there's no way you're getting away.'

Alex took a deep breath, conscious of the students milling around outside the nearby pub. He sniffed against the back of his hand trying desperately not to break down into tears, but no matter how hard he tried, he couldn't stop thinking about her. The best thing about building up her confidence, had been the knock-on effect for him.

From the day they met, his confidence had been at an all-time high. The obvious pleasure she had shown making love to him made him feel fantastic. He knew he could satisfy her to such an extent that she cried with joy. And that was a heady aphrodisiac.

Alex had known when he first arrived in Durham that his own confidence and self-worth were low following the break-up of his marriage. Although he was certain that he wasn't to blame for his marriage ending, it was understandable that a failure of any sort automatically knocked a person's confidence. He thought of Sally and how since their wedding day she had seemed to lose interest in making love to him. And, how he'd known for certain on more than one occasion that she'd faked the orgasm.

However, in those days, even though he had understandably been just as tall and big boned, he'd been trim and lean, whereas he had gained nearly a stone over the last year. Now he had a gut, that although it depressed him, never seemed to bother Kim. 'It's just the way you are,' she'd said and grinned then hugged him tight.

Remembering her kindness, Alex choked back a sob and swallowed hard to stop the tears that threatened to run down his face.

A tiny old lady walking with a stick passed by and stopped. She looked up at him. 'Are you all right, pet?'

Alex wiped his wet eyes and gazed down at her old, wizened face. He gave her a crooked smile and pulled his shoulders back. The kindness and generosity of northern people still surprised him. 'Yeah, I think so,' he mumbled.

'Good, lad. Just keep going. Whatever it is will right itself in time,' she said then carried on hobbling up the road.

Alex shrugged his shoulders knowing the old woman was right. He would eventually get used to Kim not being in his life, but at the moment everything still seemed so raw and painful. He continued slowly along the road remembering the night before when he'd stood outside Kim's bedroom window and groaned in shame. Although he hadn't meant any harm, he'd just felt so desperate to see her again. But when her sister had come outside to scold him, Alex knew that he had sunk to his lowest point.

Alex remembered Kim telling him how stern and forbidding Patricia was and how she and David had called her Mary Poppins. But the impression he'd got from Patricia was different. Alex thought she seemed to believe in him more than Kim did.

And, yes, Patricia had looked severe and fiercely protective with her arms crossed over her matronly chest, but she mellowed when she listened to what he had to say. When he'd walked back down the street, he thought that if he could have sat down and talked to Patricia, he might have got to the bottom of what had gone wrong in his relationship with Kim.

Even in the streetlight, when he first looked across at Kim standing quite still and composed, his mind had reeled with the hopelessness of the situation. Kim had looked forlorn and wretched. And by the time he'd reached his apartment he knew he was being grossly unfair to her.

Alex grimaced with the thought that if Patricia had arrived last week, he would have been desperate to make a good impression. She was Kim's only family and he'd have wanted her to like him. Now, in a mindless sense of humour, he wondered if she could create some Mary Poppins magic to get Kim to at least talk to him again. Or maybe she could transport them back to the happy state they were in last week.

He grunted and pushed his hands deep into his pockets and walked up the side street towards the studio.

***

Alex opened the studio door and took a deep breath to brace himself. He knew by the tone of Sidney's voice on the phone earlier that there was trouble brewing. Alex had agreed to call in and see him before driving down to Scunthorpe to visit the boys. He had a sixth sense that this encounter was not going to be pleasant.

When he walked through the empty reception, he could see Sidney sitting at the table waiting for him and felt his insides sink merely at the expression on the older man's face. He muttered good morning and Sidney gestured for him to sit down on the chair opposite.

Taking the seat, Alex's first thoughts were how exhausted Sidney looked. His usually pale face looked almost ashen and drawn to the extent that Alex thought his cheeks were sunken under his cheekbones. A fine layer of perspiration stood on the ends of his coarse moustache and his eyes were wide, as though he was in fear of something that was about to happen.

Alex stared down at the large portfolio spread out on the table in front of them. He noted how the skin on the back of Sidney's hands looked red raw and was even broken in places, as though it had been scraped with a razor. Alex had noticed in the past that Sidney had reddish hands but had thought this was a dermatological complaint.

Sidney patted a portfolio binder on the table in front of them. 'I just thought I'd show you the portfolio now that I've put all the shots together in sections,' Sidney muttered.

Alex nodded and silently watched him turn each page over. He was amazed at the collage in front of him. Although he had taken all the images separately this was the first time he'd seen them grouped together. Unable to stop himself being absorbed in the work, he whistled appreciatively between his teeth. They looked fantastic. Automatically he pulled his shoulders back and grinned with pleasure at the work he had accomplished.

When he'd first started the food project, he had been unsure if he could translate his skills into this new area, but with Kim's help, and he had to grudgingly admit, Sidney's assistance, Alex knew this work was worthy of high praise. He ran a hand through his hair and couldn't help but preen himself just a little because he'd done such a great job.

Alex noticed Sidney's hands tremble as he turned the last page and wondered if his hands were hurting. He felt obliged to ask, 'Are you okay, Sidney?'

Sidney nodded but didn't speak and closed the portfolio. He slid a white envelope across the table towards Alex. 'This is for you. It's your wages up to the end of the month because I'm going to have to let you go, I'm afraid...' he paused and looked past Alex towards the front door of the studio as though he was expecting someone to enter.

Alex swung his head around quickly wondering if someone had done so, but then realising they were still alone, he whipped his head back to glare at

Sidney and the unwelcome news that he had just been fired.

'You're sacking me? But you can't,' he growled. His top lip began to sweat with the thought of having no work, and worse still, no monthly income. Sidney hadn't answered so he pushed on. 'May I ask on what grounds you're firing me?'

Sidney clasped his red hands together and his shoulders shivered slightly. 'It just hasn't worked out,' he murmured. 'I mean, me and you working together, it's not been the satisfactory outcome I'd hoped for.'

Anger, hurt, and embarrassment flooded through Alex's mind while he glowered at Sidney. The anger, because he knew with absolute clarity and certainty that the loathsome creature sitting opposite with the power to hire and fire, would never have managed to pull a project like this together on his own, especially without his IT prowess, and of course, Kim's food expertise. He also felt hurt that he was being treated in this way after he'd done such an amazing job. If he had made a botched-up mess of it all he could understand this happening, but not after all his hard and excellent work.

Alex thought about Sidney's reason and sighed heavily. He knew they were totally different types of men and would never be bosom buddies, as Kim had once joked, but he thought he deserved more than this.

With the thought of his lovely Kim, Alex's throat constricted at the memories and he wondered what she would make of this embarrassment. Because that was the only way he could think of it. He felt humiliated at losing his job to a lesser professional like Sidney, who possessed a quarter of his knowledge and would never have coped with this depth of imagery on his own.

'Well, Sidney, I don't see how you can say that. I thought you were pleased with my work and I have done everything you've asked of me,' he said, pulling his shoulders back. 'I'm warning you now that I won't go easily. Not without some further explanation or recompense for all the hard work I've done.'

Sidney swung around on his seat and set his fingers on the computer keyboard. Alex watched him open the folder they had all worked from and leant further across the table as Sidney's finger hovered over a document he hadn't seen before named, Alex only.

With one exaggerated press of the key the folder opened, and Alex couldn't stop his mouth from dropping open. He craned further and stared with disgust at images of naked women with huge breasts, handcuffed and staring morosely into the camera.

'What the hell!' Alex shouted. 'Where have they come from?'

Sidney turned to face him. The trembling and fear had left his small beady eyes and his hands were perfectly calm as he folded his arms triumphantly across his thin chest. 'I don't think you are in any position to argue with my decision to fire you. Not when people see what you've been collecting in here.'

Alex's throat dried and he felt quite light-headed. 'But I haven't downloaded them. I know nothing about those images,' he raged. 'I've never seen them before in my life.'

'Aaah,' Sidney beamed, and a high flush spread up his neck beneath the blue and white spotty cravat he wore. 'Who is going to believe you over me, a pillar of the community and the life-long owner of this studio without a blemish on my name?'

Alex shook his head violently. What he was hearing and seeing was all a bad dream. His mind raced to think how the images had got into the folder. With a speedy process of elimination, he figured that, as he hadn't put them there and was one hundred percent certain that Kim would never have done so, it had to be the worthless piece of crap sitting opposite him. Temper raged in his chest and he clenched his fists, ready to spring across the table and throttle Sidney's scrawny neck.

Sidney's eyes were cast down on Alex's fists and involuntarily the older man flinched. He simpered, 'If you lay a finger on me, I'll have you arrested and then we'll see what your solicitor has to say. You can kiss goodbye to seeing those kids of yours ever again!'

Sidney's words settled into Alex's mind and he knew he was beaten. He couldn't risk anything like that, especially where the boys were concerned. He felt as though someone had put cold fingers around his heart and squeezed it hard. He gulped deeply and took a deep breath to steady himself.

Sidney tipped his head to one side and smirked. 'And another thing, Kim was disgusted when she found these images and all about your murky little secret. But funnily enough she was the one who didn't want me to fire you. She knew how disappointed you'd be because you've loved every minute of the food photography,' he said and sighed happily. 'Yep, she's certainly a classy lady and deserves so much more than to be pawed over by a big oaf like you.'

Alex had to get outside. He needed fresh air to calm himself or he wouldn't be responsible for his actions. He gripped the edge of the table until his knuckles whitened. Slowly, he stood up towering over Sidney. The older man looked up at him with eyes full of spite.

Alex leaned down menacingly close to Sidney's face. 'You really are a revolting specimen of a man,' he spat. 'I may not be able to do anything to you now, but my situation won't always be like this. Whether it is in six months' time or six years' time, I will come back and very slowly tear you limb from limb.'

Alex grabbed the white envelope from the table, and turning on his heel, he strode out of the studio slamming the door behind him.

Chapter Twenty

Alex stormed down the side street then stopped abruptly and leant his back against the wall of the fish shop. His chest heaved and his heart raced with a rage that encompassed his whole body. He wanted to go back and punch Sidney's lights out, but the solicitor's words rang in his ears and he knew that for now, he was helpless. The solicitor's words: squeaky clean, did not include images of naked women.

Feeling helpless wasn't something Alex was used to, and he seethed grinding his back teeth. Slowly and steadily, he took deep breaths, filling his lungs with fresh air until the temper cleared from his mind. Eventually his heart rate slowed to normal and he hurried along to the car park near the apartment then climbed into his Audi.

Leaving the city, Alex turned onto the motorway heading for Scunthorpe. There were a few tailbacks following the morning traffic, but once the road cleared a little, he put his foot down. A long fast drive would help him clear his head and give him the time he needed to think things through. He moved his shoulders up and down and cranked his head from side to side to release the knotted tension in his neck as he drove.

Flying past countryside on either side of the road, Alex began to think about what had just happened. It's blackmail in its simplest form, he raged, it's God-forsaken blackmail. But he couldn't think of a way around the situation. His insides roiled in turmoil at the thought of not seeing the boys again. He swallowed a huge lump in the back of his throat, knowing he wouldn't be able to bear it because he still missed them so much.

Imagining their happy faces, Alex indicated and pulled over into the next lay-by, stopped the car and rested his head back on the seat. He had a dry throat and reached for a bottle of water in the glove compartment and gulped greedily. He thought about the boys and their dark unruly hair, and big chocolate-brown eyes. They were good-looking lads, but if Alex had to admit to a likeness, he knew they looked more like Sally than him.

This didn't matter one jot because now they were both slim and short in height. Alex was pleased they were going to have a normal-sized physique like Sally's side of the family and not like him and his father, Jack, who was also a noticeably big man. He knew this would benefit them as they grew into adulthood and at least they wouldn't suffer the same issues he had because of his huge size.

Alex glanced at the clock and finished the water in long gulps then manoeuvred out on to the motorway. If he were late to collect the boys, it would aggravate Sally and he knew he would have to conform if he wanted to see Josh and Jamie that day. She had used this emotional blackmail since they'd split up and wielded his boys against him like a weapon.

Alex sighed, if only she could be more reasonable because separation didn't have to be like this. He had seen it work well with other couples whose marriages were over. If only Sally could put her jealousy aside and do what was best for Josh and Jamie, which in his eyes was to have the love and support of two parents. Just because as man and wife they didn't love each

other anymore this shouldn't mean that the boys had
to suffer. Why couldn't she see that?

Alex flew passed the ten-mile sign to Scunthorpe
and tried to concentrate on the week's happenings.
Mainly the puzzling things that now began to fit into
place. Jeez, he groaned, he was more than used to
feeling trapped by Sally and her demands, but now he
also had to submit to Sidney's ultimatums. Alex felt
his stomach churn with frustration. And all this upset
was simply because he worshiped Josh and Jamie. He
struggled to see the fairness in any of his situation and
thought of Kim again.

No wonder she'd run off and didn't want anything
more to do him. Any decent woman would have done
the same after seeing those images. He groaned aloud
thinking of the impression she now had of him. Alex
spotted a cautionary speed limit sign and eased back a
little on the accelerator. But in another way, it
gladdened him to know that her leaving wasn't
because their actual relationship had gone sour. And,
he figured, if she knew that he was innocent and held
no interest in looking at naked women, she would still
be by his side now. Which, he decided, was a
smidgen of consolation.

Alex thought of the handcuffs and huge breasts on
the images and wondered why Sidney had chosen
them. Did he have a fetish about big breasts and
thought all men hungered for them? Alex tutted
knowing Sidney couldn't be further from the truth
where he was concerned because he'd never liked
anything big, brash, or outlandish in a woman.

That was the main reason why he was so into Kim.
Although she was tall and very slim with small

breasts her body was completely natural. There was nothing false or exceptional about her; she was all woman from the top of her head to the bottom of her feet.

He remembered their last day together and how she had looked at him as if he had grown two heads overnight and was a monster. Alex sighed, this was understandable now as it must have been a huge shock, seeing the photos. But at the same time, he wished she'd trusted him enough to talk about it instead of running off.

Alex pulled up at a junction and tapped the steering wheel while waiting in a line of traffic. However, he didn't know what twisted or warped version of the truth Sidney had told her, and realistically he had to concede that they had only been together for a short time. Whereas she had known Sidney for over thirty years.

After seeing him this morning, Alex could tell that he was more than just an eccentric old man. He was a peculiar oddball who was quite capable of making up weird and whacky stories. For all he knew, Sidney could have cast him as the next Yorkshire Ripper with a history of ogling pornographic images. He could have told her any manner of things, but whatever he did tell Kim was enough to scare her because she'd certainly looked afraid that last afternoon in the apartment.

The suggestion that he was intimidating really upset Alex. He understood some rugby men had a reputation for being handy with their fists, and although he would never shy away from provoked confrontation, he had never once used his size as an advantage.

He remembered when she'd flew along the hall to the front door of the apartment. Alex gripped the steering wheel now and cringed as he remembered grabbing her arm. But she had been so upset and in such a hurry to get out that she'd caught her heel in the seam of the carpet and he'd thought she was going to fall, so he had grabbed hold of her.

Now, he felt mortified at his own inadequacy. The weak join in the carpet had been on his snag list for the landlord, and he'd meant to tell him about it along with a broken hinge on the fitted wardrobe, but he had never got around to it. 'You should have fixed it yourself,' he cursed aloud. And it would never have happened.

Alex sighed as the traffic in front began to creep forward. He knew he was a big guy, but had never, and never would, harm a hair on her head, or any other woman for that matter.

He thought of his father and one of his old sayings, 'If a man has to raise his fist to get what he wants from a woman then he's not a real man.' And he had always lived by this rule.

Alex smiled with fond memories of his father and decided to call and see Jack after he had taken the boys out. Alex chuckled. Maybe he would let him win a game of chess.

As Alex approached Scunthorpe, he smiled at the familiar sight of the skyline, dominated by the tall chimneys and buildings of the steel works. Businesses had grown up around the works over the years and most people who lived in Scunthorpe worked in them.

All Sally's family did, and Alex knew his wife
thought he prided himself as being a cut above
everyone else for not doing this. But Jack had worked
in the steel works all his life and often told people
he'd hated every single day. Alex smiled
remembering his father rant when he was a child.
'The town of Scunthorpe is the steel works, the same
as Durham is the coal mines. The last thing I want for
you is to follow in my footsteps.'

His father still lived in the family home. When Alex
married Sally and began to work for an old
photographer on the outskirts of Scunthorpe, he'd
known his father had been tempted to sell the big
house and move into a smaller bungalow.

Jack had told him at the time that it would free up
equity for him and said, 'The old photographer
wouldn't last forever and if there's a chance for you
to buy into, or take over the business, then I want you
to have the cash ready.'

However, when the time came to put the house on
the market, his father had found leaving the place
where he was surrounded with memories of his late
wife much harder than he'd expected and changed his
mind. The old photographer had died suddenly,
leaving the business to his nephew and Alex had been
made redundant, so he'd been glad Jack had stayed in
their home.

Later that afternoon and with mugs of steaming hot
tea and chocolate digestive biscuits, Alex sat opposite
his father in the leather armchair and smiled. The pair
of identical chairs sat either side of the marble
fireplace and both men fitted comfortably into the
only two large seats in the room.

A bright blue chaise longue stood in the Victorian bay window where his mother had loved to sit or lie down as her leukaemia had progressed. Alex closed his eyes, imagining her still there with her arms open wide for a cuddle. He gulped down emotion in his throat that seemed like the size of a golf ball and felt his eyes moisten.

Alex loved the fact that the lounge was just the same as it had always been because it preserved his memories of them as a family. Familiarity was a great comfort, and he adored his father for many things in life, but especially for not making any changes over the years.

The coffee table to the side of Jack's chair held the old Vienna chessmen in red and white set out on the board. Alex knew the figures were polished every Sunday morning by Jack, as his father had done before him, and Alex knew he would be honoured to continue the tradition.

'Okay, what's up?' Jack said, drawing his eyebrows together. 'Is Sally creating more havoc?'

Startled, Alex shook his head. 'Nope, in fact, she was fine when I arrived to collect the boys. And was almost pleasant when I took them back after the cinema and their MacDonald's treat.'

Jack nodded and sipped his tea, 'Well there's something eating at you. I can see by the sadness in your eyes and you should know by now there's no fooling me.'

Alex shrugged his shoulders, knowing his father was right. He'd always been able to read what was in his mind, a little like Kim had done. He sighed, missing her all over again. Alex knew his closeness to Kim was the same as he felt for his father and miserably sank back in the chair. He crossed his long legs. He didn't want to worry his father about what had happened, especially while he was away from home in Durham. But now that he had no job to return to, Alex frowned. Maybe it was time to cut his losses and move back home?

'Aw, Dad,' he said. 'If I tell you I'd only worry about you knowing and how much you will fret about me...' Alex paused and nodded towards the chess set. 'How about I let you beat me at a game instead?'

Jack leaned forward in his chair. 'Well, we can play if you want to, but I'd much rather know what's going on. Not telling me will make me worry twice as much because my imagination will run riot. And you never know, I might be able to do something to help.'

Alex shuffled in his seat and felt his chinos stick to the leather as the warm sun streamed through the window on to his face. He took a deep breath and told Jack all about meeting Kim, the project, and the events with Sidney that morning.

Jack didn't interrupt, just listened gravely and when Alex finished, he nodded.

'Okay. Well, I think you have two issues to sort out here. First, you'll have to do something about the job, because your professional integrity and reputation are at stake. Moreover, you cannot allow this creep to get away with what he's done. Then you need to sort things out with Kim,' he said. 'But I suppose once the Sidney issue is rectified it may go a long way to helping your case with Kim. Have you any idea why Sidney's done this? Did you say something to make him angry?'

Alex tutted. 'I can't believe you need to ask that. You know I'm always polite and respectful when I am working. It's how you taught me to be from way back,' Alex said then helplessly lifted his hands. 'So, why Sidney implicated me is a mystery, unless of course, he's jealous but I can't think of any other reason.'

Jack laid his cup down on the hearth and got up from the chair. Alex knew he would start striding around the room now. It was what he always did when he was thinking.

'So, Sidney doesn't know you've been seeing Kim?'

Alex watched Jack walk to the corner bookcase and back with his hands thrust down deep into his trouser pockets. He shook his head. 'No, we decided it was best to keep it to ourselves and not tell anyone, with the solicitors and Sally breathing down my neck.'

Jack passed by him and nodded. 'Good move, son. You did the right thing. There's no telling what that crazy mare would do if she found out.'

Alex saw him continue to the window and pace back and forth in front of the chaise longue. It was almost as though he was talking it over in his mind with Mum, Alex thought.

He had seen his father do it numerous times over the years, when he was worried or had a problem to solve. And, especially on the night when he'd told him about his forthcoming marriage to Sally.

Jack hadn't wanted him to marry her straight away and had advised they wait a year or so before starting a family, but at the time Alex had thought he was doing the right thing, and they were in love with each other.

Now, he knew, his father had been proved right and wished he had listened to his advice.

Alex took a deep breath and spoke to his father's back. 'Kim is lovely, Dad. She reminds me a lot of Mum because she is so kind-hearted and has a loving personality. Contrary to popular belief, or the rumours that Sally spread around about me, Kim is the first proper relationship I've had since the day Sally packed my bags and threw me out.'

Jack turned towards him and raised an eyebrow. 'No one believes a word Sally has to say about you, Alex. Your family and true friends know the gossip she has tried to spread is nothing more than lies. She should count herself lucky because there are not many men who would have been brave enough to do what you did by working so bloody hard to keep your family together. Many men would have been off like a shot when she started telling all her lies.'

'I know,' Alex said and sighed heavily. 'But you know the old saying, mud sticks…' he looked down at the floor. 'I don't know why Sally would never believe me, because I did absolutely nothing to provoke her mistrust and jealousy. According to her I was sleeping with every model that came into the studio, at least two of my mate's wives, and she even accused me of doing it with the new female GP. The sad truth of it was that not once from the day I met her was I unfaithful, although there were always plenty of opportunities at the rugby team parties. I never looked at another woman. In fact, since we parted, the most sex I've had is a one-night stand at a drunken stag weekend, until I met Kim, of course.'

The memory of Kim in her orange underwear tore through him and he smiled. 'She's special, and I miss her so much. It wasn't until she'd gone that I realised how much she meant to me, and now I can't stop thinking about her. It's as though she's in my blood, she's in my every thought and I'm not sure the ache in my gut will ever go away.'

Jack pulled the long grey cardigan he wore around his chest and Alex noticed for the first time that he'd lost weight and how thin he seemed. Jack had always been the same height as him, with similar big, muscled shoulders and arms, but now Alex thought he looked shrunken. Was this simply a feature of getting old, or was there something wrong with him?

It had been his greatest fear for years now and the thought of losing him was horrendous. It had been just the two of them for such a long time. Alex stared down at his shoes and anxiously began to tap the toes together.

His father had done everything for him from the day his mum had been carried from the house in her coffin. Jack had been both parents to him and from a small boy until he was a young man, Alex had wanted for nothing. When he was fourteen and had his head turned with a bad crowd of lads from school, Jack had pushed him through the doors of the junior rugby club. They had given him a new set of friends and an interest. When he was sixteen Jack had bought him his first camera for Christmas and Alex had become absorbed by photography.

He had known from the first few weeks with his camera that it was all he wanted to do, and as he often told people later, without seeming big-headed he'd known that he was particularly good. He found it easy to look for the best in people, especially their faces and expressions, which in turn, portrayed their personalities. Alex loved colour, scenery, and backgrounds. He prided himself in keeping up to date with new ideas, hence the level of his digital expertise.

Yes, Alex thought, all of this wouldn't have happened if it weren't for the man who was striding around the room now. His father. The man who had made him what he was today.

Alex settled his feet and looked up. Jack walked towards him and stopped by his chair. He put a hand on his shoulder and squeezed it. 'So, have you told Kim all of this?'

'Nooo,' Alex hedged. 'She won't speak to me or even see me. And now I know the reason why, I can't really blame her. She must think I'm some sad pervert that likes to ogle naked women with big boobs.'

Jack settled himself in his chair and laid his elbows on the arms. He slotted his fingers together. 'Hmm, I've always been more of a leg man, myself,' he said with a twinkle in his eyes.

Alex groaned, 'Aw, Dad, give over. I'm serious about her. I've never felt like this before about any other woman, not even when I first met Sally.'

'Well, you must go back and talk to her, Alex. My advice, for what it's worth, is if you feel like this about her then go and get her.'

Alex swelled with hope and optimism. He jumped out of the chair. 'Do you think she'd see me again?'

Jack grinned. 'Well, if she felt the same when you were together, she should at least give you the chance to explain what's happened, and more importantly, how you feel about her. She's either going to believe Sidney or you. But it's worth one last shot,' he said shrugging his shoulders. 'I mean, what have you got to lose?'

Alex hurried through the lounge towards the hall with Jack following him. Alex turned and threw his arms around his father in a bear hug. 'Thanks, Dad,' he said and felt Jack hug him close then clap him soundly on the back.

'If I'm lucky and she gives me a second chance, the first thing I'll do is bring her to meet you. I know you'll like her.'

The two men parted. 'Well, if it doesn't work out,' Jack said. 'You can always come back home to live.'

Alex thanked him and ran up the path to his car where he stopped and waved. Jack gave him a thumbs-up and Alex pulled away from the kerb. He headed out of Scunthorpe with his father's words ringing in his ears: Go get and her.

***

At just after seven, the drive was quieter on the way back to Durham than it had been earlier, giving Alex time to think. He wavered at his dad's offer to move back home. If Kim still wouldn't listen to his explanations and didn't want to see him then he might have to go back home to live for financial reasons. With five month's rent on the apartment still to pay he'd be virtually back at square one.

Alex gritted his teeth in frustration at what Sidney had done. The envelope contained enough money to pay for two months' rent ahead, but after that, then what? If he had lost Kim for good, as much as he liked living in Durham, he knew he couldn't bear to stay there without her. The thought of losing her forever and never seeing her eyes filled with desire for him made his chest feel tight. He swallowed hard.

Alex felt it was like been torn in two opposite directions and longed to explain to Kim what had happened and that it was Sidney who'd planted the images in the computer. But if Sidney found out he had told Kim he would run the risk of being estranged from Josh and Jamie.

He remembered their faces earlier, munching their way through burgers at MacDonald's, and grinned. It had been pure delight to be with them today and when they'd both run down the path to greet him, he'd nearly hugged the life out of them. Alex's guts twisted knowing he wasn't able to play Russian roulette and risk the chance of having this happiness taken away.

His thoughts were broken by the ring on his mobile, but he couldn't pull over quickly enough to answer and let voicemail take the call. It was Sidney on the line and Alex groaned. What the hell does he want now? He heard Sidney's gloating voice and could imagine the smirk of triumph on his weasely little face.

Just wanted to let you know that Kim is in love with me now and we are having a candle-light supper tonight. I know once she gets here, she will never want to leave me again! Ha! Ha! The joke is on you, klutz.

Alex indicated and pulled into a lay-by. He put his mobile on to hands free and replayed the message. It wasn't necessarily the content of Sidney's message that needled him; it was more the tone of his voice. He sounded weirder than normal, even dare he think, more unhinged. Alex knew Sidney cared about Kim and classed her as a great friend. Sidney wouldn't hurt her, would he? He started the car again and sped off.

Alex remembered the first time he'd met Sidney for his interview and how the older man had asked him to be extra nice to Kim because she'd had a few tough years since losing David. Alex had this request in mind on the first day they'd met, when he had mentioned meeting for an Indian meal one night. He'd simply thought he was extending the hand of friendship in a casual, relaxed manner. But from the first time they'd walked along the riverside together, Alex had known spending time with Kim wouldn't be a problem. Although she was a little older than him, she had a young outlook on life and was great company.

Did Sidney know that he had been sleeping with Kim? Alex supposed she could have told him, although they had agreed not to tell anyone. So maybe in Sidney's warped mind he thought they had arranged and planned their affair, which really, Alex mused, couldn't have been farther from the truth. None of their relationship had been planned, it had simply happened from a mutual attraction to each other. She was an elegant, beautiful woman and from the moment he'd put his lips onto hers, the fire in his belly had been lit and there'd been no holding back.

However, Alex pondered, there was one thing that had happened which certainly hadn't been planned and that was how he'd fallen in love with her.

Alex played Sydney's message again. He sounded highly charged and unstable. His words, we are having a candle-light supper, seemed to hang around in the stuffy atmosphere of the car and Alex repeated them over and again.

Kim wouldn't be naive enough to go to his house, would she? She had told him in the past that they'd often met for dinner in Durham. If this were the case, he wouldn't be worried as she'd be surrounded by people, but on her own in his house. No.

Alex felt his guts churn with anxiety as he imagined her gentle, vulnerable face and how defensive she always was about Sidney. If he did intend to make a pass at her she would go along without question. Alex put his foot down harder and raced up the motorway as though the devil was behind him. He had to make sure Kim was safe.

Chapter Twenty-One
Like a lamb to the slaughter

Kim sat on the edge of the desk in her office while Patricia typed on her laptop. She swung her legs along to a song on the radio that she'd known and loved when she was with Alex. She told Patricia how they'd danced to the track in a Newcastle nightclub one weekend until the early hours of the morning.

Patricia raised her heavy eyebrows and gave Kim a quizzical look.

'Yes, I know,' Kim said. 'Me in a night club, in a short cocktail dress, until three in the morning. Dancing, drinking, and having the time of my life.'

'Hmm,' Patricia mused.

Kim could tell Patricia was only half-listening and trying to finish the sentence she was writing.

With her mind transported back to the nightclub, reliving the memories, Kim started as her mobile tinkled with a text.

Patricia closed the laptop and leant forward towards Kim. 'It's maybe a text from Alex. I'm surprised we haven't heard anything since the night I chased him away from outside the house.'

'Are you?' Kim murmured taking the mobile from her clutch bag. 'I doubt it'll be from him. I think the stalking, if that's what we should call it, is well and truly over. Thank God.'

Kim read the text and then handed her mobile to Patricia. 'It's from Sidney, asking us to his house for supper tonight. He's bought a fresh salmon.'

Patricia read the text and hooted with laughter. 'It'll take a lot more than a whole salmon to tempt me,' she quipped. 'To use a Jack Nicholson saying: Quite frankly I'd rather stick pins in my eyes.'

Kim sniggered as she replied to Sidney, accepting his kind invitation but telling him regretfully that Patricia wouldn't be able to make it.

Patricia pushed her chair away from the desk. 'I'll pack my things while you're out and be ready to leave tomorrow morning. Even though I think you're crazy, you go and have fun with the strange little nerd,' she said and exaggerated a shudder with her shoulders. 'For some reason he makes my flesh crawl.'

Kim sighed heavily. 'Oh, Pat, he's not so bad when you get used to him. He has been kind to me and makes me feel safe like David used to. And, well, he just has his own way of doing things.'

Patricia pursed her lips. 'He's a bloody creep, Kim.'

Kim paused and slid from the side of the desk. Brushing aside Patricia's remarks, she felt the need to defend Sidney and pouted, 'Well, I like him, and just because he's not good-looking doesn't mean we should think less of him.'

Patricia tutted, 'Not good-looking! Now that's what I call going from the sublime to the ridiculous. A hunky good-looking man like Alex as opposed to ugly pintsized Sidney.'

Laughing at her own comparison, Patricia pulled the zip along her laptop case while Kim gently shook her head in rebuke.

Kim sighed. She often thought her sister got confused between the suspicious characters she made up for her books and normal people. She tended to forget that there were simply everyday people living everyday lives, and Sidney was one of them. Just because he wasn't run of the mill didn't mean there was something dubious about him. Kim decided that she knew her own mind and trusted her own judgement about people.

Patricia continued, 'And, Kim, whether you like it or not, I do believe that Alex loves you. In my opinion that night when we were outside the house he was in earnest when he said he loved you. I couldn't help thinking that he meant it. He wasn't drunk and seemed genuinely upset.'

'But…' Kim murmured.

Flouncing towards the door, Patricia said over her shoulder, 'I didn't say anything at the time because I knew how upset you were. But there you have it; my opinion, for what it's worth.'

Kim held her hands over her ears as Patricia left the room heading for the staircase. Was her sister, right? Was he in love with her? Up until now her mind had been full of Alex's wrongdoings, the disgusting images, and the stalking behaviour.

Following Patricia upstairs Kim tried to push those thoughts from her mind to determine how she felt about Alex. She remembered the deep understanding they had found with each other, whether at work or at home together. Their silence was easy. It was comfortable, like two old friends not needing to fill in gaps in the conversation. It had been special just to be close to each other. It had been enough.

Kim shivered at the memories of their physical intimacy. Towards the last couple of days when they'd been together, he'd often given her a proper smile, not his usual cheeky mischievous smile, but an open, honest smile that she knew was heartfelt. It had

been as though he was defenceless with her and she
had secretly hugged herself with pleasure.

Kim remembered how simply the touch of his hand
or a certain look in his eyes would give her goose
bumps and a quivering sensation in the pit of her
stomach making her whole body scream out with
longing. On the last night when they'd been making
love, she'd yearned to tell him how she felt. After
he'd brought her to a shattering climax she had
wanted to blurt out, I love you, Alex. I love every
inch of you. But his mobile had rung, disturbing their
closeness and he'd grunted, heaved himself from her
and hurried through into the lounge.

She had been left with tears of emotion in her eyes
and had pulled the sheet up over her body, missing
his warmth. She'd wiped a tear from her cheek
listening to him talk to his boys and had known how
deep her feelings for him were. She knew for certain
that she was in love with him. Kim sighed, if all this
mess hadn't happened, deep down in her heart, she
knew she would have long since said those three little
words and told him exactly how she felt.

She began to apply her make-up sitting at the
dressing table and gave herself a shake to force the
sensible rationale to the forefront of her mind. The
images of the naked women seemed to swirl around
in the mirror, and she sighed, but at what cost? Kim
knew it was stupid to stay with a man whom she
couldn't wholeheartedly trust, even if she did love
him. She felt like weeping at the thought of what she
had lost in Alex but knew if Sidney involved the
police then God knew what their enquiries would
find.

In a white cotton dress, Kim hurried from her
bedroom and popped her head around Patricia's door.
'I'll only be a couple of hours and then we can have a
hot chocolate before we go to bed.'

Folding a sweater into her bag, Patricia looked
towards Kim in the doorway, 'Okay, I'll put the kettle
on around nine. Is he still living on Mistletoe Street?'

Kim nodded and left her sister, calling, 'Yeah…'
over her shoulder as she ran down the stairs and out
of the front door.

Chapter Twenty-Two

Sidney sat in the dark basement, waiting. He sat patiently on his swivel chair staring at Kim's photographs and hoped she wouldn't be late. He had known that Patricia would not come, so hadn't been surprised when he read Kim's reply. So far, he grinned, all was going according to plan.

Sidney had also known that if he invited Patricia then Kim would feel more comfortable and definitely turn up for his special supper invitation. It would all seem totally above board and simply an innocent invite to share good food and wine. He grinned once more at the thought of her arriving soon and tried to remember the last time she had been in his house. It was probably with David years ago, he decided, although the time since Freda had left was a little hazy.

After David died, on the few times he'd taken her out for supper she had always eaten fish, so yesterday he had decided the temptation of a fresh salmon cooked to perfection would be the ideal bait in his trap.

His stomach grumbled with hunger and he cried aloud, 'Damn and Blast!'

He had been in such a fluster that he'd forgotten to buy the salmon. However, when his thoughts lurched back to the morning's meeting with Alex, they darkened, and he imagined for the hundredth-time Kim having sex with the big oaf.

He shook his head, hoping to dispel the tortuous thoughts, and looked at the photographs of the sweet, innocent Kim as a young girl at university. These thoughts were fleeting because, as hard as he tried, he couldn't stop his mind coming back to the present and how she wasn't this coy young lady anymore.

He groaned aloud, thinking of her flaunting around the city in her new shorter skirts with Alex. She had changed into a harlot. His mood darkened thinking of Alex and remembered how foolishly, when the younger man had first arrived, he had asked him to be extra nice to Kim as she'd been through a rough time since David died.

Sidney glowered at the recent photographs of her. The one thing he had never expected was that she would have jumped straight into bed with Alex. The image of her in the red cat suit seemed to jump out at him and Sidney sighed. He had to reason, however, that not all of this was down to Alex as it was as much her fault as his. She had behaved like a dirty alley cat on heat, sniffing around him from day one.

Sidney reckoned it was understandable that she was desperate for sex after the years of abstinence since David had been diagnosed, but it was grossly unfair as he had been the one to take her out after the funeral and spend lavish amounts of money on expensive restaurants.

He grimaced at her face on the cat suit photograph and cried aloud into the silence of the room: 'Why not me?'

It was beyond him how she could have gone with that big klutz so easily. Although she'd lied and said they were simply great friends, he'd known from the first week that she was shagging him. He could practically smell it on her. He had watched Kim's eyes follow Alex around the studio with her tongue practically hanging out as though she was gagging for him.

He groaned, she'd obviously been horny as hell, eager to spread her legs, and once again Sidney, her oldest friend, had missed out.

'Well not anymore,' he growled. 'I'll have her now, by God, if it's the last thing I do.'

He paused and wondered if he should nip out and buy a couple of salmon fillets instead but shook his head. No, she didn't deserve the cost of fresh salmon, he thought. Beans on toast would do nicely for her, he grinned. And the beans would give him the energy for the night's sexual activities. Sidney shivered with excitement.

Chapter Twenty-Three

Kim walked down Mistletoe Street and glanced uncomfortably at the gang of young lads hovering in the walkway. Patricia is right, she thought, this area had gone downhill since they were young. When she reached the end of the terrace, Kim ignored the lad who made a slurping noise and curled his tongue while performing a hand gesture. The other lads all laughed at their friend's sexual implication and began to copy him.

Nervously, Kim knocked on the white door, praying Sidney would be waiting on the other side and wouldn't dawdle.

At the same time, a woman in her late fifties walked up to the door next to Sidney's and pushed her key into the lock. This must be his neighbour, Kim thought, and she gave her a friendly smile. But the woman raised an eyebrow at Kim and puffed between her big lips. She gave Kim a look as if to say, you must be mad going to that house. They both heard Sidney sliding a bolt across the door. The woman put her head down then hurried inside her own front door.

The stench hit Kim as soon as she stepped through the door into the hallway. Sidney bent towards her timidly and kissed her cheek. She returned his kiss on the other cheek and smiled. She couldn't decide what the smell was, certainly not fish or any type of food cooking. It was more of a pungent, stale smell, reminding her of mothballs but intensified a hundred times over.

'How good of you to come,' he said with his back to her.

He slid both bolts back across the door and tinkled the chain into place.

Kim stared at his back in bewilderment. Why did his door resemble Fort Knox? She tried to recall if Sidney had mentioned a burglary or trouble in the neighbourhood with break-ins. He turned to her and ushered her along the small hallway.

The hall was as Kim had remembered it, but when Sidney pushed open the door into the lounge and she entered the room, Kim gasped in shock at the piles of debris and mess.

She followed him slowly along a path he had cleared through the room towards the kitchen door and shook her head in dismay. Kim was appalled at how he was living.

When she'd left home earlier, she had done a calculation and decided it was over ten years since she had been to Sidney's house when she had joined David and him for supper one night. Freda had been there, Kim recalled, and the house had been spotless, almost to the point of what would be called minimalist nowadays.

Kim gulped as she stood in the doorway to the small kitchen, not wanting to step over the threshold into the room. The pervading stench caught her throat. It was much worse in the kitchen where the mothball smell was mixed with dirty grease and a decaying food smell. The last thing Kim wanted to do was offend Sydney, especially as he'd been so kind to her over the upset with Alex.

She took a deep breath and smiled at him as though she was oblivious to the state of his home. As always, Sidney was the perfect gentleman when he walked round to the back of the table and pulled out a chair for her. The kitchen was piled high with what she thought of as rubbish, but there was a small clear circle around and up to the table, so she carefully walked towards him, trying to avoid stepping in the mess, and sat on the chair.

Kim could see Sidney's cheeks were flushed with what Patricia would call a high colour, and she sighed with gratitude that her sister had declined the supper invite. Although she had the good grace to be careful not to hurt Sidney's feelings, she knew Patricia would not have been able to hold back when faced with this situation. Kim felt her mouth twitch uncontrollably as she imagined Patricia in full Mary Poppins mode chanting, 'Best foot forward, spit spot!'

As Sidney busied himself at the gas hob with a small saucepan, she wondered what he was cooking. It certainly didn't appear to be fish, but the dirty stench in the room could conceal any manner of cooking smells, fish or not. Kim stared around the kitchen as Sidney made excitable conversation about an Indian family, he had photographed earlier that day and the colours of the women's sari dresses.

Kim made small comments where necessary but allowed her thoughts to drift. How could he live amongst this filth and mess? She shook her head in confusion, unable to understand his behaviour which was at total odds to how he performed at work.

In the studio he was fastidiously clean with all his equipment. In the two areas where they worked the carpet and floors were cleaned every Friday before he left for the weekend. Especially when she was working with food, Sidney was always meticulous.

His small fridge and freezer were spotlessly clean, and he was more controlled than she was at rotating stock and binning unused food. Kim sighed.

Although she had noticed a decline in his personal standards and attire of late, she would never have dreamt he was living in a hovel like this. How had he got himself into this mess?

Suddenly, he spun around to face her. 'Now, if I had one of those posh kitchen-diners I could talk to you properly while I prepared our meal,' he said.

Kim looked at his face properly for the first time. She had been so appalled at the state of the house that she hadn't given him any attention. His pink jeans looked grubby, with an unrecognisable stain down the front, and his grey T-shirt, which she could tell had once been white, was now frayed along the edges. But it was his face that was the biggest shock. He looked ashen to the point of alabaster and his eyes were glassy with huge black pupils. It was as if he was highly charged up and at the point of releasing something big.

Maybe he was nervous about her being there and embarrassed at the mess of the house. She stared down at the greasy marks on the tabletop and wanted to run a clean cloth over the area.

Kim silently groaned when she saw him lift two dirty plates down from the rack on top of the cooker. Oh, God, she prayed, hoping he didn't expect her to eat off one of them.

Sidney placed four pieces of bread under the grill, talking all the while. It was mainly excited chatter about how great it was to see her, how much he enjoyed their little cuddle in the studio, and how if he'd had more time he would have tidied up for her visit.

Kim recalled the time in the studio and cringed. She remembered how she had laid her head on his chest and had felt comforted in his embrace. If she had known he was living in this mess she wouldn't have gone anywhere near him, let alone allow him to touch her.

Kim shuffled uncomfortably on her seat, hoping the chair was clean and hadn't marked her white dress. She looked towards the back door, and although it didn't look as if it had been opened for years, she felt a sudden urge to rush outside into the warm evening for some fresh air. The smell in the kitchen seemed to be choking her.

'Kim,' he said. 'I'm afraid I've more bad news to tell you about Alex.'

She shook herself back to the present and looked at him expectantly.

'Apparently, when I rang the police to tell them of my new assistant's somewhat bizarre activities, it seems that he is well known to them. Seemingly they've been watching Alex for a while and I've been asked to help them build a case against him. There was a mention of other photos with, well ...' he paused, rescuing the toast from under the grill. 'with children if you know what I mean.'

Kim gulped hard and felt her heart begin to thump uncomfortably. She couldn't believe that of Alex, not now, not ever. She shook her head in abject disbelief, staring at Sidney's back. Alex loved his boys to distraction and fathers who adore their children would never entertain such thoughts.

When she did speak, her voice was choked. 'N...no, Sidney, that can't be right. Surely they've got him mixed up with someone else?'

Sidney half turned while he buttered the toast and looked over his shoulder. 'I know, it's hard to take in, Kim. But that's what they told me. And you know, I've often wondered why his wife was being awkward about his visitation rights. Maybe she knows things about his past that we don't know.'

'But Alex loves his boys,' she said. 'I cannot believe he would do anything detrimental to them, or to any other child.'

Nervous feelings fluttered in her chest and she gulped at the wine to steady herself. It had an unusual, bitter taste and she pursed her lips looking at the label on the empty Chardonnay bottle. Sidney had previously poured the wine into a decanter which he'd told her came from a car boot sale and had seemed rather proud of the crystal glass. Kim thought this was ridiculous amongst the disgusting mayhem in the kitchen.

Dolloping a large spoonful of baked beans onto the toast, he placed a plate in front of her with an exaggerated flourish and then joined her with his own plate.

He sat opposite her at the small table and his knees bumped into hers. She automatically shrank back and drew her long legs further away from his scruffy pink trousers.

'Sorry, it's not fresh salmon,' he tittered. 'I was going to buy one, but I got flustered with excitement about you coming and totally forgot.'

Kim was still reeling from the grotesque remarks about Alex and frowned. She looked down at the food on the dirty plate. All she wanted to do was get up and run.

Was Sidney telling the truth or could he be making this up about Alex? She'd never had cause to distrust Sidney before, but that was when she was working with him and having the odd dinner in a restaurant.

Patricia's words, an odious little creep, came back to her mind and she shuddered as her mind raced with questions and doubts. Kim had always classed Sidney, although not conventional, certainly an innocent in life. Nevertheless, now she'd seen him living in this manner, maybe he wasn't the harmless oddity she had always thought he was. Could Sidney's dislike for Alex be strong enough to tell lies and say things that would discredit him?

She looked up from the beans and stared at Sidney who was drinking large mouthfuls of his wine. Kim decided to go with the flow until the meal was over and then make a hasty excuse to leave. She reassured herself that the wine couldn't be off as Sidney was drinking it down rapidly and she took another thirsty mouthful trying to relax the tension in her shoulders.

There was an intense atmosphere at the table and Kim felt as if they were both waiting for a crack of lightning and thunder. Sidney's eyes darted from side to side as he ate and tapped his shoe against the table leg in time with the loud tick of the kitchen clock.

Kim tried to shake off the feeling of impending doom, but she couldn't, and her stomach churned as though she was in the dentist's waiting room. The last time she'd sensed something like this had been the day David had finally passed away and her hours of sitting by his bedside were over. Although the district nurse had said his death could be weeks away, she'd known that morning something was going to happen and hadn't been surprised when by the early evening, he'd been taken off to the undertakers.

Kim felt the same stirrings of unease and panic now as her legs began to tremble and she clamped her knees together under the table as tension built up inside her. Sidney shovelled the beans on to his fork and crammed them into his mouth, eating noisily with his mouth open. Kim watched him intently as he started to blink rapidly. She saw a wild look in his eyes that she'd never seen before.

Suddenly, he laughed out loud. Kim was startled and dropped her knife to the floor. As she bent over to retrieve it, she realised he hadn't even noticed the slip.

Sidney threw his head back and started laughing loudly again, although now she decided it was more of a devious cackle than a jolly laugh. Her heart raced and could almost smell the tension surrounding them, although Sidney seemed unperturbed. It's as though he is not here, she thought. She could tell his mind had gone elsewhere.

Kim looked down at the old food stains around the rim of her plate and her stomach heaved. She knew she simply couldn't eat the food in front of her. However, she was wary of saying anything about the dirty plate and upsetting him even further. She picked at the beans on top of the pile, hoping they hadn't touched the plate. She took a deep breath then gulped at the wine.

When she put the glass back down on the table
Sidney lifted the decanter to top up her drink. But she
protested, 'No, thanks, Sidney, I've had enough.'

She felt the hairs on the back of her neck prickle and
could tell he wasn't listening. His eyes were wide
open and totally glazed over as he stared down at his
plate. Sidney seemed lost in another world, as though
he was playing out a story in his isolated mind. He
began to ramble his incoherent thoughts aloud.

**'The beans will give me the energy for later and
I'm so pleased I didn't waste my money on the
bloody fresh salmon. The bitch doesn't deserve it.
I was right not to spend the money on Miss High
and Mighty, Kimmy.'**

Kim's mouth dried with fear as she realised, he was
talking about her. He looked quite deranged. Panic
flooded through her. It dawned upon her how
dangerous this situation was. 'Sidney,' she cried.
'A...are you okay?'

**'The bloody cow didn't give a toss about me all
those years when she was with her beloved David.
What an idiot he was. Spoilt rotten by his filthy
rich parents who cushioned him all the time we
were at university. He'd try to give me money
while all the time looking down his nose at me.
Christ, I hated him. And he wasn't the bloody
saint everyone he thought he was. I saw him the
night before he got married screwing a young girl
in an alleyway up against the wall. With his
trousers around his ankles, he was giving it to her
hard and howling like a bloody wolf! And my poor
innocent Kim knew nothing of it on her wedding
day, although snotty Patricia did, because she saw**

**him at it too. I hated him so much that on the day
he died I danced a jig around this very kitchen.'**

Kim gasped and put her hand to her throat. He must
be talking about someone else. Her mind grappled at
his words about David having sex with a girl and
Patricia seeing them. Sidney must surely be deluded
now. Even if David had been doing that, there was no
way Patricia would have let her go ahead with the
wedding if she had seen him. Kim concluded that
Sidney had to be mixing his memories up with
someone else.

Nevertheless, she cursed herself for being so naïve
over the years under the impression that Sidney had
looked upon David as the brother he'd never had.
They'd been inseparable at university and well into
the first few years of their marriage. David couldn't
possibly have known Sidney's true feelings about him
because if he had, her husband would have been
devastated. David used to feel sorry for him, and
when anyone poked fun at Sidney because of his
antiquated mannerisms and personality, he stood up
for him. He'd often said, he was just a poor little chap
in an anorak. David had believed in Sidney as a true
friend and confidant.

Sidney began to wring his hands together on the
table. He licked his lips repeatedly and made short
rasping noises as though he was gasping for breath
and then began to wail again.

**'It wasn't fair because I'd loved her for years
when we were at university, but she had her head
turned by that good-looking, useless clown. I
should have been the one she married, not him.**

My whole life has been spent loving someone who couldn't give two hoots about me.'

Kim could almost feel the colour drain from her face and the few beans she had eaten rose in her stomach. Her legs shook uncontrollably, no matter how hard she tried to ram her knees together, and her shoulders shivered.

She'd had no idea that Sidney had been keen on her at university. Yes, it was true she'd had her head turned by David when he swept her off her feet.

David had been slim, blond, and handsome in a navy blazer and white shirt. He'd been the perfect gentleman with faultless manners, and she'd fallen in love with him instantly. But she hadn't the remotest idea that Sidney held loving feelings towards her. She had only ever believed he was a good friend. The claims Sidney now accused her of were true, but justifiable. She hadn't knowingly spurned him for David. If she had known she would have been more considerate and accommodating towards Sidney's feelings.

Kim heard Sidney give a groan and watched him run his hand over the bald patch on his head. He smoothed the patch backwards and forwards, as though polishing his head for a special occasion. She shivered. The comforting safe feeling she'd always had around him vanished. It was replaced with fear; cold, unforgiving fear.

'Bloody women! Then of course, because I couldn't have her, I got the consolation prize in Freda and had to put up with her all those years with those bottles of bleach sanitising every darn thing in the house. I suppose if she could have

**scrubbed me with the bloody stuff she would have.
No wonder we couldn't have kids she was so cold
and sterile. Ha, bloody, ha!'**

Kim tried to reason with him, 'S...Sidney, can I help
you?'

Maybe he is on some type of medication, she
thought. 'Do you have any tablets or something I
could get for you?'

She scraped her chair back to make a run for it when
suddenly he clamped his hand down over her
forearm, pinning her to the table.

**'And that was another woman who messed up
my life, although she began at a much earlier age
when I was a little boy. She was a raving nut-case
and totally humiliated me when she went doolally
and ended up in the asylum,' he yelled. 'My
godforsaken MOTHER!'**

Kim jumped in the chair with shock and fright.

Sidney grimaced and Kim trembled at the twisted
look on his face, He looked evil. Pure and terrifyingly
evil. Her arm was stinging under the force of his grip
and she was amazed at the strength in his small hand
and thin arm. He looked over her shoulder and she
wondered if he was imagining his mother in the
kitchen behind her chair.

Kim felt his grip slacken slightly. Slowly she started
to try and ease her arm from under his hand, but he
jerked his head back and sneered across the table near
her face. He tightened his grip and twisted her skin.

**'Ha! Chinese Burns. Can you remember them?
And you, Miss Kimmy, you turned out to be worse
than the other two put together. How could you
have sex with that big gorilla? When I think how**

you've repeatedly rejected me in the past and treat me like a leper, only conceding to go out with me through pity because I was David's friend. And then after a few days with Alex you had dived straight into bed with him.'

He twisted her arm again and she cried out in pain.

'Do you know how many nights I've sat here thinking of that oaf mauling your body? Well, it makes me feel sick. Bloody well sick to my stomach.'

Kim started to feel dizzy and queasy then her head spun. Her arms and legs felt numb. They slumped as though she'd lost all feeling in them. Pins and needles began to prickle her toes. Get out of here now, she thought, but struggled to push the chair back. She had no energy in her calves to move her legs. Again, she tried to push herself back from the table but couldn't shift an inch. She managed to croak, 'W...what have you done to me?'

Sidney seemed to loom back into the room. She watched his eyes clear while he shook his head and his features returned to a semi-normal look. He released her arm from under his hand as though he'd been in a trance and the spell was broken.

Kim watched him chew the corner of his fingernail then lean across the table and trail his fingers up her arm. She looked down at her arm where his fingers had left a red raised weal, but she couldn't move to drag it away from him. The hairs stood up on her forearm and prickled with fear and panic.

'I just gave you a little something in your first glass of wine to relax you, my dear.'

Her focus began to wane. Her vision seemed to be bright under the lights, but then dark and grey colours clouded around the mugs and plates on the table. Tomato sauce was stuck in a thin line along Sidney's coarse moustache and she wondered stupidly if the tiny globules were shining at her.

Kim now knew that she'd been drugged. She couldn't find any control in her body, or in what was going to happen next. Her thoughts were sluggish like when she had a general anaesthetic in the hospital. She could still feel and hear things around her, but it all seemed in slow motion.

Kim watched him get up from his chair and come to her side. She groaned in disgust as his small sweaty hand clamped onto her breast and she saw a tiny pool of saliva collect in the corner of his mouth. Pain shot through her breast as he groped it hard through her thin bra. But still, she couldn't move to push his hand away. Her arms and hands hung limply by her sides.

Muffled sounds filled her ears, the kitchen clock ticking, a tap dripping in the sink, but Kim blocked them all out. There was only her and him, wrapped in a huge circle of fear.

Suddenly Sidney darted away from her chair and left the room. She heard him move around in the lounge and then outside in the hall, where his footsteps progressed towards the front door. She could hear him re-sliding and pushing the bolts across the door.

She looked to the small window in the kitchen and glimpsed the neighbour in her back yard through the torn blinds. It was a shared yard with no wall between the houses and Kim could see the woman pegging out jeans on the line.

This is my chance, she thought, and knew it was up to her to fight as she'd never fought before to get herself out of the kitchen. With all the energy Kim could muster she tried to move her legs, but the inert muscles refused to budge. She struggled once more, making every effort to move her right arm. She felt sweat form on her forehead as she puffed and panted, but it would not move an inch.

If she could catch the neighbour's attention, then the woman might be able to help her. This time Kim took deep breaths, straining once more to make her arm move. Her fringe stuck to her forehead as she sighed and panted without success.

Kim heard Sidney's footsteps coming along the hall towards the lounge. Oh hurry, be quick, she panicked, he's coming back. She had to make the neighbour see her before he got back to the kitchen.

Her heart was pounding in her ears, and bile rose in the back of her throat. Sick with fear, she tried to find her voice, but even her throat and voice box seemed stuck. 'Help me, please,' she whimpered, 'Pleeeeease, help me.' She struggled to make her voice louder.

Now she could see the woman pegging out a jumper. Kim glanced over her shoulder as she heard Sidney nearing the kitchen door. Wildly she looked at the blind again, but her insides sank as she saw the woman go back into her house just as Sidney leapt excitedly back in front of her chair.

Sidney followed her gaze to the broken blind. 'Now that's not going to help matters, is it,' he smirked. 'She wouldn't hear you anyway, she's deaf as a post.'

Kim looked at him beseechingly and tried to speak again. Her voice was a mere whisper, 'Please, Sidney, just let me go h...home.'

Sidney threw his head back and cackled. 'Go home? But anyone would think you didn't want to be here with me and hadn't enjoyed your candle-light supper,' he snarled. 'You stuck-up bitch!'

The venom in his voice as he said the word made her gulp. She stared into his beady eyes which now glared at her with hatred.

Chapter Twenty-Four

Her nostrils filled with the strong odour of photographers' developing fluid. At the sound of his cruel twisted voice, which she now thought of as pure evil, her eyes looked towards him sitting at a desk at the other wall. Kim swallowed hard and her mouth dried with fear as she realised the depth of his obsession.

Where was Kim? It was nearly nine, and the fine hairs on the back of Patricia's neck stood up. She frowned; it wasn't like Kim to be late. Knowing her sister so well and spending so many years in her company, Patricia knew Kim's habits and personality as well as she knew her own.

She switched on the kettle and placed two mugs on the island in the kitchen then rubbed her neck and puzzled. Kim hated being late for anything and usually organised her activities by the clock.

This was the total opposite to her. She often lost track of the time when writing and ran to appointments an hour late or missed them altogether. Patricia thought Kim was becoming more like their dad as the years passed. Whereas she was the double of their mam both in character and appearance.

Patricia sighed, that's how it had been when they were young girls and their parents had been alive. She'd always hung out with her mam and Kim had trailed around after her dad for hours. The family unit had been split down the middle, but not in a bad way, just a companionable drifting of two people together with a close child on each side.

Even after all these years Patricia still missed her mam. Kim claimed her memories of their mam had dramatically faded over the years, but hers were as clear as if it were only yesterday that she'd been with them. Kim had certainly inherited their father's kind and easy-going personality. He'd made friends easily and was generous and loyal to them.

Whereas she was more self-centred and introverted, taking time to make friends. She knew she was classed as standoffish when first meeting people. She sometimes tried to be more like Kim and often wished she'd inherited more of Dad's genuinely nice character. However, her efforts over the years had been unsuccessful and she remained reserved and guarded with people.

Spooning hot chocolate granules into the mugs, Patricia remembered the day the policeman turned up at the front door with their aunt and told them about the accident.

He'd said, 'They were both killed outright.' And these words had haunted her for years afterwards.

'Why did it have to be both? Why not just one of them,' she'd raged at the startled policeman while her aunt had tried to gather her up in her arms.

She'd broken down in floods of tears while Kim had cowered on the settee hugging a cushion to her skinny chest with terror shining in her wide eyes.

From that day onwards Patricia had known her main objective in life would be to look after Kim. It hadn't been a problem because Kim had been such an easy, happy-go-lucky girl right up until she was a young woman and married David.

This had been in stark contrast to Patricia who'd suffered from no confidence and low self-esteem in her teens, mainly due to her large, overweight figure. Kim had been the tall, willowy, skinny teenager who loved to play any type of sport. Whereas, at just over five foot, stocky, with a spotty complexion, she had always sat on the side-lines, wishing she were able to join in the games. The more she had wallowed in self-pity, the more she'd eaten, which meant that by the time she had left university she was a staggering thirteen stone. When she'd left university, Kim met David, or Mr Wonderful, as their aunt had called him.

Patricia shivered now as the long-forgotten memories of what she had done the night before Kim's wedding day flooded through her. She hadn't thought about that night for years and wondered why it had entered her mind now.

She wrapped her thick cardigan around her chest and plonked herself onto the stool next to the kettle. She gazed at her reflection in the stainless-steel and sighed. It was the only secret she'd ever kept from her sister and even today, after all the years Kim had been happily married to David and since his death, she consoled herself that she had made the right decision.

On the night before her wedding, while Kim had been sharing a few quiet drinks with her bridesmaid and friends in the house, she had been in the student union bar. At closing time she'd taken a short cut home from the car park and stumbled across David in an alley having sex with a girl up against the wall. The shock had sobered her up instantly and she'd crouched behind the wall with her hand over her mouth, choking back tears for her sister.

With his trousers around his ankles and amidst the
girl's passionate cries for more as he grunted and
shouted in gleeful abandonment, David hadn't seen
Patricia when she crept back to the car park. It had
been when she'd walked the longer route home that
she had seen a small figure in a hooded anorak turn
out of the car park in the opposite corner and had
wondered who it was and if they'd seen David in the
alleyway too.

Patricia had racked her brains all the way home
deciding whether to tell Kim. She had wearily
climbed into bed listening to Kim sleep soundly in the
twin bed beside her. Patricia had known that night
would be the last occasion they would do things
together as single girls and would probably never
share a bedroom again.

Although the large double bedroom had stood empty
since their parents died, they'd agreed to stay together
in their twin room and leave their mam and dads
room as a shrine. It had been left exactly as it was for
years, as though any moment their mam and dad
would suddenly come back into their lives and settle
comfortably back into their old routine.

Patricia had also decided that although she'd
discovered David wasn't the knight in shining armour
her aunt thought he was, he could just have been
having his final fling before getting married. Even
though the girl with David had obviously been
engrossed in him, Patricia had seen her face and was
convinced she wasn't in their circle of friends. She'd
decided the girl was someone David wasn't serious
about and could well have been just a one-night stand.
She'd made her decision mostly with Kim's welfare

in mind and had baulked at the idea of shattering her sister's happiness the following day.

She sighed now as the kettle clicked itself off. She also knew that a large part of her decision had been made with her own welfare in mind, because if Kim hadn't married David, she would have had to stay at home to look after her sister. She wouldn't have been able to chase the job she wanted in London.

The guilt had eaten away at Patricia for the first few years of her sister's marriage until gradually, when it was obvious how happily married Kim was, she'd congratulated herself on doing the right thing.

Patricia slid off the stool and consoled herself with the fact that it was a different way of life back then and she'd had no experience of dealing with relationships. If David had continued to be unfaithful to Kim it would have been a different story and she would have hated herself for not being honest.

She reached inside her handbag for her mobile and frowned. But now she did have the experience and knew she would always tell Kim the truth to make sure she knew exactly what she was getting herself into.

Patricia worried as she scrolled down the list of contacts to ring Kim. Where on earth was, she? Patricia began to pace back and forwards in the kitchen while Kim's phone rang out and then went straight to voice mail.

Chapter Twenty-Five

Sidney raised his hand and slapped Kim hard across the face. She felt her head loll to the side. With the force of the blow, she fell sideways off the kitchen chair onto the piles of bags on the floor which did help to cushion her fall. Kim heard her mobile ring in her handbag and a small tinkle letting her know someone, probably Patricia, had left a message.

Although Kim had no recollection of the time, she did wonder if it were nearly nine o'clock, and if she didn't arrive home soon, whether her sister would come to look for her.

Kim remembered how she had been singing Sidney's virtues before she left home, and it was possible that Patricia would think she was okay and enjoying her supper so much that time didn't matter. She should have listened to her sister in the first place. Kim sighed at the fact that once again Patricia had been proved right all along.

Sidney stood above her and grabbed a handful of her hair. Twisting the strands around his fist, he began to drag her along the floor towards the door. 'The best is yet to come, you dirty whore,' he growled.

Her cheek stung and the tearing pain in her scalp where he twisted and dragged the length of her hair made her sob and choke back secretions in her throat. Her useless legs bumped off the cartons and bags in their path through the lounge. She closed her eyes in terror, trying hard not to imagine what was going to happen next. Was he going to rape her?

She wondered how long the drug would last and prayed to God he'd given her enough to die. If she remained conscious through this, she knew she'd rather be dead than live the rest of her life with the memories. Her mouth was dry, and she tried hard to swallow to rid herself of the bitter tasting wine.

Sidney pulled her into the hallway and towards the back of the stairs where she heard him open a door. With her head lolled to the side all she could see was black darkness. Is it a cupboard, she thought, and was he going to throw her in there?

She felt him put his hands under her armpits and begin to drag her backwards down a flight of stairs. The first bump hit the base of her spine and she groaned in pain. In the dark, it took a second for Kim to realise they were stone stairs that he was dragging her down. She felt the rough stone scrape the skin on her bare legs and absurdly wished she'd worn her jeans.

Kim could hear Sidney heaving and puffing as her legs now flattened out and she realised they were at the bottom on a stone floor with a piercing strip light on the ceiling. His face and chin were on her shoulder as he dragged her, and she felt a droplet of his sweat on the back of her neck.

In between puffing and panting, he shouted, **'Welcome...To...My... Den...'**

Kim's vision blurred and faded. Sometimes she could see things in the dark room and then she would lose her vision altogether for a few seconds. But she could still feel his hands as he pulled and tore at the neckline of her dress.

Kim wondered if he felt more settled down here, because his crazy rambling had stopped, and his voice reverted to his normal manner of speech.

'This is my secret place, Kim, where I have your photographs from over the years. You'll see that I started with your pictures full of love and tenderness. But I've waited so long for you that now I'm not sure if my obsession hasn't turned a little warped. I feel as though I've headed down an avenue that is a mixture of pure hate and love for you,' he said then roughly rolled her over, pulling down the zip on her dress.

'Sometimes when I'm down here, Kim, and am surrounded by you I get a little mixed up and I'm not sure if you are here in real life, or I'm just wallowing in my fantasies.'

Kim's mind raced as he flipped her over and she felt the cold atmosphere around her body as he dragged the dress down her legs.

'Aaah,' Sidney sighed and gave a low whistle of appreciation. 'I love this silky underwear. In all the times I've looked at you in the studio and imagined what you had on underneath your clothes I would never have thought you would wear something as sexy as this, Kim. I thought you'd be a plain white cotton sort of lady.'

Instantly, she wanted to wrap her arms protectively over her white silk bra and panties, but she couldn't move. In her mind, she howled with disgust that he was ogling her body. The underwear was for Alex and me, she wailed silently. Certainly not for you or anyone else to see.

'You know, Kim, you are gorgeous,' he said and put his head to one side.

She saw him stand over her now with a foot planted on either side of her hips and watched him devouring her body with his eyes. He bent forward to stare closely at her breasts. With his face directly in front of hers she could see him licking the saliva formed around his lips.

Revulsion flooded through her. She tried to think rationally and wondered if she could talk him into loving her again then he might not hurt her? Depending upon how much of the drug he'd given her and how long it would last, there was a slim chance that she could talk him around and back to normality.

This notion was quickly dismissed as he dragged down her bra and twisted her nipple cruelly between his fingers. She recoiled in pain.

'Hmm, I just wanted to check that you're actually here with me and you're not one of my fantasies,' Sidney sneered. 'I can see that you've come appropriately dressed in your silky things ready to join in the fun.'

Kim felt her vision swirl again and blackness overtook her.

When she opened her eyes, she realised she must have blacked out and could feel that she was now sitting on a chair. She looked down at her white bra and panties on the floor and felt the cold wood on her bare bottom. He'd stripped everything from her.

Her shoulders felt strange and shivery. They were pulled backwards in a different position and although her head wouldn't move very much, she could lower her eyes to see that he'd tied her ankles and wrists to the sides of the chair. The nylon cord he had wound around her ankles and wrists dug cruelly into her skin but still she couldn't move an inch.

Kim shuddered involuntarily as she felt him behind her, gripping and squeezing her breasts. When he began to pull brutally hard at her nipples and the pain shot through her body, she wondered how she could still feel the pain when everywhere else was numb and inert. Kim then felt him remove his hands and heard the click of his camera and with a sickening realisation, she knew that he was photographing parts of her body.

'Oooh, I've made your nipple huge and dark purple. I'll have to get a shot of that,' he cried excitedly.

She felt his brittle moustache along the back of her neck when he bit hard into her flesh and sucked. The smell of sweat and stale urine from his trousers made her stomach heave.

He left her again and she managed to turn her head ever so slightly to the left where she saw the two walls covered with photographs. Kim was surrounded by herself. The images on the left-hand wall were of her face smiling up into the sunshine, her long bare legs in a summer dress and a close-up shot of her small cleavage in a V-neck T-shirt.

Her nostrils filled with the strong smell of photographers' developing fluid and at the sound of his evil twisted voice her eyes looked towards him sitting at a desk in front of the other wall.

Kim swallowed hard and her mouth dried with fear as she stared wearily at the two other walls. The photographs here were classy shots of her body dressed in elegant clothes, but they were covered with marker pen.

One close-up shot of her bottom in a tight-fitting white pencil skirt now had a red thong drawn onto it, and other photographs included black stockings on her legs. The largest poster in the centre of the wall was of Kim wearing a blue silky dress that he'd overridden with a red leather cat-suit from another image. The front of the cat-suit was open, revealing small pert breasts with blown up images of huge purple nipples and lower down the suit had an open crotch showing a wave of blonde hair. Kim whimpered in absolute terror as she realised the depth of his obsession.

Sidney was in front of her now and bent forwards with his hands on his knees. 'What, are you not enjoying it,' he cackled. 'I didn't think it would hurt with the drugs I gave you, but maybe I can give you some more mixed with wine and then you might be able to enjoy it as much as I am!' He smacked his lips together. 'Because, believe me, Kim, I'm having the time of my life.'

Suddenly he dragged her hair back roughly and tried to force her to drink more wine, but she coughed and spluttered. Defiantly, Kim moaned, he had controlled all her movement with the drugs, but he couldn't get inside her body and make her swallow. She let the wine run down her chin.

Wiping her mouth with the back of his hand he pushed his face into hers and pressed his thin cold lips on to Kim's then tried to kiss her.

She couldn't respond even if she'd wanted to, which she didn't.

'You, bitch,' he yelled. 'Think you're too good to kiss me back, do you?'

She tried to shake her head and looked imploringly at him. If she had been able to speak, she would have told him that she couldn't move her lips and would have tried to cajole him to stop hurting her breasts again. But Kim knew that in his deluded state he didn't realise she couldn't respond to his advances. She closed her eyes and braced herself for what was to come next.

Suddenly, Sidney mimicked a manly voice sounding so much like Alex's deep tones that Kim's heart leapt. She snapped her eyes open, expecting to see her big strong man in the room but felt her insides sink when all she saw was Sidney's weasel face grinning at her and felt his spittle on her cheek.

'Aah, now that got a reaction,' he snarled. 'Well, he's not here for you to have sex with now. I soon got rid of him by planting the images of the naked women in that computer folder for you to find. I knew Alex would like big breasts because of his huge clumsy hands,' he spat and grabbed her left breast roughly then brutally twisted the flesh in his fist. 'Whereas I like a neat handful.'

She saw him pull down the zip on his trousers and felt his other hand push roughly between her legs, snatching at her public hair. Oh, please God, take me now, she trembled.

Kim wanted to die. She felt all her resolve drain from her body and mind knowing she didn't want to live through anymore. Her mind swirled in terror and she tried to imagine her husband's lovely kind face. At least if she died, she would see David again.

As her vision started to blacken again and dizziness took hold, she hoped and prayed she would pass out. However, it wasn't David's face she saw in the black swirls of her mind, it was Alex's. She choked back a sob, knowing she didn't want to die without telling Alex how sorry she was for not believing in him. And that she did love him. The blackness took over and she lost consciousness once more.

Chapter Twenty-Six

Patricia hurried down Mistletoe Street, hearing her squat-heeled shoes click loudly on the pavement. During her walk through the city and around the back of the bus station her feelings of anxiety had increased tenfold. When she neared her destination, she hoped her wish would come true and she'd see Kim happily wandering towards home.

Patricia decided that she would be well within her rights to reprimand Kim for causing her worry, and for having to take this venture out into the seedier part of Durham. But when she arrived at the bottom of the street, she knew that just the sight of Kim would be a blessed relief, and she'd break with her usual standoffishness to hug her tightly.

When she arrived outside Sidney's house, Patricia gasped in surprise as a large black car pulled up and she saw Alex jump out. Her heart began to thump when she saw the look of panic on his face.

'Alex!' Patricia called. 'What the hell's going on?'

Alex swung round to face her as she marched up to him.

'I know Kim is in there,' he cried and began to pound on the front door with his huge fist.

Patricia looked around to see if the noise was causing a disturbance.

Alex ran a hand through his hair. 'Sidney left me a message saying Kim was in love with him now. He sounds completely off his head!'

'Dear godfathers, when was this? Kim left home at seven to come here for supper and hasn't returned. I told her he was a weird creep, but she wouldn't listen.'

With no answer at the door, Alex stopped pounding and took hold of Patricia's hand. 'Look, it was Sidney who downloaded those images on the computer, and he threatened me this morning. He said he'd expose our affair to the solicitor which would scupper my chances of seeing the boys.'

Patricia breathed out deeply and felt her mouth dry with fear. Her hand trembled in Alex's tight grip. It was as though he was drawing as much strength from her as she was from him.

She nodded. 'So, the little creep has blackmailed you, why doesn't that surprise me? But if that was this morning, where have you been all day,' she gabbled. 'A…and why didn't you stop Kim from coming here?'

Alex shook his head wildly. 'I've been down to Scunthorpe and only got the message as I was driving back. Look, there's no time for that now. He's dangerous and I'm scared about what he might do to Kim,' he shouted. 'Let's try around the back.'

Alex tore off down the walkway and Patricia scuttled along behind him until they reached what they presumed to be the back yard adjoining the two houses. Lifting his foot to aim at the old lock on the wooden gate, Alex rammed his shoe hard against it then heaving his shoulder into the old gate, it splintered and the lock broke. The gate opened and he hurried through.

Patricia gasped at his actions and strength then followed him. 'I'm going to call the police,' she cried.

Alex peered through the glass in the kitchen door. 'I can't see anything for the dirt on the glass,' he yelled, trying the handle on the door, and calling Kim's name again.

Patricia made the call and gave the address as calmly as she could, trying to steady her voice while her stomach turned somersaults with worry.

'We're going to have to break the glass in the door so I can get my hand inside to turn the key,' Alex panted. 'It looks very rusty, but fortunately it's hanging in the lock.'

Just as Patricia started to say that the police had told her to wait until they arrived, Alex picked up a half brick lying in the corner of the yard. He pulled the sleeve of his hoodie down over his fist then smashed the glass above the handle.

The glass breaking in the night air seemed as loud as a firecracker and she cried out while Alex used his elbow to create a bigger hole in the shattered glass.

He began to chatter nervously as splinters of glass flew from the hole and he warned her to stand back.

'I love her you see, Patricia,' he said. 'I've fallen in love with her. It wasn't something that was planned or intended to happen, it just did. Your sister has got right under my skin and I just can't stop thinking about her. Please God, let her be okay.'

Alex put his hand through the window and after a few attempts successfully turned the old key. 'If that creep has harmed a hair on her head, I'll kill him,' he shouted and pushed the door wide open against the rubbish piled on the floor.

He looked back at her. 'Look, you stay here and wait for the police. I'll be back shortly with Kim.'

Patricia shook her head defiantly. 'Oh no, I'm coming with you, she's my sister.'

Blood ran from a cut on his finger, but Alex merely wiped it down his jeans. 'Kim…Kim,' he called charging through the kitchen wildly looking around at the piles of debris.

Patricia tried at first to push the bags of rubbish aside with her shoe but gave up and rushed behind Alex striding out over the top of it all. While they hurried through the lounge she couldn't help exclaiming about the mess and joined Alex in calling Kim's name loudly.

'I'll check the upstairs,' Alex roared, charging up the stairs two at a time shouting, 'Kim, where are you?'

As she heard Alex upstairs charging through rooms, Patricia began to shake from head to foot. She looked around at the chaos of the hallway and inhaled the smell of decay then gasped when she saw the huge bolts across the door. This, she thought, even for a slightly dodgy area in Durham was excessive. She knew with sickening dread that this was not the home of a normal man.

Further down the hallway was a line of hooks on the wall with coats and jackets that looked as though they had been hanging there forever.

Patricia stared around and moaned, 'My God, what a way to live…'

She shivered with disgust as she moved two very smelly duffle coats aside to glimpse an old black anorak hanging on the hook by its hood.

Patricia remembered her earlier thoughts. Could it have been Sidney that she had seen in the car park all those years ago before Kim's wedding? And if so, what had he been doing snooping on David in an alleyway?

And, furthermore, she sobbed, what is he doing now with my lovely sister? With all the psychology research she'd done for her course and writing characters in crime novels, the pattern of abnormal behaviour she could see around her didn't bode well for Kim.

At the thought of her sister being hurt she began to choke back huge racking sobs. How dangerous was Sidney? Was he simply a harmless weirdo hung up on the past, or was he crazy enough to do Kim actual harm?

*

Alex tore down the stairs claiming the bedrooms were empty. One look at Patricia told him she was struggling to hold it together. He took both her hands in his. 'Come on, don't give up, we'll find her,' he cried and squeezed her hands reassuringly.

Patricia saw the blood still oozing from the gash on his finger and rummaged in her handbag. She pulled out a Kleenex and tied it round his finger tightly. 'Well, m...maybe Sidney took her for a drink after they had supper and they could be in one of the city bars?'

Alex looked into her eyes. Although she didn't have Kim's eyes, he could see likeness in the two sisters, and it tore at his gut. He had to find Kim and get her away from Sidney to safety.

'I don't think...' he said and paused looking down at his shoes. He didn't know how to answer Patricia without further upset because he did not think they were in the city.

Out of the corner of his eye he caught a thin slither of light along the bottom of a door under the stairs. A large old padlock hung from the outside lock. 'Is that a cellar or a basement?'

Patricia followed his gaze and grabbed his arm. 'It looks like it,' she whispered.

Already Alex was pulling the door wide open.

'Do you think he's down there,' Patricia asked. 'I mean, Kim could have already left to walk home and gone by a different route and that's how we missed each other. But do be careful, Alex, you don't know what this idiot is capable of doing.'

Alex had already begun to creep stealthily down the stone steps. Patricia was right behind him following slowly on her tiptoes. The strip light was bright as they reached the first old room and that was when Alex smelt it - photographers' developing fluid. He would know that smell anywhere and instantly remembered Sidney telling him once that he had a small dark room at home where he'd learnt his craft as a young man.

Alex walked slowly along the length of the room and then cried out. The sight before him shocked him to the core and as he stopped dead in his tracks. He felt Patricia do the same and tread on his heel.

Sidney was standing defiantly with a large kitchen knife in his hand. Kim was stripped naked and looked as though she'd been drugged then tied to a chair by her ankles and wrists.

Patricia screamed and Sidney took a step towards them waving the knife in the air. 'Don't come any closer or I'll kill her,' he warned.

Time seemed to stand still in the eerie silence as Alex's heart hammered against his ribs. He assessed the situation. Kim was alive because he could see her slim chest moving up and down slightly. She looked semi-conscious and her eyelids were fluttering, but other than that she seemed physically unharmed.

But now he had two women to protect and make sure no further harm came to either of them. Trying to stay calm, he took long, slow deep breaths while he decided what to do.

His eyes took in the basement walls covered with Kim's photographs, her lovely face, her cleavage in a summer dress, and her long bare legs where she looked to be in her twenties. This obsession appeared to be longstanding and Alex breathed hard, realising how unbalanced Sidney really was.

He has tied her down like a bloody chicken, Alex thought, her lovely gentle body shouldn't be exposed to a perverted nutcase like Sidney. He spotted the recent photographs pegged up above a tray of developing fluid and realised they were close-up shots of Kim's breasts and nipples. Alex felt everything inside him snap.

His chest filled with such rage that he couldn't control it. He growled, 'If I don't see the boys again then so be it. But I love you, Kim,' he yelled.

He lunged at Sidney, grasping his skinny neck between his large hands, and knocking him to the ground.

Alex felt pain tear through his left arm as Sidney slashed at him with the knife, but as Sidney's face reddened, his grip on the knife slackened. Alex growled once more, but this time with satisfaction. The knife dropped to the floor.

Alex could feel sweat standing on his forehead as he glared down at Sidney's face going purple. He kept the same amount of force in his hands around his neck. The red dots on the silk cravat around Sidney's neck seemed to be merging into one and all Alex could see was this pathetic excuse for a man who had caused him so much grief and had nearly destroyed his darling Kim. He wanted to keep going and squeeze the life out of him.

Once again time seemed to stand still in the silence of the room as if they were all suspended in a tableau at the theatre. He felt Patricia's hand squeeze his shoulder.

'Don't, Alex,' she whispered. 'He's simply not worth it.'

Alex dropped his hands from the older man's throat and let his head fall back on the ground just as two police offers bounded into the room shouting at everyone to stay calm and keep still.

*

Kim heard a coarse loud noise in the room. It was like a bear roaring and it reminded her of something. Was she awake or asleep? She couldn't quite decide. The growl sounded like Alex had made once when they'd watched a western together and he'd been messing around.

The happy memory roused her a little and decided she was not asleep, just dozing. She knew she wasn't in her bed because she felt too cold to be under her quilt. Then she heard more shouting with voices urgent and sharp with fear.

Her memories of where she was and what Sidney was doing crashed back into her mind. But it felt different now, as though she wasn't alone. Was that Patricia's voice, or was she imaging it? She could feel strong but gentle hands moving over her, patting, comforting and then she felt someone cradle her head. She coughed and stirred. Eventually the dirty ceiling came into focus, but then blurred again. The slight scent of sandalwood filled her senses. Was it Alex? It was certainly his aftershave, or maybe it was another ruse by Sidney.

'A...Alex,' she moaned.

*

Alex heard Kim say his name and snapped back into action. He bounded over the top of Sidney, who was thrashing around on the floor gasping for breath while a police officer pinned him down.

The other policeman had gone to Kim's side. Using his right arm Alex helped him release the nylon cord from around her ankles and wrists.

Kim's thin body trembled as she fell forwards into his arms and he dropped to his knees on the stone floor. She lay across his chest as he cradled and rocked her gently. Her skin felt cold and clammy. When he looked into her eyes, they were wide in terror. Alex murmured into her shoulder. 'You're okay now, sweetheart. I've got you. No one will ever hurt you again!'

Patricia tore off her jacket and covered Kim's modesty away from the police officers' view. They all heard the siren sound of an ambulance screeching to the front of the house.

Patricia dropped to her knees on the other side of Alex and tenderly stroked Kim's hair. 'Oh, God, I can't believe this has happened,' she murmured. 'Has he hurt you anywhere else, love?'

Kim gently shook her head and managed a faint, groggy answer. 'N…no, I don't think so. But I…I couldn't move because he'd put some drugs in the wine.'

With tears streaming down her face, Patricia soothed, 'We know, but don't worry. You're safe now we're here.'

Blood had soaked through Alex's shirtsleeve and was flowing down his hand when a paramedic knelt beside him. Opening his box and tearing the sleeve apart the paramedic applied a strong pressure dressing. He wanted Alex to let go of Kim with his other arm.

Alex shook his head stubbornly. His eyes were awash with tears. 'I'm not letting her go again.'

The other paramedic unfolded a large blanket and removing Patricia's jacket, he draped it around Kim's back. He asked Kim to unlock her arms from around Alex's chest.

But she shook her head cuddling further into him. 'Nooo, please don't take him away from me again,' she whimpered. 'I need him.'

The paramedic shrugged his shoulders with a helpless look towards Patricia. 'She's very cold and in shock. We need to get her temperature up and take her to Casualty. They'll want to assess what drugs she's been given and if she's been…' he paused and nodded his head slightly with a knowing look to Patricia, 'You know?'

Patricia took a deep breath, deciding she would have to take charge of the situation. She scrambled to her feet and dusted the dirt from her tweed skirt. 'Kim, sweetheart, you have to take your arms away from Alex just for a few minutes while the guys here sort you out. Alex isn't going anywhere. He'll be right here,' she said purposively. 'But Sidney has cut Alex's arm and it's bleeding, so we need to get him to the hospital to have it stitched.'

Kim raised her head from Alex's chest and gasped. 'Oh no, has he hurt you too,' she murmured, sitting up and allowing the paramedic to wrap the blanket firmly around her.

Alex looked up at Patricia and smiled. With the back of his hand, he wiped the tears away from his eyes and grunted in the back of his throat. 'I'm okay, Kim. Don't worry, it's just a graze. But Patricia is right; we need to get you warmed up.'

The atmosphere was interrupted when the police officer assisted then half-dragged Sidney to his feet while he whined and complained that Alex had tried to choke him. With handcuffs on both his wrists held out in front of him they marched Sidney out of the room and up the stairs.

By now the first paramedic who'd treated Alex's arm had returned with a folded stretcher. As he opened it out Alex gently persuaded Kim to let them lift her on to it.

'But I can feel my arms and legs a bit now. Let me try to stand up.' Kim said.

Alex held on to her hand all the while and squeezed it reassuringly. He shook his head. 'All the same, let's go with what these guys say. They're the experts, sweetheart.'

Kim nodded. 'Oh, Alex, I'm so sorry. I should have at least talked to you and listened to your version of events about the images on the computer,' she muttered, 'I'm truly sorry you have been hurt. This is all my fault because I put my trust in the wrong man.'

'Shush,' Alex soothed, following the paramedics who carried Kim up the stairs. 'Everything's going to be okay now.'

Chapter Twenty-Seven
The Aftermath

Kim lay against the pillows in bed on a ward at Durham hospital with Patricia sitting on one side and Alex on the other. After blood tests and dressings of soothing balm had been applied to her wrists and ankles, she was feeling much better. The doctors had assured them that there would be no lasting effects of the drug and all she needed physically was peace, quiet and plenty of rest. Psychologically it would take a lot longer to get over what Sidney had done, but as Patricia kept reiterating, she and Alex would be with her every step of the way.

Kim kept taking huge sighs of relief every time she looked from Alex to Patricia. The two people she loved most in the world were close and she knew she was blessed to have them in her life. If it hadn't been for their love and concern, she would still be tied to that chair at Sidney's.

Although the doctors had told her that intermittent memory loss following this type of traumatic experience was quite common, Kim knew her mind had blocked out certain aspects of the time she had been at Sidney's. Some of the things he had done were blurred as she'd mostly been in a trance-like state.

The first question the doctors had asked before examination was if he'd raped her. She was reasonably sure he hadn't got that far, and Kim was relieved when this was confirmed on examination.

The small ward where Kim had been admitted was apparently used just for short-stay patients. An old gentleman left shortly after she'd arrived, and the other three beds were empty. Although there were nurses scurrying up and down the long corridor outside, the room itself was quiet and they looked at each other in silence.

Kim stared at her sister's face and could tell by the redness of her eyes that she'd been crying. Kim couldn't remember the last time she had seen Patricia cry and felt guilty for causing her upset.

'Well, Patricia,' she murmured. 'You've certainly had an eventful visit home this time. I'm so sorry I made you worry. I should have listened to your warnings about Sidney. If I had, none of this would ever have happened.'

Patricia squeezed her hand and tenderly rubbed the back. 'Shush, don't be silly. Try not to think of it now. There's plenty of time to talk about all of that later.'

Alex nodded. 'Patricia's right. Don't talk about it until you're stronger.'

Kim could see they both had her best welfare at heart, but she needed to talk. 'No, I want to talk about it,' she pleaded. 'I need to hear your versions of events because there's so much I didn't see or hear when I was drugged. I'm trying to piece things together in my mind.'

Kim snuggled down the bed under the clean white sheets, ready to listen to Alex. She'd loved the tone of his voice from the very first time she heard him speak in the studio when they'd introduced each other.

Alex sighed in agreement and told her all about his meeting with Sidney. How he'd threatened to expose him to the police and that his solicitor would be notified. He described the following events in Scunthorpe.

They discussed every inch of his visit to his father and how his advice had been to sort Sidney's threats out in a professional manner. Alex explained how he hadn't got Sidney's deranged voice message until he was driving back to Durham.

He also told Kim how Jack had advised him not to give up on their relationship and finished by saying, 'Dad's words were, if you love her then go and get her.'

Kim was delighted that Alex's father seemed to approve of her. She turned her head to face him and grinned. 'Which thankfully, for my sake, is exactly what you did.'

He sighed and gently caressed her cheek. 'Thank God I made it in time. If it had been an hour later, then who knows…' he paused and looked across at Patricia.

Patricia cleared her throat. 'Please, let's just not go there,' she murmured lowering her head.

They began to talk about Sidney's obsession. She told Alex about her friendly chat and cuddle with the older man when she'd broken down in tears after finding the images on the computer. 'I…I thought he felt trustworthy and safe like David always did,' Kim said. 'But I'd no inkling about what he was really like and what his twisted and warped feelings were.'

Patricia looked up and nodded gravely. 'I know from my research that psychotic people can be very deceptive and manipulative,' she said.

Kim breathed out slowly and shook her head. 'Well, he certainly had me fooled and especially how much he hated David. That's the one thing I'm struggling to come to terms with. I mean, Sidney always spent Saturday afternoons with David. Especially in the summer when they would take the train through to Chester-Le-Street to watch Durham play test cricket. Or they'd go down to The Rowing Club on the riverside and watch the club practise. I thought it was all a perfectly harmless friendship and I presume David did too.'

Alex squeezed her hand and gave her a little wink from the corner of his eye to encourage her to talk it all out of her system.

Kim smiled, loving the familiar gesture, which was one of many she'd missed. She continued, 'Of course when David became ill and couldn't get out of the house Sidney was, dare I say, a great help. He would come around every week and sit with David, reading him sporting stuff out of his magazines and books, which gave me a couple of hours to clean the house or go out shopping,' she paused and sighed heavily. 'I'm glad that David didn't know how much Sidney disliked him because he'd have been really upset.'

Alex frowned and raised an eyebrow. 'Okay, but the one thing I can't get my head around is how someone could be so two-faced for all of those years,' he murmured. 'Maybe it was all a ruse so he could get closer to you, sweetheart.'

Patricia shook her head and looked at Kim. 'I agree, Alex,' she said. 'And because quite a few of those photographs were taken while you were at university, had you no idea back then that Sidney was, for want of a better word, besotted with you?'

Kim cast her mind back to the first few weeks at university and pursed her lips. 'None whatsoever. I met him in the canteen a few days before I met David and figured that he was just being friendly to a new fresher. And after that I just looked upon him as one of David's friends.'

Kim could see Patricia's face redden and she knew her sister was going to say something important.

'Kim,' Patricia said. 'I have to tell you something that I must confess I should have done years ago. Even though I'm struggling with myself that maybe I should wait until you're stronger, I really want to get this off my chest. The guilt seems to be burning a hole in my insides. And if anything more was to happen, and I didn't get the chance to tell you I'd feel even worse.'

Kim let go of Alex's hand and took a long drink from a glass of water on the bedside locker. She nodded. 'Okay, we don't have secrets, Patricia. Just tell me now.'

Patricia sighed. 'Well, on this occasion we have had a secret and I'm sorry for not telling you,' she said then continued to tell her sister about the night before her wedding and what she had seen David doing. 'I'm now convinced that the anorak I saw hanging in the hall belonged to Sidney and how it must have been him that night creeping around the car park.'

Kim gave a sigh of relief that this was all Patricia had to confess. Her mind had conjured up more ghastly stuff that she would need to deal with.

'Actually,' Kim said. 'That makes sense now. I remember Sidney rambling on about what David had done before the wedding.'

She took Patricia's hands in hers. 'That's an awfully long time ago, and it's over and done with. Although it was a shock, I'm sure David was faithful when we were married. I'd have known if he hadn't been and that's the main thing.'

Kim saw Patricia's face twist slightly and her eyes wash with tears. 'But you see, the main reason I didn't tell you was because if you hadn't married David, I would have had to…' she swallowed hard as though she was struggling to say the words and having to admit how painful her guilt was. 'Well, I…I wouldn't have been able to go to London. I would have had to stay at home and look after you.'

Kim gasped at her sister's honesty and knew how much it had taken for Patricia to admit this. She opened her mouth to offer words of comfort, but Patricia dropped her forehead onto the back of Kim's hand.

Patricia began to sob and to repeat over and over how sorry she was. 'To think how near I came to losing you. My lovely little sister,' she sobbed loudly onto Kim's hand. 'I'd g…gladly spend the rest of my days looking after you now.'

Kim watched her sister's heavy shoulders heave as she cried, and it hurt almost as much as the torture that Sidney had inflicted on her.

She ran a hand over Patricia's hair, murmuring, 'Shush, just stop that. You're the one being silly now.'

Alex got up and muttered, 'I'm going to find us a strong cup of tea.'

Kim smiled at Alex over Patricia's head and mouthed the words, thank you.

When Alex left, Kim stared down at Patricia's bent head. Kim's insides twisted with sadness at her sister's distress, and even though her scalp was sore from being dragged across the floor, she leant forward and rested her chin on her sister's head. Draping an arm along her shoulders, she said. 'Look, we were just kids ourselves back then. If I'd been the older one and was in your shoes, I would probably have felt the same.'

Patricia snivelled. 'No, you wouldn't, because you're a much kinder person than I am. Looking after me wouldn't have been a problem to you.'

Kim could feel her sister's tears run between her fingers as she cried. She tried again, 'But that's utter rubbish. You are one of the kindest people I know, Patricia. Look at how you cared for me when David died. And all the trips you made up and down from London when he was having his treatment. I couldn't have got through that time without your help and support.'

Patricia's sobs lessened. She lifted her face up to Kim, who removed her arm and flopped back onto the pillows, exhausted.

'I will look after you properly now,' Patricia said, rummaging in her handbag for a tissue.

Wiping her eyes, Patricia sat up straighter in the chair and patted her fringe back into place, just as Alex entered carrying three polystyrene cups of tea.

He put them on the table and swung it over the bed for Kim to reach then placed small packets of custard creams and jammy dodgers for them to share.

'But I don't need looking after,' Kim exclaimed. 'I'm a grown woman now and since I met Alex I've changed.'

Kim sipped the hot tea and sighed with pleasure. 'Aah, that's heaven. My mouth is so dry and I've a raging thirst,' Kim said, smiling fondly as she watched Alex dunk a biscuit into his cup while Patricia stirred three packets of sugar into her tea and whizzed it around with a plastic spoon.

'Don't go changing too much, Kim,' Alex muttered through a mouthful of soggy biscuit. 'Because I'm pretty fond of the woman I fell in love with.'

Kim grinned. She was so pleased to see Patricia pull herself together and drink her tea while she nibbled on a custard cream and stroked Alex's big arm that lay on the bedcover.

'Nooo, I just meant that before this happened today, being with you had changed me into a more confident and capable person. I was more spontaneous and open-minded in my newfound confidence. I felt more willing to try new interests rather than hang back in the shadows as I'd done with David and was up for having some fun. I knew where I was going in life and the exact countries I want to visit on holiday,' she said.

Alex and Patricia both nodded in agreement. She knew they'd both noticed the change in her.

Kim suddenly shivered when her mind flashed back to the basement and the chair then wondered how it was going to affect her. 'Well, that was until today of course. Maybe this might set me back a little,' she said.

Alex squeezed her hand and she looked longingly into his eyes.

'But,' she said. 'If there's one thing I've learnt while being tied to that chair and thinking I was going to die at the hands of a maniac, it is that we've all got a hell of a lot of living to do.'

Alex whistled through his teeth and happily sighed. 'Kim, you're amazing.'

Patricia smiled and looked over towards Alex. 'I don't think I've said this, Alex, but I will always be eternally grateful to you for saving my sister,' she said and then nodded to Kim. 'This man saved your life, darling. Alex has rescued you in more ways than one,' she paused and smugly folded her arms across her ample chest. 'And, as I've never been able to resist a told-you-so, I'm saying it now.'

That's more like it, Kim thought, delighted that Patricia was back to her normal self.

'Actually,' Kim grinned. 'Patricia's right. She was the one who could see that you loved me, more than I could myself. I was the one with all the doubts, especially as Sidney kept saying there was something not quite right about you.'

Alex shrugged, grimaced at the mention of Sidney's name, and dunked another biscuit.

Kim continued, 'So, I think you should be more grateful to Patricia than me because she was the one who believed in you, whereas I stupidly put my trust in the wrong man.'

Chapter Twenty-Eight

The following afternoon Kim lay soaking in warm bubbles with Alex sitting behind her on the end of the bath while they talked. The steamy bathroom was filled with a scent that Alex thought seemed relaxing and refreshing. He read the name, jasmine, on the bottle of bubble bath Kim had used.

Patricia had flatly refused to leave until she was certain that Kim was going to be all right and had also agreed to the suggestion that Alex would stay with them in the house for the next few days to help with the further police investigations.

Alex glanced down at Kim's bruised nipples and the teeth marks on the back of her neck. Rage swept through him once again at the thought that any man could hurt Kim like that. The anger in his chest engulfed him and he felt as though it was choking him.

She was so slender and lovely that he couldn't bear to think of Sidney having his hands on her body, let alone inflicting those awful wounds. There was still a large part of him that wished he hadn't listened to Patricia, and when he'd had his hands around the maniac's throat, he had kept going until he had choked the life out of him for doing this.

'They'll heal,' she whispered looking up at him. She took her wet arm out of the water and stroked his cheek.

Alex moaned in annoyance at himself for letting his mask slip and allowing Kim to read his thoughts. From the minute they'd brought her home from hospital he'd been able to keep up his cheerful banter, but now he cracked under the strain. His eyelids felt moist and he wasn't sure if it was the steam in the bathroom or the emotional upset. He croaked, 'Is your head still sore?'

Patricia had washed her hair gently with baby shampoo and massaged her scalp with scented oil then wrapped it in a warm towel.

'Not as much now that Patricia has worked her magic on it.'

'That's good. Just let me know when you need more painkillers,' he soothed and picked up the soft sponge. Soaking it in the bubbles he tenderly washed her back while she leant forward.

'It's a strange feeling,' she said. 'Although I can see the bite mark on my neck and my nipples are very sore, I've no recollection of him doing it. Or, for that matter, what he actually did. I mean, I can imagine why they hurt, but I just can't remember it, which is different from my hair. I remember him twisting my hair in his hands and dragging me along the floor. So, it's strange how some of my memory has gone, but not all of it. I can only remember certain bits of the ordeal.'

Alex gritted his teeth. 'Well, I'm glad you can't remember, and I pray you never do,' he seethed. 'I hope they lock the cretin up and throw away the key.'

'Oh, Alex,' she whispered. 'Thank God you came for me or I could still be there...' she paused and shivered.

Alex could feel emotion build up in his throat like a huge ball of misery as he stroked her back and she sighed. Nobody will ever hurt her again, he determined, and of course if she would have him. He remembered the days last week after she had walked out and how much he'd missed her.

Suddenly it all became too much for him and he blurted, 'It was terrible when you left me in the apartment. I couldn't believe I would miss anyone like I missed you. I just couldn't stop thinking about you day and night. I know the old saying, you never know what you've got until it's gone. And boy, was that true!'

Kim took his big hand in hers and interlocked her fingers in his. 'I'm so sorry. I should at least have talked to you about it, but I was so shocked!'

Alex stared down at their hands and nodded miserably. 'Of course, you were. Any decent woman would be. But surely, you would know that I'd never look at trash like that. No man in his right mind would, well, not if he were lucky enough to have you by his side.'

Kim twisted around in the bath to face him.

Looking down at her, Alex felt his eyes wash with tears. His chest constricted as he tried to suppress the upset that engulfed him. 'Once you'd gone, I realised how much I love you, Kim. You were in my thoughts and my body constantly and I couldn't bear living there without you.'

A big tear slid slowly down Kim's face and Alex wiped it away with his thumb. He took a deep breath, trying to gain hold of himself knowing he had to be strong for her. But when she sat forward and gently placed her lips on his, he let go and crumbled.

'C…Christ!' he spluttered, grabbing a towel, and sniffing his tears into the soft material. 'I'm meant to be the strong one helping you through this, but it's the

other way around. Here I am blubbering like a little
boy!'

Kim put her arms around his shoulders, and he
buried his face in her wet neck while she sobbed
along with him.

Eventually they both stopped crying and he lifted his
head. 'I...I think they're tears of relief and joy to
have you back in my arms again,' he paused. He saw
the bruise low down on the base of her back where
Sidney had bounced her down the stairs, and
grimaced, 'I just wish I could have got to you before
that monster did. I feel I've let you down.'

'Shush,' she cooed, running her hand through his
hair. 'As hard as it is, try to let that go in your mind.
It's my own stupid fault that I was taken in by the
maniac. At least you got to me before he did anything
else. And another thing, not being strong for me is
utter rubbish. Isn't this what couples do when they are
an item, Alex? There will be days ahead when I'm
not strong and will lean on you and vice-versa. But
we'll get through it together.'

Alex nodded and wanted to crush her to his chest but
was conscious of the pain in her body, so he settled
for stroking her back. 'I'm fighting the urge to slide
into that tub with you and if you weren't in pain, I'd
crush you in my arms,' he said.

'What,' she giggled, 'with our Patricia downstairs?'

He grinned then whistled through his teeth. 'Yeah,
she's certainly a formidable lady, I'll give you that,'
he smiled. 'But I like your sister. She's got plenty of
guts.'

Oh, Alex,' Kim whispered into his hair. 'I do love
you. I've never really had the chance to say it to you

properly. But I do. I love you so very much and have done ever since we first met.'

Epilogue

It was a dull afternoon in winter when Kim stood at the large bay window in her lounge and looked over to the cathedral thinking of David. It had been nine months since her ordeal at the hands of Sidney, and although David's memory had loomed large at the time of the assault, she rarely thought of her dead husband now. Her life had changed so much, and her daily thoughts were now wrapped up with Alex and their future.

It hadn't been an easy time. The first few weeks had been the worst, but with Alex's love and support she'd managed to cope. Her hair had fallen out in handfuls. Many of the long strands were broken and split, so following the advice of her hairdresser, she'd had it cut into a short shiny bob which she liked, and Alex loved.

Immediately after the assault she had private counselling sessions which Patricia had arranged. Although the counsellor was a genuinely nice woman who talked through all aspects of the trauma, it was talking with Alex that she'd found the greatest comfort. The counsellor had confirmed what the hospital doctor had told her about periods of memory loss and how it might never come back or that she might experience flashbacks in the future.

However, the most important piece of advice that Kim kept uppermost in her mind was that she was determined not to become a victim, and she strived most days not to allow the memories, and Sidney, the chance to ruin her life. There were some days that this life-plan was still a struggle and she would chant repeatedly like a mantra, 'I'm not going to be a victim. I am a survivor.' But most days now she was able to believe in herself and put it into practice.

The nightmares had been dreadful at first. But since Sidney had been safely locked away in a secure psychiatric unit, they had begun to diminish. The dreams usually centred on the basement chair, the ties around her ankles and wrists, and although she still couldn't remember exactly what Sidney had done, she often thought her imaginings were probably more grotesque than the actual events.

When she'd woken screaming and soaked in sweat with her heart racing, Alex would wrap her into his arms and big chest. Stroking her back, he would murmur tenderly into her hair, 'You're safe now, it's all okay.'

And, no matter how tired Alex was he'd never go back to sleep again, until sometimes clinging to him for dear life, she would relax and doze off into a sound sleep.

Patricia had returned to London two weeks after the assault, but she still rang Kim every night. They'd become closer, with a deeper understanding between them and Kim no longer thought of her as the older bossy sister. Instead, as well as knowing she owed her life to Patricia, she valued her as a close friend who she could confide in and talk through her innermost thoughts and feelings.

Kim had taken Alex with her on their first weekend visit to London and helped Patricia celebrate the launch of her crime novel on publication day. They'd both loved the capital and Kim had coaxed Alex, who admittedly didn't like heights, into ascending the 95-

storey skyscraper, Shard of Glass, to look at the
amazing views.

Kim sighed at the pleasant memories and tore her
eyes from the view of the cathedral. She'd returned to
her house today to clean the two top bedrooms for
new tenants arriving the following week.

After her ordeal, Kim had immediately moved into
the riverside apartment with Alex and readily agreed
to his plan that they remain until the six months' lease
had expired. However last month, when they'd
discussed the idea of returning to live in the house,
she'd decided against it. As the value of the five-
bedroomed rental capacity was so good, and she did
love the apartment by the river, they had decided to
stay for another six months.

'Well, you're the sexiest landlady I've ever seen,'
Alex had said, and she'd dissolved into fits of giggles.
They now called the pool of rental money she made,
the holiday pot. And when Alex finished his work
contract in Newcastle, they intended to take a month
off and travel extensively throughout Italy, first
stopping off in Provence, to visit Vicky.

Kim lugged the hoover upstairs, remembering her
previous day's outing to York with Alex's dad and
she smiled. Jack had taken to coming to Durham once
a month on the train to stay with them for weekends,
but during the weeks in between she often met him in
York for the day. Yesterday they'd visited the Jorvik
Viking Centre and The National Railway Museum,
followed by lunch near York Minster.

Kim mused while plugging in the hoover, not for
one minute was she interested in Vikings or trains,
but she did enjoy Jack's company and loved to listen

to his stories of Alex growing up and his childhood antics.

While hoovering the carpets, Kim grinned as she thought of Alex. It could, she supposed, have been easy to end up with depression after the assault if she hadn't been with Alex. But as the months had gone by, she could tell her lovely big man was incredibly content. She saw the happiness in his eyes every day. And no one could help being carried along with someone who was so cheerful every day. It was infectious.

Alex was thoroughly enjoying his new job photographing Christmas hampers for a large company on the outskirts of Newcastle. The photographer was an old client of Kim's, and when he'd mentioned that he was looking to expand his team, Kim had sent over the portfolio of the fruit and vegetables project that Alex had put together. He'd eagerly invited Alex for an interview.

On the morning of the interview, Kim had printed out the photographs and bound them with a blue leather portfolio before he set off. When he returned after lunch, grinning from ear to ear, she knew he had been a success.

His divorce from Sally was progressing easier now because she'd met a builder in Scunthorpe and was only too glad for Alex to take the twins every other weekend.

After their first visit, when Alex had returned from driving the boy's home, he'd hurried into the apartment and scooped Kim high up into the air. 'I think I'm the happiest man in Durham now,' he'd cried. 'No one could have been a bigger hit with my boys than you were.'

Kim had loved having Jamie and Josh for their two-night stopover, so much so that she hadn't wanted them to leave that Sunday evening. In her past life ten pin bowling, bike rides, and skate boarding had never loomed high on her agenda of pleasurable interests to fill a weekend. But as she'd whispered to Alex in bed the night before, it had been a barrel of laughs and she'd loved every minute.

She draped her arms around his neck and hugged him tight. 'I couldn't agree more, Alex, life couldn't get much better.'

If you have enjoyed this story - A review on amazon.co.uk would be greatly appreciated.
You can find more from Susan Willis here:

His Wife's Secret https://amzn.to/2DDhlci
When David meets old school-friend, Erin again he falls head over heels in love. He leaves his wife and their sixteen-year-old daughter to marry Erin. But, in a small village people have long memories and they move south for a fresh beginning. Erin's behaviour starts to change in a very strange way and David wonders if she is punishing him for something he's done?

Ebook Cosy Crime Short Reads:
Christmas Intruder https://amzn.to/38ZpyZj
Megan's Mistake https://amzn.to/2pl88Sf
An Author is Missing https://amzn.to/2N1DAOX

Food Lover's Romance Novel, 'NO CHEF, I Won't!' https://amzn.to/3j1HiGn
A fruity, explosive story with all the right ingredients!

Website www.susanwillis.co.uk
Twitter @SusanWillis69
Facebook m.me/AUTHORSusanWillis
Instagram susansuspenseauthor
pinterest.co.uk/williseliz7/

Printed in Great Britain
by Amazon

16526746R00160